Rebel in Blue

Liam English

This is a work of fiction. The events, characters, places, and incidents are used fictitiously. Some of the historical figures who lived through the period of history in which this work of fiction is set have a place in this story. Their real names are used but the scenes, dialogue, and characterisation are created by the author for fictional purposes. Any resemblance of other fictional characters to actual persons, living or dead, events, or locales is entirely coincidental.

Copyright © 2022 by Ciaran English

All rights reserved. No part of this book may be reproduced or used in any manner without written permission of the copyright owner except for the use of quotations in a book review. For more information, address: lenglishwriting@outlook.com

First paperback edition May 2022

Book design by Andy Bridge

ISBN 9798414599227 (paperback)
Independently published

www.liamenglish.com

In loving memory of Liam English

Thank you for giving us a way to keep talking to you.

PROLOGUE

OCT. 1861

He didn't have to cross the Ballyhouras – strange, looming hulks completely unlike his beloved Knockdrisna – but, being the unlikeliest route, 'twas the surest way of avoiding police, militia and soldiers.

Before the hills, he had survived by cadging bread and potatoes from safe houses - a meagre diet, supplemented by snared rabbits. But there were no safe houses and few rabbits on the Ballyhouras. On his second evening in their tenebrous embrace, he had snared a scrawny doe which he'd half cooked over a slow, damp fire. Since then, apart from melted snow, there had been no sustenance.

Snow and driving rain, multiplying the debilitating effects of hunger and injury, whirled around the peaks and valleys whipping skin which received no protection from the tattered rags he wore. He took what shelter he could: behind boulders, inside caves and crevasses, underneath branches of stunted trees and in scooped out snow hollows, but those four days and three nights of his flight were epochs of enduring hardship.

Finally, in the glowering light of a late October afternoon, he stumbled down from the peaks separating east Limerick from north

Cork and staggered towards a safe house outside Mitchelstown. Within sight of the church spire, he took a muddy path winding back west. The ground was wet and it became harder and harder to pull one leg after the other. He teetered and would have fallen face first in the ooze, but an inherent pride kept him upright.

'Easy boy, easy,' he spoke to himself, like he was a shying horse, and the sound of his voice had a reassuring, calming effect; for days, struggling soullessly along the heights, there had been nothing but the rattle of his breathing to punctuate the howling wind.

When he spied the crumbling, dishevelled cottage his eyes filled with tears of relief and joy. He lengthened his stride, anxious to avail himself of its sustenance. An axe protruded from a block, filling him with the hope of a welcoming fire once he was within. An irregular line of flat stones sunk into the soft ground led to a flaking green door and he rapped his knuckles on it. For a few moments he thought he'd have to break it down to get shelter. Then a shuffling sound announced a presence and the door was pulled open a crack.

'God bless! I'm looking for Dan O'Leary,' he announced.

A woman peered at him through the sliver of space she'd allowed. 'He isn't here, he took two cows into the mart at Fermoy a few days ago, I'm not expecting him back until tomorrow. If he got a good price, who knows when he'll be back; the more he'll get, the more he'll drink. And every penny needed to pay the rent and they the last two beasts to call our own around the place.'

'God save Ireland!' He assumed this woman was Dan O'Leary's wife and as likely to help as the man himself, which was why he said his half of the Fenian watchword.

'Oh Christ! One of them, are you? Well, I don't want you or your kind. I want my husband home from the mart with the money that might enable us to stay on in this hovel for another year. I don't want any of his fancy boys prancing around – fighting this, liberating that, and sleeping off hangovers the following day while the Ireland they were so determined to liberate the night before carries on exploiting its people same as ever.'

Though it wasn't the welcome he'd hoped for; he was desperate. 'Missus, I'm not a fancy boy. I'm a patriot, after trekking sixty odd miles from West Limerick through all kinds of weather. I'm freezing and starving. If you don't let me in, I'll have to break in.'

She studied him. Tall, thin, and dirty. His only possessions a pathetic bundle of rags tied by strips of cloth to a hazel stick. His hair was matted with damp mud; a scraggly beard failed to attenuate a sloping chin. Even in these times of poverty and hardship his appearance was uninviting. Yet a spark in his greenish eyes hinted at warmth capable of being fanned into life.

'Do ye all talk as tough as that in Limerick?'

'Please, Missus, just let me come in for a bit of heat, will you?'

'Sure come in for a small while, you can't be worse than my husband's other accomplices. Or himself, for that matter.'

Inside was dark and smoky – the jagged hole in the roof providing no more than a miniscule up-draught. He made out a roughly hewn table, a few *súgawn* chairs and a straw pallet near the open fire. She held out a bucket of water and a ladle.

'Have a few scoops of this – it'll revive you, while I fix something to eat.' She'd opted to be friendly. Smiling, she said, 'I'm Mairead.'

He raised the ladle to his lips and slurped. He choked like he'd swallowed a draft of strong whiskey. When his breathing eased he had another slurp and considered the woman. She wore a dark cardigan and green woollen skirt. A grey shawl was draped over her shoulders. It was hard to put an age on her, though more stooped, she was of a similar height to his Kathleen, with a face covered in freckles.

'That'll do you for now,' she said walking away into a gloomy annexe with her bucket. When she reappeared she gestured towards one of the chairs next to the table. He ate chunks of griddle bread washed down by warm buttermilk while she sat across from him and watched.

She asked his name.

'Seamus O'Farrell.' He didn't add that to the authorities in West Limerick he was also known as 'Captain Rock.' That was how he signed the notes threatening the lives, livelihoods, and families of deserving recipients within the authority.

'Do you have any children?' He spoke to deaden the sound of his chewing but immediately regretted asking, realising they'd surely emigrated or died.

'We had six. Three died, one joined the army and the other two emigrated. We haven't heard from any of those three since they left. Sure, why would they want to contact us? Times were always hard around here and Dan O'Leary was never very kind to them.' She stared at the fire, like it was a mere speck in the far distance. 'I wasn't as kind as I should have been myself.'

'It's hard to show love when you're struggling to survive,' he said.

The woman looked at him through narrow eyes. 'What about yourself? Do you have family?'

'I'm betrothed.'

She guffawed. 'A fine catch she's got in you then, traipsing all over the countryside when you should be putting food on the lady's table and warming her bed.'

Feeling the need to justify himself, he spoke slowly, resolutely. 'She told me to go. Life is intolerable back there. After the Great Hunger a local Catholic farmer, name of Nolan, became landlord. He took over from the bankrupted English one, but instead of supporting his own, he's proven a worse bastard altogether. He's got the constables – old, doddery fellows - eating out of his hand and he has employed a bunch of young thugs as militia men to terrorise the rest of us. They say things have improved in many places, even in West Limerick, since the Great Hunger, but not in our corner – Kilgarry. People are evicted and left to die on the roadside in the blink of an eye. It could be anyone. The landlord's mood decides. A group of us got together, called ourselves the Kilgarry Crew and decided to strike a blow.'

'How?' She asked, her tone laced with scepticism.

He needed to be circumspect, but he was lonely after the Ballyhouras. 'We heard about a new movement stirring, some called it the Phoenix Society, others, Fenianism, but what could *we* do but follow the old ways of agrarian protests? Maim a few defenceless beasts, write threatening letters, rough up the agent, that sort of thing. One night, after they were drawn away to a disturbance at the other end of the parish, we broke into the constables' barracks and stole guns. A week later we went to fire shots over the landlord's house. Just to frighten him. Put the pressure on. But we were expected. When we crept out of the woods surrounding the house, the militia opened fire. I took a musket blast in the side. The others managed to get me away, barely, and I had to recuperate in a cave near the top of the local peak, Knockdrisna, like an animal. They say Fionn MacCumhaill and the Fianna sleep beneath it, resting, waiting for the day when they will return and liberate Ireland. I must say they are fond of their sleep as they appear to be postponing their return indefinitely.'

The woman rolled her eyes, either at the stupidity of the actual mess he had gotten himself into or his exposition of the legend of the Fianna. But there was humanity in her gesture and it was good to feel any sort of connection with another human being. He continued with his tale.

'Their presence or absence was no consolation to me. I couldn't go home. I was a wanted man. My mother was terrorised. Only for Padraic, my cousin, anonymously threatening the severest recriminations on the families of every militia man in the locality it's certain she would have been evicted or worse. As it was, her life was rendered intolerable. This, a woman who lost her husband and all her children, bar one, to the Famine.

I thought I was to die in that cave. Only for the attentions of Kathleen and Padraic I would have. My betrothed and my 'blood-brother cousin,' as I call him. Eventually, Padraic somehow made contact with other Fenians in the region and I was provided with money and names that would help me get to America to gain military experience and return with an army of experienced fighters. I was also provided with directions to safe houses like this. Kathleen agreed that it was our only hope. There is no point in trying to settle down in Kilgarry as it's now governed.'

When he reached the end of his soliloquy, the woman merely snorted.

'Will your husband really not be back until tomorrow?' he asked.

'He'll be back when the money runs out or he's barred from every pub in Fermoy, which thankfully is likely to happen first.'

'Doesn't sound like the sort of man to get involved in Fenianism.'

'Sure he'd get involved in anything that'd allow him brag and act the big man.'

'Has he taken part in any action?'

She laughed – a hollow, bitter guffaw. 'My sister warned me not to marry him. He was always a Fancy Dan – cavorting at the crossroad dances, singing at wakes, telling tall tales, all that stuff. Ignorant me never saw beyond the showing off to the mean-spirited drunk lurking beneath. He was going to take me to America and buy hundreds of acres of land for next to nothing; sure I was going to be a regular Lady of the Manor. Then one night I opened my legs to him and next thing I knew I was living in this hovel on half an acre of rented land subdivided from his father's. Lady of the Manor!' She guffawed once more. 'Sure, I was worse not to see it coming.'

'None of our kind will ever be Lord or Lady of Anything or Anywhere until we drive the English and their lackeys out of our country.'

'Wisha good luck to you! You think you'll be able to achieve that by teaming up with people like my husband?' she sneered.

'I'm just passing through. I'm not teaming up with your husband or anyone else in Ireland until I return with a well-trained Irish American army. Then we'll really achieve something.'

'Catch yourself on, will you? Someone has spun you a right yarn. Irish American Army? It'll be the usual bunch of idealistic eejits who'll cross the Atlantic and be betrayed, arrested or slaughtered within a few hours of landing.'

'There's a civil war going on out there with thousands of Irish on either side. Most are members of the Fenian movement, sworn to use the martial experience gained to invade Ireland and drive the English out. I intend to lead one of those regiments into my local area and free my people.'

She looked at him pityingly. 'I thought you looked intelligent. Thousands of Irish involved in a war?' Again, she did that laugh – bitter and sarcastic. 'They'll waste their energy and lifeblood fighting each other, like they always do – the only difference being they'll do it thousands of miles from home this time.'

A horrible basic truth at the heart of her scepticism riled him. 'If we were to listen to doubters like you, we'd never do anything but cower in our hovels all day sipping bad porter. If I wasn't desperate for shelter, I wouldn't stay in this house for another second.'

Her face lost its sneer and slackened, allowing him a glimpse of the girl she'd been before all her hope and optimism had been extinguished. He wondered with dread if he or Kathleen would end up with such disgust and dismissal of each other's ambitions.

'I don't wish you ill, Limerick,' she said. 'I just think people who pursue foolish dreams end up being more hurt than if they'd accepted the reality of their life to begin with.'

'And to accept the reality of our life is to accept defeat and slow death. Trying is better than accepting,' he responded.

She was finished debating. 'There's a barrel of rainwater outside that you can have a proper wash in.' She rose from the table and fetched a worn blanket from a back room, which she half-threw, half-handed to him. 'You can have the cot in the room, I'll take the pallet near the fire, that way I can be about my jobs in the morning without waking you,' she sounded almost apologetic.

'After the Ballyhouras, to be under a roof will be heaven. Thank you very much.'

And he did sleep, even after he'd washed in freezing water, but his dreams were of darkness; gunshots; blood; shouts; his mother; Kathleen; cold; hunger. All mixed up. His mother was shot and Kathleen ran to tend her, then it was Kathleen who was shot and his mother who ran to tend her; he was dying in a cold mountain cave, Kathleen was dying in a cold mountain cave; they were all running from the militia, but his mother was old now, they closed in on her, slavering like wolves…

Maybe he had been shouting like a scared child. Maybe the woman merely recognised their mutual need for comfort. He never knew. But it felt good when, sometime during the night, she slipped into his cot and cuddled against his back, covering him with warm softness. Her fingers lightly stroked his chest and stomach before straying onto his erect penis. He closed his eyes, trying to empty his mind of the badness and wickedness he'd experienced and committed – there was too much to expurgate, but, as she continued to stroke his manhood, he allowed himself experience a pleasure he'd denied himself with Kathleen. He gasped and exploded into the cold darkness of the tiny room: an effusion bearing dull guilt amidst sharp pleasure; images of Kathleen and his mother once more alternating in his mind. He tried to push them away as he reached behind and, guided by instinct rather than experience, stroked her until she shuddered and gasped against him, biting on his exposed shoulder. Then they slept, huddled together under the single blanket while the cold whistled outside – two strangers gifting each other temporary comfort in a world permanently harsh.

An instinct to live started him awake seconds before the first blow landed, though he was too late to avoid it. Pain and shock stunned him.

He twisted slightly, and a second blow glanced off his cheekbone. Even in the predawn darkness, black spots suffused his vision. A stinking tidal wave of cheap liquor swept over him, nearly as debilitating as the blows.

'Bastard of a Whoremaster! Ride a patriot's wife while he's away on business, would you? I'm going to kill you and then take my time with her.' His assailant, obviously none other than the man of the house – Dan O'Leary – gripped him around the throat and squeezed.

Normally Seamus would have swatted such a feeble drunkard to one side like an annoying insect, but the blows that had landed whilst he was half asleep had their effect and, coupled with the exhausting journey and the still suppurating gunshot wound on his side, granted his attacker the upper hand. He tried to grab O'Leary, but the latter pressed on his windpipe with calloused thumbs filling his eyes with tears and swelling the lump in his throat to the size of a blackbird.

He had some awareness that Mairead was trying to help. But O'Leary could neither be dislodged nor distracted from his murderous intent. A line of drool dribbled onto Seamus's chest. Through watery eyes he could make out his assailant's screwed-up, angry red face inches from him. The nauseating stink of O'Leary's breath now the least of his problems.

Once more the icy dark of near-death swam before his eyes. His life had almost ended as he suffered from a gunshot wound in a cold, dank, mountainside cave. But he had recovered. And trekked sixty miles across some of the most difficult terrain in Ireland, only for it to end in a draughty Cork hovel. And he welcomed it – he was tired of struggling, tired of fighting impossible odds, he was no help to his mother or Kathleen anyway… let it end…

Suddenly the pressure on his throat eased, though his breathing was still constricted, and the sound of his tortured gasping filled the room.

In the developing light the scene in front of him slowly slid into perspective and he began to take in what had happened.

It was both simple and terrible. O'Leary, though his hands had released their grip, still sat on him as steady as ever. But his head was missing. Gouts of blood squirted out of open arteries in his neck. The woman lay back against the wall, the axe, that had been buried in a block of timber out front now dripped red in her hands. Naked, she stood there her mouth opening and closing soundlessly.

Eventually, he summoned sufficient will to throw O'Leary's headless body off him, toppling it sideways like a felled tree stump. He went to her, naked himself and smeared with blood. But she pushed him away.

Without cleaning himself he pulled on his clothes and, ignoring the decapitated body and bloody lump of a head thrown against the far wall, went to her again.

This time she let him hold her. Though she didn't speak, she whimpered, while he tried to soothe her with shushing sounds. He stroked her hair as he whispered. Apart from tensing straighter and lowering the axe, she reacted to neither words nor strokes. But when he asked: 'Do you want to come with me to America?' she shook her head.

He stayed three days. Then had to move on, he had only a week left to get to Queenstown and board the *Victoria Star*. By then he'd cleaned up most of the blood and washed the sheets in the river. He'd dragged the body to the bottom of the garden behind the cabin and dug a hole that he hoped was deep enough to deter rooting scavengers, then he fetched the head wrapped in a soiled sheet and placed it near the shoulders. After filling it in, he tamped the earth down firmly to try and approximate it to an ordinary lazy potato bed.

Throughout this time neither he nor the woman spoke much, nor did they lie with each other, though she'd recovered sufficiently to help with cleaning up the mess and to say she'd persuade people her husband never returned from Fermoy. She didn't think they would question too much after some initial probing. When he asked again if she wanted to come with him, she reiterated her desire to stay around in case any of her sons returned – she'd find the money for the rent somehow. Her neighbours were good. He thought about asking her for O'Leary's shoes but couldn't bring himself to do so. His own were holed and paper thin.

On the afternoon of the third day, he shook her hand and walked away, not looking back, knowing that any possibility of fulfilling his dreams and those of his loved ones lay elsewhere; fearing he was fated to leave death and misery in his wake.

CHAPTER ONE
NOV. 1861

Watching and listening to the elaborate presentations, First-Sergeant Michael O'Rorke's lips formed a thin line of distaste – he had no time for judges, generals, archbishops, or any of that ilk.

The 69th Regiment, New York State Volunteers, Irish Brigade, stood at ease in the grounds of the Catholic Archbishop of New York - an Irishman from the bogs of Tyrone: John Hughes. Though the Archbishop himself was absent in Europe, an array of Irish American dignitaries was present. Judge Daly, a gentleman distinguished in political and legal circles, was eulogising Irish soldiers and Irish men in general, relating how their skills had contributed to the success of their adopted country and exhorting them to use these attributes now in the Union cause. The occasion was the presentation of regimental colours to the 69th who were on their way to Virginia and to representatives of the two other Irish Brigade regiments - the 63rd and the 88th - who would shortly follow. And where was more appropriate for its hosting than that epitome of Irish American success and power: the grounds of the doyen of New World Catholicism?

Judge Daly presented a huge silk flag of deep emerald enclosed by a saffron border to Colonel Nugent of the 69th. The dominant feature was an ancient Irish harp suspended between bright rays of sun bursting out beneath a heavenly cloud and a wreath of shamrocks. Along the bottom, across a crimson scroll, in the Gaelic mother tongue, was the motto - *'Who Never Retreated From The Clash Of Spears'* - a tribute to the legendary Fianna warriors of Fionn Mac Cumahaill, who'd stormed the very gates of hell. The whole was hung on a spiralled, silver-coated staff.

'Colonel Nugent,' Daly extolled, 'in committing to your charge these colours, I need scarcely remind you that they are pregnant with meaning. This green flag with its ancient harp of Brian Ború, its burst of sunlight, and its motto from Oisín, in the old Irish tongue, recalls through the long lapse of many centuries the period when Ireland was a nation, and conveys more eloquently than words how that nationality was lost through the practical working of that doctrine of secession for which the rebellious States of the South have taken up arms.'

Applause surged through the crowd, making the heatwave ripple and the soldiers rock on their feet. Still, they looked keen, expectant as puppies, for surely now they would get their opportunity to inscribe the annals of glory with Irish valour.

After the disaster of Bull Run the previous July, the Union had turned to the engineer and railroad magnate, General George McClellan, 'Young Napoleon.' This redeemer had remodelled the Northern war machine into an unstoppable, indestructible force. Within weeks it would crush the rebellion by marching into Richmond, the capital of the Confederacy, and cleansing the secessionist vipers that nested there. And the Irish Brigade, consisting of the 63rd, 69th and 88th New York, intended to be in the vanguard of that advance. Afterwards, they would use their experience to sweep into Ireland and liberate 'the Old Dart.'

Acting Brigadier-General, Thomas Francis Meagher took the stand. O'Rorke grimaced. 'Meagher-of-the-Sword,' he was titled, but as far as O'Rorke could judge he would have been more aptly titled: 'Meagher-of-the-Whiskey-Bottle.' In his youth he had given some fiery speech or other in defiance of Daniel O'Connell's exhortation to seek repeal of the union with Britain through peaceful means. Meagher and his cabal were christened 'Young Ireland'. But their supposed penchant for violence merely resulted in a dust-up in Tipperary so pathetic it was titled: 'The Battle of Widow McCormack's Cabbage Patch.' Meagher - though he was nowhere near the fighting - and other ringleaders were rounded up and transported to Van Diemen's Land. Eventually he managed to escape to America where he became its most famous Catholic Irishman.

Whatever his revolutionary credentials had been in his youth (and they never, as far O'Rorke could figure, extended to any actual fighting) they certainly didn't extend now to anything beyond speechmaking and the contents of a whiskey bottle. He had seen Meagher in action at Bull Run - galloping all around Henry Hill like a headless chicken, waving his sword over his head, shouting platitudes, 'Advance boys and remember Fontenoy!' That sort of ould shite. It was the kind of windbaggery that had Ireland where she was. What she needed was not noise and high falutin' speeches, but clear heads and cold steel. And by Christ and his Holy Mother that was what she was going to get.

O'Rorke bit on his frustration. Love of Ireland and hatred of England was a noble thing, but mawkish sentiment was an Irish weakness, it led to the bottle and foolish romanticising.

Meagher was in full flow now - rambling on about Oisín and the Fianna - folk tales of a thousand years ago. Now that was going to win them battles in the nineteenth century, wasn't it? O'Rorke had heard a story about the Confederate general, Thomas Jackson, at Bull Run: while Meagher was galloping around like a madman fuelled by God knew how much officers' whiskey, Jackson had sat motionless as a stonewall on his horse at the opposite end of Henry Hill. When asked what he would do if his position was overrun by the Federals, he replied tersely: 'We will give them the bayonet.' Just that. And who won the day? Not the windbag, Meagher, that was for sure. Jackson was a Protestant heathen, but his fighting beliefs would do for O'Rorke.

Meagher was, thankfully, coming to an end. His speech was spiralling off into ever fancier realms and the timbre of his voice was flying towards the clouds. Always finished with a flourish, did Meagher. In case you'd forget him. Typical of his class. All wind and no substance. They played at being soldiers; even organised themselves into Fenian Circles, held weekly meetings where they served wine and had poetry readings. Like that was going to free Ireland. It seemed to O'Rorke that not only should the English be run out of Ireland at the point of a blade but the class, typified by the senior officers of the Irish Brigade to whom freeing Ireland was just another high-stakes poker game, should be sent scampering with them.

Michael O'Rorke did not play games, but he did wear a shiny clean uniform and carried a shiny clean musket which granted him permission to kill – a chance to practice for the day when those who had wronged him would be on the receiving end of his too long delayed vengeance. God help anyone, on his own side or the other, who got in his way. They would taste his cold steel.

At the thoughts of such bloodletting, he finally smiled.

CHAPTER TWO

'Five hundred dollars?' Seamus attempted to grasp the enormity of the sum, but it eluded him. He could conceive of it only by imagining how many years' rent it would pay. At least ten. Certainly enough to allow his mother live out the rest of her life in peace.

The recruiting agent smiled as he recognised his wonder. 'You get half now and the other half six weeks after you join your regiment; after that, you get your regular monthly pay. You'll never want for anything again. The army knows how to look after its own. Fix you up with a good job when you leave, then there's the pension.' The agent shook his head in disbelief at the wondrous bounty of the United States Union Army.

And Seamus was tempted. He sought to take in more of his surroundings while he considered the proposal. Maybe if he could grasp their exoticness, he could grasp the enormity of the agent's offer. He was in the grounds of Castle Gardens, in New York Harbour; the *Victoria Star* had negotiated its passage through the world's busiest shipping lanes on a tide of hope and trepidation. It had taken her three weeks to voyage to the New World. She was a steamship, far superior to the coffin ships of the Famine era, yet Seamus and his ilk were tossed hither and thither in their cramped steerage quarters until the stench of vomit and bile permeated every pore. Though it was no longer strictly forbidden for steerage passengers to go on the upper decks, it wasn't encouraged, and after one trip where his presence was greeted by cold stares and supercilious sniffs, Seamus's pride confined him to the stinky, overcrowded lower deck and quarters.

If he hadn't been treated like a beast of the fields, he would have been pleased to be on solid ground. The passengers' entry was processed in the imposing round, dark building now behind him – its size and corridors reminded Seamus of the Newcastle West Workhouse - an association that did little to boost his confidence on arrival in the New World. As he followed the line into the cavernous building, he wobbled on legs that expected the ground to shift at any minute. He was asked all kinds of questions about where he was going, how much money he had and what kind of skills he possessed. The man who'd asked sat at a long wooden desk and, though a small man himself, the tone of his interrogation left no doubt that he had the power to refuse entry to America; to command Seamus turn around and go back to where he came from. And if he hadn't insisted that he had come to fight in the Union Army, he undoubtedly would have. The Yankee nation was no longer accepting poor, dirty, malnourished Paddies.

Seemingly accepting his professed desire to fight, the small man with the big power looked him up and down before asking him to lean forward to look into his mouth and then waved him along to another queue. Here Seamus's pathetic bundle was examined with distaste. Then he'd suffered the humiliation of stripping alongside dozens of other men and washing communally in an iron trough, before being examined by a man with cold eyes and a long grey coat who lingered briefly over the mish-mash of scar tissue left by the musket ball wound in his side. Mercifully, it had dried up during the voyage and, though it still throbbed, he was not about to betray any discomfort to his examiner. At last, he was waved ahead and he could put on his filthy rags again. With clean skin and good intentions, he was allowed enter the New World, wondering anew about the arbitrary power that so many seemed to hold over him.

The recollection reminded Seamus of the vulnerability of loved ones and neighbours and that money was not the prime reason behind his coming here. An ability to pay the rent for however number of years would still see them slaves at the end of the period and just as liable to eviction at a moment's notice in the intervening years. Even if this bounty was forthcoming, which he doubted. To attain a military training and help raise an invading army to free Kilgarry and Ireland: those were his reasons for being here. If he was to have any hope of achieving these, he needed to be amongst his own. Which meant sticking with the original plan.

'I believe I will go up town to find the Irish Brigade.'

The agent smirked contemptuously. 'It's up to you. You can join up here and get good money up front and be set on a path to glory or go up there and be lucky to see money in six months, if you haven't already drunk yourself into an early grave.'

'I'm sure I'll find decent, brave Irishmen up there like can be found wherever we gather.'

The agent shrugged. 'Whatever you think, Pat. Just don't say you weren't offered a good opportunity when you arrived in America.' And he turned away with a veneer of nonchalance that failed to conceal his anger at not milking a commission out of the bog-thick Irishman.

Fighting off myriad offers of expensive lifts in carts and carriages, places to stay and recommendations for work, he eventually found the thoroughfare of Broadway and commenced walking up it. The snooty recruiting officer was soon far from Seamus's mind. Although lot of what he had experienced since leaving Kilgarry had been strange, uncomfortable, and frightening, they had at least occurred in a recognisable world. Even crossing the Atlantic in a steam ship had an air of familiarity from stories and newspaper articles he had heard and read and, once he had gotten over the seasickness and adjusted to the stink, interacting with his fellow passengers in steerage wasn't a whole lot different from trying to get along with his fellow parishioners in Kilgarry.

But Broadway was so different, so alien, from anything he had previously experienced that his walking up there could have been happening to another person in another world for all the sense he could make of it. He'd thought the port of Queenstown back in Ireland exotic and hectic after the isolated rural life he had led before then, but New York, and Broadway in particular, was beyond anything he had ever dreamt. No amount of skulking up to the landlord's big house or hanging around Newcastle West on Fair Day, or traipsing around Queenstown, came close to preparing him for the sights, sounds and smells he was now experiencing.

A whiff of horse dung wafted off the street and, being the only assault on his senses with which he could remotely identify, he sought to grasp its familiarity. But it was overwhelmed by a unique blend of cloying dampness, decay and sweat, tinged with unidentifiable alien aromas that could have originated in the mountains of the Hindu Kush for all he knew of their tangy, bitter-sweet currents. These foreign scents wove a blanket of strangeness that appeared intent on smothering his identity.

Then there was the traffic. The constant clip-clop of horses and swish-creak-clatter of carriage wheels as goods and passengers streamed up and down Broadway. More people than he ever thought existed, dressed in clothes that not even the aristocracy could afford in Ireland, walked, strolled, and ran along the sidewalks or dashed in and out between the traffic. Reverberating background chat filled his head with the buzzing of malevolent bees, punctuated regularly and sharply by criers promoting their wares.

And the buildings! Enormous behemoths of stone, brick, and glass, towering over the incessant traffic and activity below. He'd thought the facade of the Bank of Ireland in Newcastle West impressive, but it would have fitted into the foyer of most of the buildings he was now passing. The landlord's mansion would be unnoticed and unremarkable amidst the blocks of grandeur flanking Broadway. Unlike Newcastle West or Queenstown - his only previous urban experiences - there was not even the hint of a green field. Not a blade of grass. The ocean and harbour, with which he'd become passing familiar, now lay well behind him, out of sight. Seamus found himself in the midst of a structured, artificial environment, hemmed in by a heaving mass of anonymous humanity and, though moving, he'd never before felt so trapped, so overwhelmed.

For the first time in his life, he felt real fear.

It wasn't the fear he'd experienced when the Kilgarry Crew were ambushed and shot at by Paul Nolan's militia; there was certainly fear then, but, an accompanying adrenaline surge, even after he'd been shot, held real panic at bay.

He stood on the sidewalk sensing the smells, the crowds, the carriages, the enormous buildings, the unnerving hustle, and bustle, constrict into a tight ball at the back of his throat and he doubled over, gagging. Incredibly, he never felt so alone. Wounded, cold and desperate for visitors in his hilltop cave he wasn't this alone. Visions of Kathleen, his mother, Padraic and the rest of the gang, along with their dependency on his making this American mission a success blended with this thought. He said Kathleen's name aloud like a prayer for help.

Eventually, buttressed by notions of duty and responsibility, he swallowed the ball of strangeness, straightened slightly, and began to walk up Broadway once more.

He was heading for No. 596, where a recruiting station for the Irish Brigade had been set up. It was the last piece of information that Padraic had passed onto him - the last link on the chain leading from

Kilgarry to New York; it was up to him to ensure it worked in reverse by returning in triumph to his starting point.

Surely the existence of such a chain, extending from the hovels of West Limerick to the redbrick behemoths of Broadway, augured eventual success for the Irish. He walked more confidently, though at times it seemed the crowd pushing against him would wash him back down the street like a leaf in a mountain stream. But he had no further debilitating attacks and somehow he found himself before 596 – one of those huge redbrick monsters.

It was deserted. Seamus knew it before he climbed the steps and pushed at the door handle. He sighed. It made a pathetic kind of sense he supposed. The power and wealth it exuded was not for a peasant Irishman like him. His heart, which had been thumping high in his chest borne by the alien ambience, sank to familiar depths. There was no welcome in America, no flocks of rich Irishmen queuing up to help their fellow countrymen, no Fenian Army readying to free the Old Country. It was another of those Irish myths that materialise in perpetuity from the ashes of defeat and despondency. A tale told to ease the burden of broken hearts in tumbled down shacks. Except, he'd travelled three thousand miles across a fathomless ocean to unearth the truth of this one.

'Ah! Washed up from Erin's green shore with no one to greet you, I see.' A short, thin, shabby individual stood on the sidewalk looking up at him. The sleeves unravelling from the shoulders of his jacket, a bowler hat scuffed at the crown like it had spent too much of its life resting upside down on the counters of public houses. His demeanour and apparel, from his faded drainpipe trousers and splitting shoes to his lined, stretched face, portended fathomless time spent hanging around dingy bars with insufficient funds.

'Sure 'tis only open Tuesdays and Thursdays and only for half of each day at that.' Though underlain by an American twang, his accent and speech were identifiably Irish.

'I was looking for Colonel Robert Nugent or Colonel Michael Corcoran,' Seamus explained.

The man guffawed. 'Wisha good luck to you. What on earth makes you think either of those exalted gentlemen would deign to speak to a peasant with bog muck still clinging to their shoes?'

Seamus bridled, but he was too vulnerable, too defenceless, to react aggressively.

'I was told they'd look after me; help me enlist in the Irish Brigade.'

The man guffawed again. 'I'm sure you were. A lamb to the slaughter that's what you are. Look, 'tisn't rude I'm intending to be. I had plenty of bog muck on my shoes once and often regret wiping it off. It's just that Nugent and Corcoran aren't men who easily make themselves available to the likes of you. Nugent has stuck a poker up his arse in the hope that the Anglos will accept him; Corcoran is halfway decent but he's rotting away in some rebel hellhole down in Richmond. Didn't you hear about Bull Run?'

'The battle where the Irish Brigade saved the day for the Union?'

'More like, stood and let themselves be slaughtered while Anglo soldiers and gentry spectators hightailed their precious arses back to the Washington as fast as the overcrowded road would take them.' The man paused for a moment, seeking to give the impression that he was about to impart arcane knowledge. 'I've learned one great overriding lesson in my twenty-five years in this country, which I'll gladly share with you.'

Seamus allowed him his moment. 'What's that?'

'We Irish are every bit as thick, ignorant and stupid as our enemies say.'

Seamus sighed. He was more at sea on Broadway than he'd been on the *Victoria Star* and more defenceless than he'd been when he was wounded outside Nolan's house, but he was damned if he would continue to stand and allow himself or his race be denigrated so easily and so soon upon his arrival in the New World. 'Don't worry I'll find someone else to help me,' he said and began to descend the steps.

'Now look, there's no need to be going off in a dander and you only in the country a few hours at most. I can take you to meet people who'll ensure you'll get fixed up with the Irish Brigade. By this time tomorrow you'll be representing the green Old Country in New World blue. How about it? Sure, what do I care if you insist on finding out for yourself the truth of what I've learnt?'

Seamus stood at the foot of the steps and stared at the heaving mass of alien bodies rushing in all directions and knew he had no choice but to go with his fellow Irishman. 'Alright, take me to people who can help.'

The man brightened at the opportunity. 'Follow me, lad, 'tis Moroney's Tavern ye want. That's another thing about this country – pubs and shebeens are called 'saloons' or 'taverns.' But sure, Thomas Francis Meagher himself- the exalted hero of forty-eight and the Commander of the Irish Brigade, in Corcoran's absence - is known to have a tipple there. And if he isn't in today there will be plenty of others willing to help. Dunne is my name, Thomas, but you can call me 'Tommy' to distinguish me from the great man himself.'

Dunne led him off Broadway into its insane twin, kept hidden from the sight of decent people. They were in a maze of narrow, dingy side streets where crowds seemed to squeeze out of the pores of the smoke-blackened, filthy bricks. People in rags, even more tattered than his own, leant over balconies, crowded in doorways, gathered around waterless fountains, and hindered the entrances to alleyways. Children played in sewage running in rivulets along the gutter while men and women in various stages of inebriation staggered and tripped along the same courses. A pig, chased by some ragged children with sticks, skittered and squealed before turning up a dark alleyway in the hope of sanctuary.

And there were voices here also. Women calling, men swearing, children laughing, crying. Every so often the cacophony would be broken by something more melodious: the songs of emigrants' laments or someone sitting in a broken chair with a torn vest blowing off-key into a mouth organ. An impoverished multitude that should be tilling land, milking cows, or harvesting spuds crowded into unnatural, man-made hellholes. The rural detritus of Ireland's misfortune washed up in urban America.

As they walked, 'Tommy' Dunne, his guide and mentor, talked incessantly about himself. How his family from Galway were all wiped out in the Famine; how he made his way to New York, by working his way down through the farmland that lay between his port of arrival, Montreal, and there.

'Now I'm the gentleman you see before you.' He flicked his arms out to his side in a theatrical flourish. He turned to Seamus. 'So you see, young lad, all it takes is hard work and connections. And Tommy Dunne is your man for both.' He tapped himself on the nose.

Seamus looked at this gone-to-seed chancer and prayed that he wouldn't turn into someone even remotely like him. He'd be better off back in Nolan's Kilgarry – at least he'd have family and friends there to share his hardships.

The streets they passed through became even narrower, dirtier, and more chaotic. Now Seamus's alienation was multiplied by another factor - black people were everywhere. He didn't want to stare, after all they were God's creatures too. But, before coming to America the only black face he'd seen was in a sketched picture from a faded *Limerick Chronicle* thrown on the floor of the Widow Morrison's shebeen. The sketch was of a sailor from a ship that put into the Shannon Estuary for urgent storm repairs. There had been a few black faces fetching and carrying luggage down at Castle Gardens and he'd seen one shining shoes on Broadway. But here black people were everywhere. They lived in appalling filth and squalor and were even more crowded together than the Irish. There was still a scattering of white men and women, who mixed with the black people. Seamus saw several mixed-race children staring at him and Dunne sullenly as they passed by.

They came to a bustling intersection. Dunne gave one of his flamboyant waves to indicate the area: 'The illustrious Five Points – the only place in our glorious continent where the races mix freely and procreate. And a great advertisement for why they should be kept apart. The worst of Irish and Black, ignored by the outside world, coming together. Apologies for bringing you this way, but it's the shortest route to Moroney's. And you might as well see the worst of your new country; indeed, see the very people whose rights this ridiculous war is being fought over. Inspiring, eh?'

Inspiring, it wasn't. Yet, it was closer to his experience. He could identify with the neglect and lack of hope, the dirt, the poverty, and the associated smells, which was eerily comforting after the alien assaults perpetrated by Broadway. Still, it was far from Kilgarry's green acres and he was glad when Dunne announced they'd arrived at Moroney's. Men in tired clothing lounged against the outside of the tavern – a long barn-like structure, completely unlike the shebeens at home. The light died at the opening to be replaced by a darkness deeper than that inside the cave on Knockdrisna. Somehow, despite the sounds of human chatter coming from inside, the tavern was less inviting than the hillside cave.

Dunne hailed the men around the door. 'Boys! A great big Irish welcome to this poor soul, fresh from the salty brine. Sure the mud of the Ould Dart is still on his boots and he's lost in this great metropolis. But he's fallen amongst friends, right boys?'

The tallest, best dressed member of the group, wearing a red cravat above a blue striped shirt and shiny green waistcoat, took a few steps beyond the others and approached Dunne and Seamus. At first glance he seemed grim and calculating. A scar, faded but lengthy, ran from the side of his left eye down by his mouth was attenuated by laughter lines pushing out from his eyes and mouth as he smiled at Seamus.

'Don't tell say me Dunne has been your American guide? I suppose he has been spinning yarns about how he came over in a coffin ship and worked his way down from Canada. All lies. Born over on the east side, he was.'

Dunne spluttered with indignation, but the tall man ignored him and came nearer Seamus. 'Donal O'Hagan is my name, just off the boat, heh?'

Seamus took his hand, it felt soft, damp, like it had not done much work. He wondered how O'Hagan and his cronies made a living, it had to be at something for they seemed more confident and prosperous than anyone he'd seen since walking off Broadway. 'I've come over to join the Irish Brigade,' he said.

'The Irish Brigade?' O'Hagan smirked. 'Sure what would you be bothering with those eejits for?'

Seamus started to explain his intention to gain martial experience and return to Kilgarry with an Irish American army, but a glance at the quizzical, hard faces before him brought a realisation that he would be mocked for such romanticism, so he toned down his intentions. 'I came over to fight and my passage was paid for by people who expect me to fight.'

O'Hagan smirked again. Seamus was no longer sure that the big man's demeanour was pleasant and thought it likely his first impression was the truer one. The crinkled lines running from his eyes and mouth could betoken cruelty, not amusement. His friends shared similar demeanours, making Seamus feel anxious.

O'Hagan shrugged. 'Sure, who am I to stop you? They're a pack of fools going off with their uniforms and their guns to fight for those who want to free the black slaves. The real battleground is here.' The big man swept his arm wide to indicate the surrounding streets.

Seamus was tired, weak, hungry and his side throbbed. A debate on New York society was beyond his ability. 'Tommy was saying Thomas Frances Meagher or Robert Nugent might be in that bar – I mean, saloon.'

'Flaherty, did you see either of those exalted gentlemen enter these premises today?' O'Hagan addressed a curly red-haired man, sporting freckles and muscles that seemed ready to pop out of his chequered black and white shirt.

The downward twist of Flaherty's smirk was more overtly contemptuous than O'Hagan's. 'Wherever there's a counter doling out liquor Meagher won't be far behind it. If we go down the alleyway here and in the side entrance we will avoid most of those lumbering dock workers who've finished their shift and are now slaking their thirst. We'll come right on Meagher this way.'

Without waiting to see if Seamus, or anyone, was following, Flaherty turned and began to walk up the side alley where the sunlight quickly died a death as final as at the front door of the saloon. O'Hagan followed him, leaving Seamus to wonder who the real ringleader was, if indeed there was what could be termed a ringleader here. Rubbing his hands, Dunne also followed. 'Come on, entrance to the Irish Brigade beckons and a place in the hallowed halls of Irish rebel immortality awaits you.'

Though not taken in by such hyperbole, as Seamus watched the others with their resigned smiles and clothes that would not have been out of place in the Widow Morrison's shebeen, he felt a relaxation; he was amongst his own, he had travelled a vast distance to escape a tyranny and to seek its eradication. There were many times when it seemed he wouldn't make it, but now here he was in the great city of New York, being looked after by his own. Fellow Irishmen. Even if they were cynical about his mission, sure what Irishman hadn't the romanticism starved and beaten out of him? So, he merged with the group and entered the darkness.

He never knew if it was a kick or a blow which felled him first; just that a force from behind bent his knees to bend and sent his face hurtling towards the dust and stones of the alleyway. Instantaneously he cursed himself for allowing his guard to drop. After all, he knew that being amongst one's own was no guarantee of security. Else, why would he have had to come out here in the first place?

But then the ground hit and thought, rational or otherwise, disintegrated into fragmented recollections.

Dunne's obsequious whine. 'I want my share. I found him. I brought him to you.'

'Shut up, Dunne, you *amadán* you. I'll be the judge of who gets what. Now stand back before I stick ya. You too, Cassidy.' That was O'Hagan.

A boot in the ribs. 'Just off the boat? I fucking hate fresh fish.' Sounded like Flaherty. Agony. His wound. Must be open again.

'Please boys, I'm one of you. Don't…'

O'Hagan's harsh laugh. 'Course you're one of us. Next week you can have first go at the latest arrivals yourself. Despite your whining, I think there's a man in there somewhere. Probably more of one than is in the whisky sodden pricks helping me now.' As if testing his hypothesis, O'Hagan booted him again. Seamus felt hands like sharpened sticks scrabbling at him, scraping, and ripping him open.

'A few dollars is all.'

'Hardly worth the bother. Still, all grist to the mill.'

'Give it here,' said O'Hagan, 'sure, it will be a good lesson to him and not a very expensive one at that.'

The man had some concern for his fellow Irishman after all. To drive the lesson home he put the boot in again. Seamus sensed the familiar inky blackness of unconsciousness cloud in. 'Let me gut him.' Flaherty. O'Hagan might be overruling him.

Seamus welcomed the security of the encroaching blackness, but his final waking thought bore unsettling clarity.

Too many people to be responsible for…Too many…

CHAPTER THREE

Pain filled his awareness. He heard himself groan. No friendly faces welcomed him back to consciousness.

'Easy, champ. I've enough to do without having any more mess to clear up. There's a bucket next to the bed if you're going to puke. And if you were drinking in Moroney's, like I think you were, my advice would be to get that poison out of your system before it kills you.'

Seamus tried to focus on where the voice emanated. Yet another Irish one. But such familiarity no longer gave him hope of succour. He slipped a hand into his pocket. No money. 'I wasn't drinking; I've been robbed and beaten. A fellow called O'Hagan…'

'You were lucky – not everyone who falls into the clutches of the O'Hagan gang live to tell the tale. They must have liked you.'

He wasn't sure it was worth trying to make sense of what the voice was saying.

'How much did they get?' it asked.

'Ten pounds worth of dollars.'

A silence that might have been thoughtful.

'To be sure, not much to the O'Hagans, but surely all you had on you. They'd have found more if you had it – not that I can see where you could have hidden it in those rags. They probably let you live because they want you to join up with them.'

The world slid into a blurred focus. He realised he was in a cell. About eight feet by ten. His jailer, owner of the voice, sat with his chair tilted back, legs crossed and resting on a cluttered desk a safe distance outside. He wore a navy-blue jacket with a red trim. Seamus fixated on him, desperate to comprehend this new situation and to ignore his pounding head and muscles.

'You see that's how it works with the O'Hagans and their cronies when innocent Irish emigrants fall into their clutches,' the jailer continued. 'First they befriend them, either on the street or in some watering hole, normally Moroney's, then they rob them blind. Even the poorest emigrant will have a bit of money scraped together from families, friends, or philanthropic landlords, to get set up in the New World. If you're weak, vulnerable, too young, or too old, they'll likely cut your throat and throw you in the East River. Eventually, you might wash up on the Jersey shore, bloated and stinking, but by then nobody will recognise you and anyway it's usually more trouble than it's worth to report finding a body. You get thrown back – food for Yankee fishes. However, if they take a liking to you or think they can make use of you, they just give you the beating and steal from you. Then they get you to work for them; by then, you have no other choice.'

'Any family out here?'

'No.'

'Friends?'

'No.'

'Where were you intending to get to?'

'I want to join the Irish Brigade.'

Seamus expected the usual guffaw, but, to his surprise, the jailer said: 'That might be the best way out of the mess you're in; you're likely to end up buried in a pauper's grave out in Potter's Field if you stay, whereas with Meagher and his boys you have a shot at a more edifying burial. Take it, I say.'

'When can I get out of here?'

'Whenever you want. The cell isn't locked. A couple of Dublin men came across you in a bad state, brought you in here for your own safety. 'Twas quiet last night.'

'Irishmen helping Irishmen? That seems a rare commodity in this place.'

The jailer shrugged again. 'We're a dehumanised race. Forced off our land, washed up on this concrete jungle; disdained for who we are;

competing with the black men and women for the scraps civilisation deigns to toss at us. Sure, 'tis no wonder we're the way we are. I'm not excusing the likes of the O'Hagans. But there are bad apples in every race. Five Points, where you were last night, is a fertile orchard of bad Irish apples. Go join the Irish Brigade, you'll likely find some better ones there.'

Seamus felt pain in every joint, but didn't think anything was broken and, most importantly, by some miracle, the wound in his side hadn't reopened after all. He levered himself off the hard bunk, a bolt of pain sharp as a shard of glass cut through his head, blinding him for a moment. He staggered and grabbed the cell bars.

'You can drink the water from that tap,' the jailer indicated a metal sink on the wall near the main exit.

Seamus made his way slowly to it. The water was tepid, but he felt more refreshed - his aches were no easier but his vision was clearer after he'd splashed his face and swallowed a couple of mouthfuls. He feared his pains would be worse later, when the numbing effect of the alcohol had dissipated from his system. He turned and thanked the loquacious jailer before he left. The man didn't stir. He appeared to be waiting for the drunk in the next cell to wake so that he could begin philosophising with him also.

As Seamus left, the jailer cast out a final piece of advice. 'You want to go east, towards the river; Pier Nine, you can catch a ferry out to Fort Schuyler from there. West takes you back into the hellhole you were dragged out of last night.'

Though it was not more than three miles from where he set out, it took him hours to get anywhere near Pier 9 on the East River. He gave up asking for directions; when he did ask most people just brushed past him anyway, but even when he received information, his lack of an urban sense of direction meant he was lost worse than ever minutes later.

By the time he finally approached the pier his headache was rampant. He couldn't recall the last time he'd eaten; there was nothing but tepid water in his system. The walking; the lack of food; the beating; the night in jail; the overpowering sense of disappointment; hopelessness even, weighed heavily on him. He was still two blocks from the pier when he started to stumble. He had invested so much hope in America - the New World - only to find it a larger more debilitating version of the tyranny, corruption, and poverty back in Kilgarry.

It was too much to bear.

'Whoa! Steady white man. This ain't a neighbourhood to go staggering and falling in. If a man goes down here, especially a white-ass, he's likely to get the very eyeballs stripped out of his head.'

Seamus understood that two dark skinned men – one much older, the other quite baby-faced - had come up close to him. He'd never even seen a person with such skin in the flesh before yesterday, now he was about to be touched by one and he hoped, he truly hoped, the black man was reaching toward him out of kindness. He figured he couldn't live through much more of the urban hardship he'd discovered so far.

'You look all used up,' the older man said. 'Are you going somewhere in particular?' The man's breath smelled alien and exotic, hinting at lands and cultures Seamus could only dream about. Yet, he sounded *American*.

It was strange how he could think complex thoughts about this man's skin and nationality yet feel exhaustion and hunger to the point of being inarticulate. 'Irish Brigade, Pier Nine.' He mumbled.

The older man caught him under the arms as he sagged. His hands felt strong and hard.

'Don't know it. Is it a saloon - *The Irish Brigade*?'

'Army. Union Army. Irishmen.' Seamus managed to get out.

The man laughed. 'Irishmen in the Army? Heard they was a bunch of them went down to Virginny alright but didn't believe it. Why, what would Irishmen be doin' fightin' in a richman's war? Goin' to free us littlely, wittley old blacks, are you?' He cackled. 'Nope, I didn't think so. Must be plain stupid is all.'

Was he ever going to find someone in this godforsaken place who would just *help* him? 'Please…' he begged.

'No skin off my nose if you want to progress from staggering around the streets of New York to getting your stupid white head shot off. Giss a hand, Joshua.' Though he could still hear everything that was being said, Seamus was beyond helping himself.

The two carried him down the street, he hoped towards Pier 9. He smelt salty water and heard gulls crying; the hustle and bustle of riverside activity was all around. People, lots of people, pushed past in both directions. Seamus felt the activity and riverside air revive him. He began to straighten.

'Ye bastards! Let that white man go!' The shout was harsh, the hatred explicit, the accent Irish.

'It's alright. They're helping me.' Seamus tried to say, but the words wouldn't come out. He mumbled incoherently.

'Jus' tryin' to help the man out,' the older man said.

'There ain't no such thing as blacks helping out whites, unless it's helping him out of a job you are. Now get your filthy hands off him. If he needs looking after we'll look after him.'

'Suit yourself. Wants to go and get his foolish ass shot off in the war anyways. Don't want anything' to do with such stupidity. Hey buddy, don't push me.' Seamus's saviour's voice suddenly took on a hard edge.

'You going to stop me?' There was ominous mumbling from others gathering around. Seamus tried desperately to pull himself together. The two black men had let him go and he was standing wobbly on his own, but none of the white people moved to help. They were more intent on causing trouble for the black men than in helping him.

'Now look, I don't want no trouble,' the older man was saying, 'just tryin' to help the man to his destination - to his own kind. Looks like we succeeded. Now we'll be on our way again.'

'Coming down to the harbour to see what jobs you could filch; whose mouth you can take the bread from, more loike.' This was the first voice again, the one that had spoken so bitterly, the fellow who seemed to be the ringleader of the whites. It sounded familiar. Seamus forced himself to look up. Flaherty. O'Hagan's right-hand man. His freckles and red hair should have belonged to a jolly Irish farmer, but a leer of hatred and suspicion hardened his eyes, twisting Flaherty's mouth and lower jaw into an ugly rictus, leaving no doubt about his true personality.

Seamus staggered as he continued trying to focus, then, at last, he found a voice strong enough to project. 'It's true: he was only trying to help. I...I haven't had much sleep or anything to eat and...'

Flaherty continued to stare at the men but pointed a finger back at Seamus. 'Shut it!' he commanded; the harshness in his voice grated Seamus's skin. 'We need to teach them to know their place. And it sure as hell isn't here.' A chorus of approval for what he was saying wafted from the crowd. Flaherty didn't look at Seamus. If he realised this white man was the emigrant he helped to beat and rob the previous day - he didn't care.

There was a moment of silence when everyone seemed to draw in their breath; eyes flickered, but nothing else moved. 'Grab em!' Flaherty shouted. Though he didn't move himself, his supporters responded instantly. The black men didn't stir. If they felt fear they weren't going to show it by running. The older one lashed out at the foremost white man and sent him sprawling back onto his companions, tangling a bunch of them up in each other. Then the man caught another Irishman with a sidearm swipe to the jaw, bringing him up short. The young one, presumably the son, no more than fourteen or fifteen, kicked and scratched like a wildcat. For a few moments, Seamus dared hope they were going to hold their own. But the odds were impossible, and they were soon overwhelmed.

'Bring 'em here!' Flaherty commanded above the furor - Irish accent prominent. Though only a sidekick of O'Hagan's, it was clear he carried a lot of authority with the mob – there were twenty to thirty altogether, mainly men, a good few women; half a dozen children – without having to lift a finger, he got them to do what he wanted.

They swarmed around Seamus as they dragged his despairing escorts towards the docks.

His presence forgotten along with the fact, if it was ever remotely recognised by the mob, that the two captives had been assisting him. Feelings of helplessness and cowardice changed to horror as he realised what was about to happen. Flaherty stood under the beam of a steel hoist, pointing up to where a transept jutted out a couple of feet. A length of rigging rope was flung around that part of the beam; a looped knot secured it in seconds. They were going to hang them.

The captives were raised aloft by the crowd and passed lengthways towards the hoist. The younger one kicked and scrabbled furiously, resisting his captors. The older one was strangely muted; seemingly determined to portray the same defiance-through-dignity that he'd shown when first challenged.

They'd gotten the young one to the noose and were trying to

force his head in. His eyes were popping with fear and he screamed in a high voice. He peed on the two men holding him up to the noose and the others laughed uproariously.

Seamus summoned his voice and called out for them to stop. But they took no notice. He tried to push through the crowd to get in near the front and stop what was happening. A woman spat at him and a burly bloke shoved him roughly.

'Maybe we should hang you too seeing as you love them so much,' he said.

'Better get out of here, buddy - no traitors welcome.'

'Time the blacks were taught a lesson,' a woman screeched, 'taking the bread out of our babbies mouths, they are. Getting so a white man cannot get an honest day's work for an honest day's pay because the blacks are taking all the jobs, working for almost nothing.'

'String those defending 'um up as well,' the burly bloke said. 'Where are you from? Just off the boat are you? Coming to take our jobs as well?' he asked Seamus. 'I didn't survive the Famine and the coffin-ship to starve in America because of some so-called Irishman who swanned over in a posh steamship.'

A murmur rose. The mainly Irish mob were in agreement; Seamus felt the anger and hatred boiling in them as they moved closer;

desperate to lash out at whatever was keeping them poor and downtrodden in America - the New World of which they had had so much hope.

A sigh of satisfaction rose from the front of the mob - they'd succeeded in getting the noose around the head of the young boy. He swung from side to side, kicking furiously as he dangled from the end of the hoist. The older man's head was shoved towards a second noose. Seamus never forgave himself for hoping that the mob's thirst for vengeance would be sated by the hanging and that they would consequently forget about him. He was thinking of slinking away and going back down to Castle Gardens to sign on with the snooty Anglo he'd scorned yesterday. It would be humiliating, but at least he'd get paid and he'd still acquire martial skills. He had to get away from here. There was nothing he could do to help his saviours.

The air rattled overhead. Musket fire. The mob froze, some of the women screamed, everyone turned towards the direction from which the balls had come. Streams of smoke pointed the way. Four soldiers in dark blue uniform stood further down the docks. Two were hastily, but methodically, reloading and two stood with muskets pointing at the crowd, one distinctly aimed at the red-haired ringleader.

'Cut him down!' this soldier ordered. 'Now!' No one moved. He pulled back the hammer on the musket and levelled it at Flaherty's head. The boy had been hanging at least a minute, though his legs still kicked – weakly.

Flaherty stared unblinkingly at the musket for a few seconds. Then he nodded to one of the men standing beneath the boy, who then produced an industrial knife from his belt and slashed at the rope suspending the young lad.

'You're not the law around here,' the redhead snarled at the soldiers.

'While we have these muskets, we are.' The soldier responded.

'Shoot yere own, would ye?' A woman called out. 'Bloody traitors!'

'Just doing what we think is right, Ma'am,' the soldier replied.

'Fighting for slaves rights, while they're taking the bread out of the mouths of yere own, who have no rights. Is that what ye think is right?'

'We've just came down to stock up on some flour and corn for the regiment above in Fort Schuyler, don't like to see anyone get hurt needlessly is all. Now everyone back away and let them go.' He gestured towards the makeshift gallows with the barrel of his musket. The older one cradled the younger one in his arms. It was impossible to tell if the youngster was dead or alive.

Some people around the edges began slinking away. But a large body of men and women stood around and glowered sullenly at the soldiers. 'Four of you and at least forty of us,' Flaherty said, 'I think you are outnumbered. Now if we were to rush you, you'd be very lucky to get four of us - that leaves more than five times your number to tear you apart.'

The soldier who had his musket pointed at the redhead was doing all the talking for his side, he was at least six foot with a droopy moustache, grizzled skin, and grey eyes as hard as flint. He exuded authority and calmness. The stripes on his shoulder indicated he was a sergeant. 'You won't do that,' he said.

'Why won't we?' Flaherty asked.

'Because we'll put our musket balls to good use. One for you and one each for your lynching buddies alongside you. None of you will live to see us torn apart and you haven't the guts for that.' The sergeant made a show of steadying his aim.

Amidst the tense silence, a gull cried on the river. Seamus sensed the crowd's hatred, but the soldier was right: the ringleaders hadn't the guts to order a charge. The older black man began to push his way out through the crowd, who gave way sullenly. His son hung limply in his arms.

'What's going on here, Corporal?' A troop of police had materialised from the streets above. And when Seamus turned to look properly, he realised yet another crowd had gathered, spilling out of the alleyways leading to the Pier. A mob of black men and women, intent on rescue and revenge.

'This scum tried to have themselves a little necktie party and we thought to gatecrash. By the way it's 'Sergeant' not 'Corporal.'

'Well, it's alright now, Sergeant, we'll take over,' the policeman said.

The soldier shrugged. 'As you wish, but I suggest you should let us keep the muskets on them until they disperse.'

'Sergeant, we're the law, we'll deal with this, go back to your barracks, or your boat, or wherever you've come from.'

The sergeant shrugged. 'Fair enough! Let's go men.' The soldiers lowered their muskets and wheeled away. Seamus was astonished to see the policeman walk up to Flaherty and cuff him viciously with his truncheon. 'Flaherty shouldn't you be at home keeping your wife off the bottle and your snotty brats off the streets?' he enquired as he did it.

The Irish mob rushed the Irish police, the black crowd poured down from the streets above and rushed both of them. He watched the man who'd helped him get swallowed up by the swarming crowd, his son still prone in his arms.

Seamus gaped in astonishment at the chaos of the New World, before realising he was cut off from the soldiers, whose sergeant had said they were from the Irish Brigade. They were marching away on the opposite side of the riot and he was losing his chance. Though weak, hungry, and emotionally drained, the utter frustration of the last twenty-four hours, along with all that had gone before, found its expression in superhuman strength. He lashed his way across the surging mobs: Irish rioters, Irish police, black rioters - anyone who stood in his path - felt the force of his pent up emotions. He kicked, punched and forearm-smashed until, finally, he broke through: breathless, weak, but determined.

He ran after the soldiers, who had turned their backs on the melee behind them and were walking down a gangway to where some boats were moored, out of sight of the chaos; though there was no getting away from the shouting, cursing, and screeching.

'Take me with you,' Seamus shouted, his voice restored by the shock of discovering he was close to missing out on his reason for being there. 'I want to join the Irish Brigade.'

The soldiers turned. One of them sneered at him. 'We have no need of the likes of you - go back to whatever shithole you crawled out of.'

'Please,' Seamus gasped, 'I've come from Ireland. The Fenians sent me. I want to learn how to fight like a soldier.' He directed his plea to the Sergeant. 'Please!' he said again.

The man stroked his moustache while he considered Seamus, who knew what he looked like: dirty, bloody, dressed in rags - the dregs of society. However bad he looked when he left Ireland, he looked a hundred times worse now.

The Sergeant's voice was gruff, but his words were kind. 'Son, you seem pretty desperate. If we leave you here, you're bound to end up fighting and dying in the streets like that lot over there - you may as well come and die like a man. You look rough, but there are vacancies in the 88th and I know the Captain of L Company, is very anxious to fill his. And at the end of the day you look no worse than Twoomey here when he first showed up. Come on. But let me down, and I'll shoot you myself.'

With his relief at being accepted and at hearing his first genuinely kind words from a fellow countryman since he left Kilgarry, Seamus's short-lived strength evaporated, and he pitched forward in a dead faint into the arms of the soldier who'd sneered at him. The man looked down with disgust, then looked up at his Sergeant who, after a moment's hesitation, nodded towards the boat. The soldier dragged the unconscious Seamus down the gangway.

And so, the infamous Captain Rock of Kilgarry joined the Irish Brigade of the Union Army of America.

CHAPTER FOUR
DEC. 1861

There was a raucous mood around the campfire. There usually was when Corporal Jer Horan was off-duty and holding forth.

'Go on Jer! Do it again. Encore!' The men cried.

'Ah! Ah! You know the drill, boys. At least you should know *this* drill.'

'Oh for God's sake, Horan, you're robbing us blind.'

'Well, I'm happy to sit here just sipping my whiskey.'

'Is that what you call this gnat's piss? I guess I may as well spend my money on watching you turning your rubber puss inside out. God knows 'tis an improvement on how you usually look.' Company L's other corporal, Sean Cregan from Brooklyn, whose ginger hair, and beard betrayed his ancestry, grumbled jocosely as he tossed a dime into the tin cup.

More dimes rattled; Horan weighed the mug in his fist and seemed happy.

'Do the one about the Whirlygig!' someone shouted.

'Well now that was back in South Tipperary; it's a great country around there, but folks are a bit quare.' Horan launched into his tale by making his polished Tipp accent thick and peasant-like, dropping aitches and doubling his a's. Seamus had heard the story several times over the past few weeks but had yet to tire of it; the inflections and gestures the Tipp man added as he went along cracked him up. But it was the denouement that made it so popular with everyone and why he'd collected upwards of ten dollars to tell this story yet again.

'...Mary, I'll skin you alive, the ould farmer said, I know 'twasn't me because I haven't been up to much ever since I got that kick from the cow out in the far field thirty year ago this Spring. So who slipped you that parcel you're carrying there, you rip, you? If it was that bastard, Murphy, I'll swing for both of ye before I put a drop of milk or a crumb of bread in the little bastard's mouth. There's many a man rocking another man's child, they say, but I'm telling you now I won't allow the little git under my roof for two seconds. I'll swing for ye, Mary, I will.' To portray the appearance of an elderly Irish peasant farmer Horan bent over as if he had a crooked back and pushed his tongue against the side of his cheek to make his voice sound even more delinquent. To complete the appearance, he twisted his army forage cap around to the side of his head.

Acted out on stage in New York, London, or Dublin by an Anglo the men would have found it racist and insulting. But here, under the stars of a Virginia sky, performed by one of their own, they laughed uproariously. It was a constant source of amusement to the company that Horan, a tall, well-built, handsome man with dark hair, verdant eyes, and a well-proportioned nose, could transform himself into all kinds of country bumpkins, male or female, in the blink of an eye.

Quick as lightning he discarded the cap and stuck a cushion under his shirt.

'Paddy, Paddy,' (in a high squeaky voice) 'will ye calm down, will ye? Sure I was nowhere near Willie Murphy. I'm telling you, 'twas a Whirlygig. A Whirlygig came to me in the middle of night and he was very rough with me. He had his way with me, Paddy.

'Hmmph. What did it look like so? This Whirlygig?'

'Sure, he looked like this, Paddy.' Horan twisted his ears inwards and, by some miracle of tissue and gristle, they remained scrunched. Then he pinched his nostrils and by the same miracle they stayed pinched. Simultaneously, he managed to widen his eyes like saucers. It was one of the best tricks Seamus had ever seen and the ugliest, most deformed face. He joined in the gales of bent-over laughter.

'Jaysus, Mary, I'll kill you - he has the exact head of that bastard Murphy...' Horan finished.

Seamus O'Farrell, now, Private James Farrell, Company L, 88th New York, lay back with his head on his haversack, and thanked the same stars that glittered over Kilgarry as Virginia that he'd found a place to belong in the New World. Now that Horan had finished his piece, Pat Gorman commenced a wistful air on his harmonica – *Tenting in the Old Campground* - and a bivouac that was noisy and boisterous became hushed and pensive. Thoughts of home and loved ones to the fore.

Seamus was as preoccupied as the others. His mind muddled over the new life he was beginning to forge for himself in the army, being surrounded by so many people with similar thoughts, and the physical distance between Virginia and Kilgarry – the images of Kathleen, his mother, and the others in Kilgarry were not as stark as before. Finally having some time to think, his thoughts wandered back to that cabin in Cork and the mess he had left behind there. He tried to take solace in the truth that O'Leary was a horrible husband – that his wife was likely free of his drunken, abusive tirades - but there was no easing of the guilt he felt in his role in the man's death. This worsened with the knowledge of his own betrayal of Kathleen in that moment of weakness. He wondered if her image of him had faded too before reminding himself that he was in a place now among good men – far from the discomfort of recovering in that Knockdrisna cave, the home of Dan O'Leary, or the street war between the Irish and the black population of Five Points. His feelings of love and concern for Ireland weren't any less, but those images had become suffused with a soft background light induced by distance and improved circumstances.

The attainment of these improvements had been touch and go, even after Sergeant Coughlan had accepted him on the pier.

He came around on the boat back to Fort Schuyler; lying on a hard flat bunk, similar to the one he'd had on his voyage from Ireland. He attempted to sit up but bashed his forehead off the underside of a bunk overhead and nearly passed out again. He lay there for a few seconds, attempting to orientate his thoughts. A raging thirst motivated him to move. He raised himself carefully from the bed and, unhooking a lantern from a nail protruding from the side of the steps, climbed the iron ladder to the deck. The Sergeant stood there talking to the soldier who'd wanted to leave him behind. The third soldier steered.

'Well, if it isn't the bold Rebel,' the Sergeant said when he saw Seamus coming towards them.

'Do you have water?' Seamus croaked. 'I'm gasping.'

'Whiskey does that to you,' said the soldier called Twoomey, scorn evident in his voice.

'There's some down below,' the Sergeant responded, ignoring the other's scorn. 'You'll find a pail of nearly fresh water in the kitchen for boiling coffee. Help yourself and while you're at it - stick your head in, we'll be at the fort shortly and you look like a vagrant.'

Touched by the man's brusque kindness, he went to slake his thirst and wash his face.

He didn't know why the Sergeant took to him - the man didn't even belong to Company L, nor was he a Fenian. But from the time they docked at the pier below Fort Schuyler to the time he was mustered in as a private in the 88th, the officer looked after him and eased his way over a lot of difficulties.

He had been born Fintan O'Reilly but he was now George Coughlan, a fact he admitted immediately on hearing Seamus's name. 'Be proud of who you are and where you came from, but don't give the bastards an opportunity to put you down before they even speak to you just because they see your name on a scrap of paper. Take my advice and become James Farelly or some such; you'll do a lot better in this country with a name like that. It's not as bog Irish as 'O'Farrell.' Don't be ashamed to change - what's a name but a moniker to suit our parents' whims? It's the man inside that matters – give him a chance to show himself and don't leave him imprisoned by chains that shackled him in the womb.'

And so he decided to muster in as 'James Farrell,' - he couldn't bear to change his name any more than this. He was to lead a new life now, at least until he'd gained sufficient wherewithal to return to Ireland and redeem his old one. A new name seemed appropriate in the short term and a small price to pay when he considered the redemption prize.

He still wasn't wanted in the Irish Brigade.

The Adjutant for the 88th made that plain when Sergeant 'Coughlan' brought Seamus to him. 'Begging your pardon, Sergeant, but General Meagher has made it plain that he only wants strong, healthy, *clean* individuals in the Brigade and Colonel Kelly has reiterated this for the 88th in no uncertain terms.'

The sneer that this five-foot nothing adjutant put in his voice when he said 'clean' hurt Seamus as deeply as any militiaman's gunshot or O'Hagan kick.

'I'm as strong and healthy as any individual forced to leave his native country due to English deprivation and, given the opportunity, I can be clean as well. You will appreciate that not having a place to stay or not knowing anyone in America, I was hoping to get a uniform and a good wash when I joined the Irish Brigade.'

The short official snorted. 'Joining the Brigade for a clean set of clothes and a wash, eh? What do you think we are running here - a doss house?'

Seamus bit his lip, before speaking. 'I can assure you I didn't cross the Atlantic for a clean set of clothes and a wash. I came here to fight. With the Irish Brigade. And when I've given my all to their American cause, I intend to re-cross the Atlantic and fight for my native Ireland.'

The small man openly laughed. 'Jaysus! Them's big ideas for a bloke who hasn't an arse to his pants. Look, there's some nuns downtown, just off 23rd, they do a bit of charity for people like you. They're who you want. Not the Irish Brigade.'

'Mr Dixon! Is Captain McMahon back from leave yet?' Sergeant O'Reilly, now Coughlan, cut in.

'No, Sergeant! He's seeing his family up in Albany and is not due back until the end of the week.'

'Goddammit! Are you going to muster this man in or not?'

'No, Sarge.'

'I am a First-Sergeant and you are a non-commissioned Adjutant, I think that gives me rank,' Coughlan said.

'I'm sorry but I can only take mustering-in orders from Colonel Kelly or Captain McMahon. I cannot muster in a man,' he looked disparagingly at Seamus, 'without at least one of their say-sos. They were both very explicit about that, Sarge.'

The Sergeant sighed. The Adjutant was an officious snob, but technically he was correct and there was nothing that could be done about it, though the 88th were more than a hundred men short of the quota.

'Right, Farrell, come with me! You can be a guest in my Company until the Captain returns and I'll speak to him about you officially filling one of the vacancies in the 88th.' With a look of thunder at the Adjutant, he turned and stormed away. Seamus followed sheepishly behind.

Even in his own regiment, Coughlan, had to pull rank to get anyone to take responsibility for his new recruit. Eventually, after some shouting and disparate abuse, he got Seamus a bunk, and detailed a short muscular looking private from Galway - John Shinnors - to take him to the Quartermaster's stores and the bathhouse.

'Just over from the ould Dart are you?' Shinnors asked on the way.

'Only landed yesterday. Though it is many weeks since I left my home in West Limerick.' Seamus replied.

'Things are still rough back there, I guess.'

'They'll always be rough while we have no rights over our own bit of land.'

Shinnors nodded. "'Tis true for you. I loved the bit of land myself, but I was starved out of it. I made my way over here to an uncle in Brooklyn who apprenticed me to his carpentry trade. A fine trade it is too, making furniture for the big nobs out in Brooklyn, and it appears that I've a knack for it. Been able to send decent sums of money home to keep them from being thrown out on the road.'

'So, why did you give up carpentry for the Army?' Seamus asked the friendly Galway man.

'I haven't given it up. Just put it on hold for a while. One good turn deserves another my father used to say, or did, until he died of the hunger and a broken heart. He'd buried my mother and six of my siblings by then. Two older brothers and a sister are killing themselves to hold onto the place, but it's only the few dollars I'm sending home that's keeping the roof - a leaky one - over their heads.'

'You wouldn't want to take a bullet then.'

Shinnors laughed. 'No, I guess not. But Uncle Sam has been good to me and I want to repay him a bit. He's paying me close to the same amount I received as wages from my uncle, so the family in Galway are not short. Though I will admit that when I joined up I thought it would be over in a few weeks. Bull Run saw to that, and Stonewall Jackson, bad cess to his black Presbyterian soul.'

They had been standing outside the stores hut door for a while trying to finish their conversation. There was lots Seamus wanted to ask his talkative companion, but Coughlan had told them to be back for supper in thirty minutes and he didn't intend on getting the wrong side of the man who seemed most likely to get him into the Irish Brigade.

'I'd better get those clothes and have that wash.'

'Oh yeah. Sure.' Shinnors said, looking up from whatever grain of dirt was reminiscent of Stonewall Jackson's black Presbyterian soul.

After his bath, following Shinnors' directions, he threw his tattered rags and broken shoes on a pile of discarded material being readied for a bonfire. Shinnors ensured that, despite the Quartermaster's huffing, he was issued with a cap of dark blue wool stiffened by pasteboard, taller at the rear than the front; a flannel, grey shirt; a woollen waistcoat, once dark blue, trousers of a similar colour, along with socks and, most welcome of all, ankle-high leather boots. Though still not a bona fide member of the Irish Brigade, or any of its regiments, a warm bath, a new pair of boots and a faded blue uniform bequeathed him no little dignity.

Adorned with his largesse, he sat at Sergeant Coughlan's campfire, feeling awkward and diffident despite a nascent self-respect, slowly he began to unwind and relax in the presence of easy-going company.

'So, you've come over to save the American Union and when you're finished, you're going to go back and sever the Irish one. Aren't you a powerful man all the same?' A private sitting on the arc of the circle near Coughlan teased.

'You'll have to take sherry with Surgeon Reynolds in his tent the first Tuesday of every month, along with the other senior officers, while you discuss Ireland's opportunities. Sergeant Coughlan? I hope you'll give him time off from latrine duty to attend,' Twoomey said to general laughter.

'Does Queen Victoria know you're here? She must be shitting herself. Here, have some beans for Christ's sake.'

And so it went on. Though there was teasing and banter at his expense, it was free of malice. He received this treatment because he was one of them. They may have made fun of his Fenian ambitions but they accepted that he was a soldier willing to fight like them. With them.

He'd done drill work back in Kilgarry. Even some marching and parading, though it was done in rough, stony fields or halfway up mountains and usually after dark. They'd observed the practices of the militia and yeomen and read about tactics in a tattered British Army training manual, donated by the grandfather of a Crew member who'd served under Wellington. They knew what they were doing was amateurish, but it was far in advance of most agrarian secret societies and it provided them with the rudiments of good military practice. However, he only realised how amateurish and rudimentary those practices were when he started going through routines with the 88th.

He was issued with a Prussian smoothbore musket, for close-in killing - the kind Colonel Meagher insisted the Irish would be doing; it was like the weapons they had acquired in Kilgarry. Familiarity didn't prevent him tripping over his feet as he was forced to move through the professional drilling programme instigated by Sergeant Coughlan and other officers of the Irish Brigade. Seamus's waking and sleeping hours were filled with short, barked instructions which regularly threw him into a torrent of confusion and caused him to wake with starts during the night. 'Stand to attention!' 'Order Arms!' 'Shoulder Arms!' Secure Arms!' 'Right Shoulder Shift!' 'Support Arms!' 'Present Arms!' Arms right!' 'Arms left!' 'Load in nine times!' 'Load in four times!' 'Load at will!' 'Fix Bayonets!' 'Charge Bayonet!'

He struggled to keep up. He bumped into everyone around him, his cap kept falling into his eyes and his new boots made a painful red mush of his feet. He loved every second of it. He was a soldier. Not a scrabbling-around-bogs-skulking-behind-rocks-with-his-musket-stowed-in-the-thatch-of-his-hovel soldier, but an out-in-the-open-up-front soldier with a proper uniform, a weapon to be proud of, and surrounded by more than a thousand men who thought like him. This was why he had left Kilgarry and crossed the Atlantic and by God he was going to make the most of it.

Captain McMahon returned from leave and Sergeant Coughlan used his longstanding friendship with him to get Seamus officially mustered-in to the 88th, Company L, whose quota was still short. And so, in front of the sullen Adjutant, he became a fully-fledged member of the Irish Brigade, specifically, Company L of the New York Volunteers, 88th regiment.

A week later, the 88th, having received their colours from Mrs Meagher, were sent down to Virginia, to join the 63rd and 69th regiments of the Brigade.

And here they were - 'Mrs Meagher's Own' - outside a town called Alexandria in a camp called 'California.' Seamus stared at the stars in the northern Virginia sky, absently scratching his newly filled out beard and listening to the banter of the others as the music and singing died away.

He belonged.

CHAPTER FIVE

'Pst! Farrell? Farrell, where are you?' The voice came out of the damp, dark mist in front. Seamus raised his musket.

'Halt! Who goes there?' He called as ordered on picket duty - whether he recognised the voice or not.

'For Christ sake, Farrell, give it a rest will you? It's only me – Eoghan Crosby. You haven't got any tobacco have you? I'm dying for a smoke.'

'Password?' Seamus asked.

'Oh, you're not serious are you? Who's going to attack us here in the middle of nowhere? The rebs aren't that stupid. They've better things to be doing with their time and so have I. Now do you have tobacco or don't you? I'll sidle on over to Twoomey if you haven't.'

'I don't care who you are or what you want, your voice is coming from in front of me and you have not given me the password. My instructions for such a situation is to shoot first. I've already delayed too long. Now, do you know the password or not?' He tried to prevent his voice trembling; he had strict orders to shoot anyone who approached his picket without providing the correct password, so what was he to do if Crosby, who was Company F from the 69th, was doing picket duty on the right flank of Company L from the 88th and whose voice he *did* recognise, continued to hold out? He pulled back the hammer of his musket as loudly as possible.

'Jesus! 'Clover' - alright? The damn stupid password is 'Clover'. Are all Limerick men this officious?' By the light of the lantern, Crosby's pinched ferrety face and wispy moustache came into misty view.

'Just following my instructions,' Seamus said with far greater aplomb than he felt. 'You shouldn't be coming in from the front like that and not saying the password, liable to get yourself shot at.'

'What would you know about getting shot at?'

Seamus sighed. There were two types of soldiers in the ranks of the Irish Brigade: those who'd been in battle and those who hadn't. Some had seen fighting with the British Army in the Crimea or India; others had fought with the Papacy in Italy against Garibaldi; some had been at Bull Run; some had done all three. Those who had, never ceased to remind those who hadn't that they were greenhorns and could never call themselves soldiers until they had 'Seen the Elephant.' Those who had saw themselves as superior to the Johnny-Come-Latelies who thought that soldiering was only about drilling, marching, singing and passwords. Seamus was determined not to let Crosby take advantage of him, just because he hadn't 'Seen the Elephant.'

'I know plenty about being shot at,' he said.

'How? Crosby asked. 'By having a bit of a ball fired after you while you were jumping over bog-holes and a few feet of ditchwater?'

In spite of himself, Seamus laughed. 'It was a bit more serious than that, and regardless of what you're jumping over, it isn't pleasant having a musket ball fired after you.'

'Farrell, whatever shenanigans you got up to back in Limerick you can't say you've Seen the Elephant until you've had hundreds of screaming Rebs using you as target practice whilst you're trying to dodge cannon-balls filled with nuts, bolts, canister, grape and God knows what, and all the while you're surrounded by the cries of mutilated men and horses. Hoping upon hope that if you are hit you will be one of the lucky ones and die quickly. Now, will we shut up about shooting and will you give me a twist of tobacco?'

Seamus was about to point out that it wasn't him who had raised the Elephant issue initially and that he wasn't sure if he did have any tobacco. But the fear he sensed underlying the bravado in Crosby's voice caused him to relent. 'Yeah, I've got a twist here you can have,' he said and, though Crosby outranked him, went on: 'but you shouldn't be smoking on duty and I'm not sure you can get it to light in this weather.' The mist swirled in cloying, drizzly, spirals that caused the moisture to drip off the peak of his cap down onto his nose, onto the rubber-coated poncho he wore over his uniform before sidling onto his freezing hands, saturating his boots, and numbing his toes worse than any downpour. There were no stars to gaze at tonight and he couldn't wait to be relieved.

'Relax, will you? I'm going to take it back to my watch and smoke it there, you won't be incriminated in any way. Not that there's any fear of being caught on a night like tonight: the Rebs are more than fifty miles away and no Union officer is going to stir a yard from his nice warm fire and glass of claret.

'Speaking of officers,' Crosby continued as Seamus searched beneath his oilcloth for the tobacco, 'are you coming to the Fenian meeting next Tuesday?'

'Yeah, I heard about that,' Seamus responded eagerly. 'Wasn't sure if I needed to be invited, or if I could just turn up.'

'Oh, just turn up. It's in that log cabin over near the 69th encampment. Sergeant O'Rorke is the Centre of our Circle. Though maybe the senior officers' meeting run by Surgeon Reynolds would be more your taste?'

'Why? Do I look as if I would fit in there?' Seamus passed over some tobacco.

'There's plenty of privates and non-commissioned who go to

that one. Especially those that enjoy their wine and poetry.'

'Don't worry. I mean business. It's why I'm over here: to meet like-minded people and to learn how to fight properly.'

'Good! You'll fulfil both objectives in O'Rorke's Circle.'

Crosby tipped a salute from the rim of his hat by way of thanks for the tobacco and turned to go back to his post. Seamus was pleased to be left alone again. Despite the weather, it gave him a chance to think; life had sped up so much over the previous weeks he appreciated any opportunity to put order on his thoughts.

Then, just before he was swallowed by the mist, Crosby turned and asked: 'On your way to the port back in Ireland, did you by any chance pass near Mitchelstown?'

He wouldn't have been more stunned if Crosby had delivered a powerful blow to his head. He paused breathlessly, Crosby's fawning manner suddenly took on a menacing, dangerous look while he stood waiting for an answer.

'No, sure that's the opposite end of the county to me,' Seamus said, struggling to keep steady. Why, anyway?'

'No why. It's just that a prominent local Fenian - name of O'Leary, I think - disappeared from there round about the time some fellow from Limerick passed through the area. A fellow called Flaherty who joined us in Company F has apparently been tasked with tracking down this renegade.'

'Oh?'

Crosby laughed. 'You should see the look on your face. It's easy to get you going, Farrell.' He turned to go again. Over his shoulder he called out: 'If you do come across a fellow county man who fits that description let us know. Flaherty has delivered instructions emanating from Cork and the New York East Side Circle for O'Rorke to cut his balls off.' With this hammer blow, Crosby finally went back to his post.

Seamus stood in solitude again, but after what he had just heard there was no hope of putting any order to his thoughts.

'I, James Farrell, in the presence of Almighty God do solemnly swear allegiance to the Irish Republic now virtually established, that I will do my very utmost, at every risk, while life lasts, to defend its independence and integrity, and, that I will yield implicit obediences, in all things not contrary to the laws of God, to the commands of my superior office, so help me God.'

He removed his hand from the Bible and stepped back from the table. The solder who'd administered the Fenian oath wrote in his ledger and indicated with a twist of his head that Seamus could go through. He had taken the oath before, but as this was his first time attending these Tuesday meetings, the corporal signing people in had insisted he take it again to prove he wasn't a timewaster or a spy, though, if he was either, he'd hardly break his cover by not taking the oath. Still, he supposed, they had to be seen to do something to filter out non-Fenians.

He looked around. The surroundings were spartan. A rectangular wooden table, not unlike a butcher's chopping block, stood off to one side. There was a pitcher of water and lemonade on it and a few chipped enamel mugs. A few stools and a couple of straight-backed chairs were scattered around. A green cloth banner with a harp and sunburst with the words *'Erin Go Bragh'* stitched in a gold thread parabola across the top hung on the far wall. Soldiers clustered in groups. The cabin was cold and the atmosphere humourless; it was geared towards transacting serious business, not frivolous drinking, singing or poetry reciting.

'Ah me oul *Segosa* – how're you doing?' Jer Horan detached himself from a group of soldiers and clapped an expansive hand on his shoulder. Seamus was never more glad to see a friendly face. 'Well, you've come to the right place to start frying your English bacon,' the Corporal expounded.

'That's good, Corporal, but I didn't know you were interested in the aims of the Fenian movement.'

Horan waved a hand dismissively. 'Oh, I'm not. Not really. But I like to know what's going on and the senior officers' do, despite the quality of the wine, is such a bore. I much prefer listening to O'Rorke's blood and gore; much more stirring than tales of the Fianna, even if I have to drink lemonade. By the way, call me 'Jer' when we're not officially on duty, James.' Horan was smiling as he spoke; Seamus couldn't always discern when the Tipp man was being his Company L Corporal and when he was being Jer Horan – joker, but, regardless which one he was now talking to, he was pleased with the companionship. Seamus felt he was on his way: beginning to reap the rewards of his transatlantic voyage to join the Union Army. He thought about the landlords and the militia men and all those - English and Irish - who had kept his people downtrodden and hungry and had to stifle welling emotions at the notion of receiving help from people like Jer Horan in smashing their power and bringing joy to the lives of Kathleen, his mother, Padraic and so many others.

Horan stood with a group that included Corporal Sean Cregan, First Sergeant Martin Brosnihan, Privates John Mulvaney and Tom Dillon - all members of the 88th's Company L and well known to Seamus. They were men that he'd drilled with and befriended in his short time with that regiment. There were several others present that he knew or whose faces had become familiar to him from the 69th, 63rd, and 88th. All lower-ranking officers or privates. All were Irish-born, except for a few like Cregan, who were American-born children of Irish parents. All would have either experienced the Famine first-hand or had family members who did. Everyone had compelling personal reasons for hating the English. He felt at home in their company.

Suddenly, he started. At the top of the room, with the organisers of the meeting stood Flaherty. When he'd heard Crosby mention the name, he thought it coincidence. Now it seemed this rabble-rousing thug was detailed to track down the killer of Dan O'Leary. Which, to all intents and purpose, meant him. The air in the cabin seemed to plummet further as he directed his sullen, gaze towards Seamus and smirked.

Crosby turned from the top of the room and shouted: 'Your attention please!'

Sergeant O'Rorke, of the 69th's Company F, whom Seamus only knew by sight, stepped out from the cluster beneath the green cloth banner. Instinctively, he had avoided the man up to now. Though he was not that imposing a figure – probably no more than five-six or seven – his cold, grey eyes and the hard set of his jaw exuded bitterness.

He spoke in a calm, unemotional, voice. 'I am First Sergeant

Michael O'Rorke, of the 69th New York, Company F. I am the elected Centre of this Circle of the Fenian Movement. It is pleasing that each time we meet our ranks grow thicker. But let's be clear: these meetings are neither social occasions nor drinking clubs. If you seek either of these, 'twould be better for you to leave now than wait to be expelled. Tonight, we are going to talk about how invading Canada, that jewel in the British crown, could be a stepping stone between the ending of this war and liberating Ireland.'

There followed a discussion on the merits of this strategy versus directly invading Ireland. It was a good debate; some maintaining it would be a waste of time and resources to invade Canada and others holding that it would be such an excellent bargaining chip, the English would capitulate quicker than on the threat of an invasion of Ireland.

Though he didn't contribute to the debate Seamus favoured the option of invading Ireland immediately after the American war finished. He stood with Horan and other comrades from the 88th while they had their say; his confidence soared with the knowledge that there was all these brave, able, military men gathering to debate and to prepare for liberating Ireland.

Oddly, Seamus could not decide what option the O'Rorke faction favoured. The only certainties about them, especially O'Rorke, were that they wanted to be in control and they wanted to kill.

'Men, there is only one proven method of dispensing justice in this world. Cold steel! Justice from the point of a bayonet or justice from the barrel of a musket. That's what will serve. No amount of talking, pleading, or letter writing will suffice like cold steel. And there's nothing like experience to improve effectiveness. Plunge plenty of steel into the Rebs and if you get a few Confederate Irishmen along the way – it'll be a small price to pay for the experience gained towards putting it into Englishmen.'

Though Seamus was uncomfortable with the starkness of O'Rorke's rhetoric and with the obvious pleasure the captain got in talking about killing, he had to accept there was truth in what was said. When, at the end, O'Rorke brandished a sword, swung it over his head and cried: 'Up boys and strike a blow!' he roared approval as loudly as anyone else in the room.

Despite the menacing shadow cast by Flaherty, he returned to the 88th's quarters with that sense of belonging reinforced. Taking a swig from Horan's canteen he found himself accepting, approving even, of O'Rorke's bloodlust. The whiskey helped to blot out the knowledge that people within the Brigade knew the murder of a Cork Fenian coincided with a Limerickman passing through on his way to join the Union Army.

CHAPTER SIX

Camp California was sited on rolling ground which, excepting certain distinctive features, mirrored the arable land around Kilgarry. The three regiments of the Irish Brigade occupied rising ground either side of the Alexandria to Fairfax Road. On the right were the tents of the 69th and the 63rd. On the left was the 88th, from where Seamus admired the panoramic view of multicoloured forests, lush grass and fertile valleys rolling all the way back to the redbrick houses of Alexandria.

Sometimes it lifted his heart to have such a view here in faraway Virginia. Other times it near suffocated the same organ by overwhelming him with homesickness. Christmas 1861 was such a time. The tents of the three regiments, laid out with the north-south, east-west symmetry of American streets, were lavishly decorated with holly and all manners of green boughs and branches plucked from the surrounding woods. At the entrances to the 'streets,' arches of evergreen had been erected reaching thirty feet into the air and straddling the gap between the rows of tents. Drill and parade ground manoeuvres had been suspended since lunchtime on Christmas Eve, giving the men time to prepare for the festivities and to partake in the religious ceremonies.

Seamus attended midnight Mass in the 88th's tent-cum-log

chapel set on one of the highest brows in the area. Father Corby, a highly respected chaplain on secondment from the University of Notre Dame, officiated, standing behind his altar - a long wooden table covered with a white linen cloth, normally used to hold food and drink at officers' parties. Father Corby spoke of duty and of the debt owed to the freedom-loving Union. They were here this blessed Christmas, instead of at home with their wives, sweethearts, and other loved ones, because of that debt. But they could be at peace with the knowledge that repayment would result in a multitudinous bounty of liberty and gratitude from the Union, that they and their descendants could draw on in perpetuity.

Shuffling up with the crowd to receive communion, Seamus recalled a similar ritual in Kilgarry twelve months before. Then, he had walked with his mother to midnight Mass; they made their way along a beaten path towards the little stone chapel standing at the furthest edge of the scattering of hovels that passed for the village. Along the route they were joined by up to fifty others from the surrounding farms, including Kathleen and her family. To Seamus, the people carrying candles or flaming bulrushes, both for their religious significance and to light their way along the rugged path, resembled a ghostly congregation condemned to tramp the afterlife in a luminous half-light. That thought, though creepy, instilled one of those feelings of belonging he regularly felt when in the company of his downtrodden neighbours and he knew that he would go to the furthest limits to preserve and strengthen that emotion.

As it did in the log and canvas chapel here in Virginia, the congregation in Kilgarry that Christmas before had bulged out the door and spilled outside where most could not hear the priest. However, all had stayed diligently to the end, content to be on the periphery of one of the holiest ceremonies in the Catholic year. Father Browne articulated the Mass in his sing-song Latin and led the congregation in hymn. Though he was elderly, and his extremities shook, the priest's voice was strong. The poor man had suffered as much, and more, hardship than the rest of them. He'd been through penal and famine times, which had been merely the lowest points in a life of enduring hardship. Even now, the religion he preached was barely tolerated by the English authorities; the contempt it was held in obvious from the poverty of the priest and the miserable draughty little church in which he had to say Mass.

Father Browne had preached against violence and secret societies many times in the past. Everyone knew what and whom he meant. But, unlike other priests, he did not discriminate against those he knew to be responsible and all were welcome to attend Mass and receive the Eucharist.

Father Corby was also a priest who had no compunction about administering to fighting men and Seamus felt an exhilarating peace as he turned from the makeshift altar with the familiar blandness of the communion wafer dissolving on his tongue. He had partaken of the body of Christ once more and hadn't realised how much he'd missed the ritual.

Content that he was seeking to fulfil his obligations to both congregations, he slept peacefully until Christmas morning. After breakfast, sitting outside the tent he shared with Pat Mangan – a large, dark, friendly Kerryman – gazing at the dusting of snow decorating the countryside, his thoughts fixated on a letter he'd received from Kathleen.

'Are you going to open that fecking thing or what?' Mangan asked as he thrust a mug of bitter coffee at him.

'Leave the poor fellow alone,' Sean Cregan said from the neighbouring fire. 'Sure he's saving up all that lovey-dovey stuff until after he's triumphed in the 'Catch-A-Greased-Pig' competition. With a flagon of Colonel Meagher's whiskey for the winner can you blame the man for not wanting ay distractions until that prize is in his hip pocket? But I'm giving fair warning: I have ambitions of my own in that regard.'

Seamus had been holding onto the unopened letter since the previous afternoon. Once they'd been stood down until after the festivities, the regiment had received a delivery of post. He had tramped along, more in hope than expectation, to the wagon where a corporal was dispensing mail for soldiers in his section. Along the way to New York, he had written notes to Kathleen, trusting their posting to strangers, but, if she had received them and replied, he had not remained in the one place long enough to receive them. Now, though he had an army base, he had still gone to the mail station only in hope and had become so used to the moniker: 'James Farrell' that it was a good few seconds before he snatched the envelope under 'O'Farrell, Seamus' from the corporal's desk.

He told himself he hadn't had a chance to read it. When he'd arrived back at his tent he'd been drawn into regimental and company preparations for the festivities: cutting branches, bending boughs, marking out ground for today's games, cooking supper, getting ready for Midnight Mass. But, this morning, apart from keeping the coffee warm, he had no further excuses.

He knew that was what he had been doing – making excuses. He was afraid to read the letter, afraid of what he might find out: did the militia take revenge on everyone for the attacks of the Crew and his fortuitous disappearance? How was his mother? How was Padraic? Did Kathleen still love him? Did he deserve that love after what he had done with Mairead O'Leary?

The questions were going to drive him insane. He had to know the answers. Pat Mangan made a playful swipe at the letter and boomed. 'Let's see what's in it. Afraid she's given you the heave-ho? Can't Limerickmen read?'

'Yeah, read it out, Pat. Share and share alike in this Company. God knows I could do with a laugh at his expense after all the money the bastard won off me last night,' Jer Horan called.

Seamus rose and walked towards his tent. 'Sorry to disappoint you boys but it'll be a dry day in the Irish Brigade before any of you ever see the contents of this letter.'

'Let's hope we never see it then,' someone called out to general laughter as Seamus threw himself on his blanket. Trembling slightly, he finally brought himself to rip the envelope and, ignoring the taunts and hootings that were still coming from outside, began to read her scrawly, but articulate, writing - forged, like his own, in the new Irish national school system they'd both attended.

My darling Seamus,

It is with great joy that I read of your arrival in America and

enlistment in the Irish Brigade. You are indeed the man I, and your family and neighbours, always knew you to be. We are all survivors, have to be, but you are a leader and a hero and one day I know you'll return a powerful man. My every wish, thought and blessing goes out to you, now and always, Seamus O'Farrell. My betrothed and rock. I am desperate for you to be here by my side but I realise that sacrificing my immediate desires will result in a greater good for us all.

Seamus, it is not my intention to burden you with greater concerns on that distant shore, but I want you to know the truth so as to steel your determination and to instil you with even greater belief in what you endeavour. Father Browne, God bless him, though knowing the truth, attempted to persuade the authorities you had died and that you had been buried in the bogland around Knockdrisna. It seems they did not believe him because there continued to be a great hue and cry after you left. Constabulary and militia combed the area for weeks after your disappearance. No evidence of your survival or anything untoward was found. That didn't stop recriminations of course. Mick Cussens was found hiding behind some bales of straw in an outhouse and arrested. He was taken to Castletown Jail and I warrant cruelly tortured, but you know Mick, tough and loyal to the core. Anyway, they obviously didn't hear what they wanted from him and he was conveniently shot whilst 'trying to escape'. When his sister went to get the body she said his face had been beaten to such a pulp that it looked as if he had tried to escape by headbutting his way out through the stonewalls of the jail. By then, Mick's wife and five children were living in ditches and begging by the side of the road, their dwelling house and outhouses were reduced to rubble and ashes. Mick's married sisters did their best to help, but they don't have a lot of their own to give and if they had they would only draw retribution on themselves. As would we all. I don't know where Mick's family is now – I think they are in the Newcastle West Workhouse. Padraic is trying to find out.

Peadar Treacy has gone into hiding and his family have been coming under fierce pressure. His fourteen-year-old brother was grabbed in Kilgarry by several militiamen, stripped of his clothes and covered with boiling pitch. That was some weeks ago and it is still not clear if he'll live. I met his mother at Mass the other day, she was in an awful state –

for both her sons. Bad and all as things are, they would be far worse if it wasn't for Padraic – God bless and spare him – the O'Farrells of Kilgarry are indeed a noble race. At the height of the crisis, with the militia and constabulary pressing in on us from all sides and every one's lives and livelihoods at risk, Padraic bought the neighbourhood breathing space. Somehow, himself and a bunch of lads (I know John Danaher and Sean Roche were with him, but there's also new younger lads) managed to get past guards and dogs to get inside Nolan's mansion. They tied the landlord, his wife and two daughters back-to-back on four high chairs and threatened all kinds of retribution on them if pressure on the tenants did not ease. They even planted the seeds of some cock and bull story about you and the rest of the Crew falling out about the division of the spoils of a robbery and you being assassinated as a result. It's certain no one in authority really went for this, but the intruders put the fear of God into Nolan. Rumour has it that, before he left, (he only laughs when I ask him to verify) Padraic urinated all over Nolan and his expensive chair and carpet.

Whether true or not, and I wouldn't hold any of this

against Padraic if it is, Nolan was badly scared and, though he has sent his daughters away to some posh English public school, he remains so frightened that things are a little better around here.

But now, I come to the most difficult part, though, darling, I know you would want to know and I know you are strong enough to turn your grief into strength and resolve. Padraic's boldness came too late to save your mother. A few days after you left, the militia and constabulary, along with a few local thugs, people like Ned Bresnihan, willing to do anyone's dirty work for a few pints of porter, came and tumbled your house with levers and crowbars, barely giving your mother time to get out. In fact, I believe, she refused to come out, but trying to keep some semblance of moral authority on their side, they lifted her out as the gable started to collapse.

Though the participation of Ned and his cronies in this dirty work was noted, there was nothing anyone, even Padraic, could do at the time – due to the presence of the heavily armed militia and constabulary. Padraic took your mother to live with his family. A couple of mornings later, they woke up to find her gone. Padraic found her amongst the ruins of the cottage, shivering and shaking (it had been a cold, wet night) and calling your father's name. He got her back to his house, where they keep a close eye on her, but her mind I'm afraid is still wandering – she seems to think she is back in hard, but happier, pre-Famine times. I wish I could have spared you this, but as she is also refusing to eat and surviving on soup that Padraic's sister forces into her every now and then, it cannot be long before the inevitable. So, darling, that's another trial you need to grid yourself for.

My father is also poorly, he spends most of his time sitting bent at the fire or the table staring at something only he can see. Though, through Padraic's efforts, we've been spared the worst. Paidín Óg is a dutiful son, and with Eileen and me doing our bit we get along. I look at Paidín Mór now and compare the shell to the man he used to be and cannot help but wonder how long he's got on this earthly coil. Your mother and him, and others of that generation survived the potato blight, only to have their very lives blighted. God help me, but sometimes I wonder what is to become of us all.

Well that's enough of my *rámeis*. I know I've gone on

and that I've depressed the life out of you, but I've not hidden things from you before and, just because there's an ocean between us, I'll not start now.

How can I end darling Seamus, other than by sending you my undying love and expressing my great hope that it will not be long before we meet in better times?

>**Your devoted,**
>**Kathleen.**

He let the letter fall onto his chest. Mercifully the others were outside sharing a bottle, ignoring him, for the distance and time separating him from Kilgarry collapsed with an almost audible whoosh and nearly crushed him in his bunk in Northern Virginia. But, he held on – he hadn't come this far to be crushed; he had come to find strength in himself and others. He was determined to see it through to better days.

So, he held on.

There were many entertainments in the encampment of the Irish Brigade that Christmas Day, including Catch-A-Greased-Pig, a three-legged race and a steeplechase organised by the officers. Seamus participated until he collapsed on his bunk about two o'clock in the morning, with whiskey exuding from every pore. Though not for one second, throughout that memorable day and night, did the fertile fields of Kilgarry feel an inch further away than the rolling grass of Virginia that he cavorted on.

CHAPTER SEVEN
MAR. 1862

It rained a lot in Kilgarry. Pregnant grey clouds blowing in from the Atlantic ripped their bellies on the jagged Kerry mountains and spilt their contents across Munster. The rain that fell in North Virginia throughout the early months of 1862 should have constituted another connection with home. But the effect this precipitation had on the terrain rendered it as alien as the buildings on Broadway.

The ground disappeared. To be replaced by a treacly, glutinous morass, whose texture somehow combined sufficient resistance to make the soldier's step feel like there was a ton of iron strapped to his ankles with a porosity that swallowed men, beasts, and artillery whole whilst churning up mud apparently stained red with the blood of its victims. A story did the rounds that a sutler's mule had taken a step off a hard track road the previous week and the beast along with the wagon of goods had sunk until only its ears stuck up. Seamus, who'd heard it from a private in the 63rd, who'd heard it from a private in French's brigade, who knew a sergeant who'd help whip the sutler off the wagon seat before he went down with his mule and wagon, was almost certain it was one of those tales that soldiers told round the campfires to leaven their gambling, drinking and homesickness. Though admittedly, based on his own experiences of Virginian mud, it wasn't the unlikeliest tall tale he'd heard since joining the Army.

He *had* witnessed Father Corby testing the mud's depth not far from the 88th's camp and watched disbelievingly as the ground swallowed the ten-foot measuring pole as surely as a man might ingest a sliver of sausage, so he didn't have to believe stories about mules' ears sticking out of the ground to accept that this was treacherous terrain. His mother and himself would often shiver for days inside their cabin, seeking to extract a bit of heat from the damp fire while the rain beat down incessantly outside. But, unlike its owners, Kilgarry soil was not treacherous. It absorbed that rain dutifully and, whilst regularly soggy and damp, seldom overflowed or flooded. Here the Virginian soil seemed to have joined the rebellion by swallowing, stalling, and depressing the invading Northerners.

Throughout the opening months of 1862 he had plenty of opportunity to indulge such thoughts and to experience close up the treachery of the ground. It seemed that he had spent most of those months floundering back and forth between Camp California and the Rebel front line twenty miles away - part exercise, part observation, part pre-emption of boredom. A few weeks earlier, approaching Warrenton from the far side, Seamus caught a blurry glimpse of soldiers moving off in the distance; their uniforms a lighter hue than the Union Army's. Sean Cregan, told him they were rebels and he wished he'd taken more notice as they were the only ones he'd seen since joining the Brigade.

The night before St Patrick's Day, they were on their way from a small village called Fairfax Courthouse to a town called Centerville, in a confused march all too typical of their recent movements. That afternoon the rain had finally ceased, but the darkness reeked of damp and the night silence was punctuated by rushing streams and the plopping of cold globules of water from overhanging trees.

The soldiers plodded along in silence. This was no more than what was expected of a night march, but in truth the post-Christmas gloom, imposed by incessant rain and purposeless marching, had extinguished the men's spirits weeks before. Even Jer Horan's jokes and facial gymnastics had dried up in inverse proportion to the amount of water that fell from the heavens. Seamus did not regret his enlistment - he'd endured far more gloom and bleakness back home, at least here there was still the possibility of a positive outcome, but his initial flush of euphoria had faded as he settled into the monotonous rhythms of winter soldiering. Like the falling rain, his life had adopted a slow, steady, incessant beat.

Company L was on skirmish duty – out in front, ensuring the

regiment wasn't surprised by non-existent rebels. Deep in thought about home, his mother, and Kathleen, it was not until the second or third cry that he registered it wasn't a vixen calling, but a human in agony. Or terror.

'Christ! Did you hear that?' he called, louder than he should have, to his nearest comrade – Tom Dillon, whose low, stocky build made him seem more gnome-like than ever in the gloom.

'Yeah! Do you think someone's in trouble?' Dillon asked.

'Definitely.' Seamus replied, as another scream rent the damp night air.

'It's well over on the left, so it's nothing to do with us,' John Mulvaney whispered from the other side of Seamus, then sniffled loudly, dragging snot up to his brain. It was an annoying habit that Seamus had become used to, but now it grated again, like it had at the beginning until Mulvaney's decency and friendliness had subsumed it. 'There's 69th folk over there, let them sort it out.'

Seamus couldn't leave it. There was a vulnerability in the cry that tugged at him. Even if it was only an animal, he'd have to investigate. 'There! Look!' he called too loudly again. Flames flickered, then slashed at the darkness, before exploding into an orange ball brightening the sky a mile to the north-east. The cry came again. This time there was no doubt. A woman was screaming. 'I'm going to see what's happening,' Seamus said and immediately started walking towards the flames and the cries.

'Farrell! Come back!' Dillon shouted. 'Our job is to walk straight ahead and ensure there are no surprises for the rest coming up behind.'

'You're going to get killed, walking across your own guns like that.' Mulvaney called, his nervous sniffling carrying far in the night air.

'I must see what's wrong,' Seamus answered and kept striding, he scrunched up tight to make himself less of a target. The officers were way over on the right somewhere, even Jer Horan wasn't close, so there was no one to immediately pull rank on him. He jogged across the field towards the source of the screams; a series of explosions and bangs emanated from the fireball, increasing his urgency. He knew, by leaving the skirmish line, he was committing a serious breach of discipline but an integral part of him insisted on reacting to injustice, whatever the consequences – a part of him that he'd badly let down in New York. So, he scuttled along, bent low to make himself less of a target to friend or foe and ignored the cries of: 'Get down you fool!' from soldiers who didn't know him and 'Farrell, come back!' from his colleagues in the 88th. He heard one guy say: 'Don't shoot, he's one of ours!' And another: 'Damn fool deserves to be shot for running across his own lines like that!'

He was vaguely aware that one or two of his comrades were following him, but the rest of the line held steady. Burning buildings, barns, conflagrations of all sorts had been common on the marches since Christmas – the surprise was that there was anything left to burn in the devastated landscape. It was likely just some rebels getting their comeuppance from the far side of the line and if it wasn't, well, it surely wasn't anything that could not be contained by the 69th – the core of whom fought at Bull Run and were experienced veterans. Yet, he couldn't stop himself rushing towards the trouble.

Nagging doubts about duty slowed his legs. Then the screaming came again. A woman's high-pitched wailing. His diagonal traverse had carried him on an ever-widening angle from the main line of advance, he felt safe in standing up and sprinting the last seventy yards or so.

He burst into a clearing where the heat and brightness of the fire seared his eyeballs - illuminating a hellish scene.

'That's enough!' he shouted - Instantly aware of how foolish and pathetic he sounded.

O'Rorke didn't look up. It was possible he didn't hear Seamus amidst the din of the exploding wagon and the screaming woman as he pounded a black man into the liquid mud with a ferocity that betokened beating him to death before he drowned. A black woman was pinioned to the ground, further along, closer to the blaze. A group of soldiers – five, no, six! – were holding her while another pummelled away between her violently kicking legs; her clothing was ripped in several places, her chest appeared to be exposed, beneath her waist there was a flash of white petticoats and a skirt of darker material billowing in the night air. She let off another scream and gave a violent buck. The man who was raping her was thrown forward towards her chest and he took the opportunity to cover her mouth with his hand. It looked like Flaherty.

'Hold the bitch will ye? God damn it!' With the help of his companions, her assailant regained his rhythm.

Seamus fired in the general direction of this group – only slightly too high. They jumped like men whose pants had been simultaneously invaded by an army of ants. The one in flagrante delicto reacted the coolest of the lot, reluctant to have his pleasure interrupted he lifted slowly back from the woman, his erect member startingly white in the half-light.

Seamus swung around towards O'Rorke, who had desisted from beating his victim and now grinned wolfishly over at him instead. As Mulvaney and Dillon ran up alongside him ('Jesus! What the...' one of them exclaimed) he became aware of more soldiers in this clearing. From the glimpses and silhouettes he garnered they were all familiar to him from O'Rorke's Fenian Circle meetings – men with whom he had hoped to free Ireland.

'Private, how dare you point your musket at a superior officer,' O'Rorke spoke calmly, but authoritatively. 'I can have you court-martialled.'

Seamus's world, which had been on a relatively even keel since joining the Brigade, careened into free fall once again as all his recently constructed props of companionship, loyalty and common purpose were kicked out from underneath him.

Keeping his voice steady, despite the fear that had parched the inside of his mouth, he responded: 'Hung for a sheep, hung for a lamb. If I'm going down I may as well go down for something big as for something small.' He cocked the hammer. 'Now step away from that man – *Sergeant*.' Putting a sneer into the title helped steady his nerve.

'Steady, Seamus,' Mulvaney sniffled beside him.

O'Rorke held out his hands in a gesture of mock surrender. He grinned. 'You're making a big mistake, Private.'

'Not as big a mistake as attacking and raping innocent people.'

O'Rorke laughed aloud. 'Oh these aren't innocent people.' There was a general guffaw from his companions. 'And you should know that they are your enemies, Limerickman. Or should I say *Captain Rock*?' A louder guffaw, maybe nervous laughter, from the others.

The woman, who hadn't stopping crying, ran across the opening, firelight reflecting off her tear-streaked skin. She fell onto her man.

'How do you know what I was called back home?' He asked O'Rorke.

'Oh, you'd be surprised what I know.'

The woman was not quite screaming anymore, it was more like screeching. She tried to pull and drag her powerfully built mate out of the quagmire he'd been pounded into. She slipped and fell backwards into the liquid mud herself. Both of them were coated in a reddish slime. She reverted to mere crying. Seamus had never seen a more pathetic scene in his life – not even amongst neighbours dying of the hunger back home.

'Is that man alright?' he asked O'Rorke.

The sergeant gave a careless shrug. Suddenly, stealthily, he drew a pistol from a side holster and fired it point blank at the man's head. A jet of blood and other matter exploded out the temple's left side, splashing onto the woman beneath, the front of whose dress now glistened darkly.

Seamus's trigger-finger reacted automatically, and his musket fired. The night erupted. For a moment he assumed O'Rorke's cronies had opened fire on him. There was a tremendous explosion and the whole clearing was filled with blinding light, the air around him reverberated with buck and ball – he automatically dived to the ground and covered his head with his hands. In the flimsy security of the damp hollow made by his body, he realised the wagon had exploded. A short relief, as he was immediately jumped on by several people. He took a punch, which felt like a kick, to the kidneys. The agony convulsed him and against all normal odds he managed to turn onto his back and lash out with desperate kicks and punches of his own. He was aware of Mulvaney and Dillon also fighting against overwhelming numbers next to him. At least, Mulvaney was still standing, his sniffling now the only noise Seamus could take sustenance from.

'Hold the traitorous scum!' O'Rorke's voice commanded. Immediately the opposition changed from punching and kicking to leaning and pressing on his limbs and pinioning him to the ground. Seamus could only move his head. Despite the presence of Dillon and Mulvaney, he felt vulnerable and alone – like he was naked in the midst of a large group of well-dressed people.

'Bring the woman and child over here.' O'Rorke ordered.

Child!

O'Rorke stood over him. The wagon continued to emit desultory bangs but the spectacle of light and sound had peaked. A sheen of sweat covered O'Rorke's face, his breathing slightly quick, like a man who'd just partaken of strenuous, but satisfying, exercise.

Eoghan Crosby appeared at his shoulder – apprentice cub to king of the pride.

'Farrell – what the hell are you doing, defending blacks like that?' Crosby spoke like he was being reasonable; at that moment Seamus loathed him more than O'Rorke, who at least didn't try to disguise his maliciousness.

The woman's screeching had descended to a keen but the girl's crying remained sharp – scintillating the nerves like fingernail flesh jabbed with shards of glass.

'Didn't seem like good odds, is all. Half a regiment against a man, a woman and a child.'

O'Rorke snorted. Crosby explained: 'Their kind are the enemy of the Irishman. If they are not at the bottom of New World society, then we are. Didn't you have enough of being at the bottom back in Limerick?'

'Doesn't mean I want to murder and rape them.'

'Do unto them before they do it unto you, is my motto.' He

gestured disdainfully at their shaken figures, 'These are contraband. Goods that would benefit the enemy if left unspoilt. They were also smuggling gunpowder, which they undoubtedly meant to deliver to their Confederate masters on the other side of Warrenton.' Crosby shrugged to imply that, having had it all explained, he was now certain Seamus understood why O'Rorke and his men did what they did.

Strangely, ashamedly, he found he didn't have the energy to argue. He'd expended it all. He laid his head down and closed his eyes – he just wanted to get on with his life. He knew it was futile to debate. O'Rorke and Crosby were certain they were right. And they held the power. So, how could there be a contest? There could only be action. And there could be no action while he was in the position he was in.

Mistaking his silence for acquiescence, or not caring either way, O'Rorke moved on. 'So, Limerickman, what do you know about Dan O'Leary?' he asked.

Dan O'Leary. Seamus had come here to escape the sins of the Old World. Indeed, to gather an army and return to expiate them. But his sins had followed him and as a result the army he'd hoped to gather around him intended to kill him.

'Never heard of him,' he replied.

'You're a liar as well as a lover of their rotten black race,' O'Rorke no longer hid his anger. He kicked at Seamus, near where he'd been punched in the kidneys earlier, but he bit his lips and refused to cry out.

'I did mention this to you,' Crosby said in his reasonable voice. 'We've had communication from a Circle in Cork – an active and well-run Circle – that their Centre disappeared around the time a Limerickman came to stay with him, a Limerickman who professed he was on his way to America to join the Irish Brigade. A Limerickman who murdered Dan O'Leary and stole the funds he'd accumulated for the Circle. They've asked us to look out for this Limerickman and requested that we retrieve the stolen funds and authorised us to deal with him as all traitors should be dealt with. Corporal Flaherty has enlisted with Company F to co-ordinate this effort and he will receive full cooperation from Sergeant O'Rorke. From all of us.'

'So, I'm a Limerickman who's a Fenian, doesn't mean I killed this O'Leary fellow. Doesn't even mean I met him.'

'Except his wife says the last time she saw her husband was when a Limerick Fenian, called O'Farrell, and him went down to the nearby village for a drink. She says you came back hours later on your own and in a mighty hurry – you threw your things together and disappeared into the night. Hasn't seen you, or, more importantly, her husband since.'

Seamus felt let down by her semi-betrayal. But what else could she have done? She couldn't just say her husband never came home, because she didn't know whom he met or when and where he met them. Maybe any number of people saw him reach his own door. Likewise, many people would have known he had stayed with her – she had to try and eliminate any rumours about what happened. Reputation was as vital as food and drink in a small community. So, she, reasonably, cast suspicions about her husband's disappearance onto a stranger to divert them from herself. He couldn't blame her really. And she couldn't have known it would have repercussions for him in America, or at least she must have thought it very unlikely.

'Still doesn't prove anything.'

'I don't need proof,' O'Rorke spat. 'Suspicion is enough for me and I've plenty of that. The Fenian movement traced you back to West Limerick, where it seems you were called 'Captain Rock' – a grand name in a two-bit outfit who mucked up their only serious engagement. You ran like a coward to America, killing a good man in Cork and stealing his money for the passage. It's traitors and cowards like you that have brought about the ruin of every attempt by the Irish to fight back. Not this time, though – suspicion is enough. Enough to cut the canker out. You and the slaves are going to die and the rest of us will be the stronger for it. No weaknesses or malignancies tolerated this time.'

'Seems to me, you intend to swap one tyranny for another.'

Seamus could see the others turn towards this new voice. Though the speaker wasn't yet within his eye line, he didn't have to see to know it was Corporal Horan. 'Killing those whom you are merely suspicious of, or who are merely competing with you, isn't that what you accuse the English of?'

Horan sounded his usual confident self.

'Corporal, I'm not going to discuss the finer points of this argument with you, not only because I outrank you, but because it is not Brigade business. Though you're right - that was how the English remained on top. Which is why we're adopting these tactics. This is not a moral issue, it's a military strategy.' O'Rorke responded.

'Well, seeing as you're such a military man, Sergeant, I'm sure you'd like to know that General Meagher, his staff and the majority of the Irish Brigade are bearing down on this spot as we speak, drawn to the commotion.' Horan spoke almost laconically.

O'Rorke said nothing. But there were noticeable stirrings within his black eyes as his brain processed this information.

'Maybe we should get out of here?' Crosby suggested.

'Kill 'em first.' O'Rorke ordered.

'I don't think so.' More soldiers had come into the grove. This last sounded like Pat Mangan. There would definitely have been a confrontation, a shoot-out even, between the different factions, but just then horses and lights entered the clearing.

'What the devil is going on?' An authoritative voice shouted. Seamus found he could move at last. Everyone around him, even O'Rorke, came to attention or near attention. The rather portly man with the bushy moustache, a plume in his hat and a saffron sash with gaudy tassels around the waist of his uniform was instantly recognisable as Thomas Francis Meagher – now Brigadier-General of the Irish Brigade. He was flanked on either side by a retinue of staff equally as ostentatious, flaunting flags and colours even in the wet darkness. Seamus was grateful for the sense of pomposity and officiousness they brought to such a barbaric place.

'You heard the General,' one of Meagher's staff called out, 'what's going on here?'

O'Rorke responded. 'We apprehended some Confederate slaves, Sir. They were smuggling gunpowder to the Rebels. Some of the men took the law into their own hands. This Private from the 88th tried to intervene. We were going to teach him a lesson too, Sir.'

Seamus was impressed by O'Rorke's leavening of the story with grains of truth.

'Sergeant, do you realise what you're jeopardising here?' Meagher asked.

'General, I'm sorry, but I only know that it would be jeopardising all our lives if I'd allowed these slaves to get through our lines and pass their ammunition to their masters,' O'Rorke replied.

Meagher ignored this. 'The reputation of the Irish, Sergeant. The reputation of the Irish - that's what you're jeopardising.' The Brigadier-General waved his hand flamboyantly, encapsulating the scene around them.

O'Rorke saw his opportunity and took it. 'Yes, General. Sorry, General. I didn't think.'

Meagher smiled and Seamus's confidence in the organisation and integrity of the Irish Brigade plummeted. 'Sergeant, you've overstepped the mark,' Meagher continued paternally, 'the Irish Brigade have been given the honour of ensuring there are no rebels between here and Centerville. And, by God man, that is what we are going to do. The eyes of America, indeed the world, are upon us. We have been starved, oppressed, and humiliated throughout our history. Now we have an opportunity to display the martial prowess that is endemic to our race. We must not Sergeant, must not, be distracted by sideshows. And above all, we must not be seen to be fighting amongst ourselves. It gives our enemies the opportunity to say they were right: the Irish cannot be trusted with anything. I am determined, Sergeant, absolutely determined, not to have this said of the Irish Brigade. Do you understand?'

'Yes, General.'

'Do you, Private?'

It took Seamus a few seconds to realise Meagher was addressing him. He felt the eyes of the clearing on him – friends and foes. 'Yes, General.' He sensed relief by all that he wasn't going to complicate things further.

Meagher smiled benignly. The wagon's firelight cast shadows, along with the torches carried by Meagher's staff. The General's face glowed red. It might have been the flames. It might have been whiskey. 'Sound men. Sound men. Get this place cleared up and see those women are looked after. Bring them to my tent in the morning. Sergeant, I will ensure Colonel Kelly hears about your brave interception. Now get back on the road to Centerville as soon as possible and let there be no more about this imbroglio.'

'Yes, General.'

Meagher stood on his stirrups and addressed the clearing. 'Men, your fearless deeds go before you, I know you will not do anything to disgrace the dear old green flag. Remember Fontenoy!' The General and his staff turned as one and wheeled away into the damp night.

Seamus saw how it was. The reputation of the Irish Brigade took precedence over any misdemeanours or atrocities. Appearances were everything and any blemishes that bubbled to the surface were to be glossed over as smoothly and efficiently as possible, regardless of their underlying putrescence.

As the horses' hooves squelched into silence, Seamus expected a resumption of hostilities with O'Rorke and wondered if the other members of the Brigade, Fenian or otherwise, who had now come up, would intervene on his behalf. But the Sergeant was clever enough to know that the situation had changed, and it was time to move on.

'Alright, men,' he addressed his cronies, 'you heard the General, let's go. Bury that body, shouldn't be difficult in this terrain, and bring those women along.' He turned to Seamus with his wolfish leer: 'We'll speak again, *Captain.*'

Crosby said: 'See you now,' as if they'd just had a chat about the bad weather.

Seamus's energy and enthusiasm had drained away, but he managed to call out: 'The women come with us.'

O'Rorke turned around again and looked at him; he looked at Horan, at Mulvaney, at Dillon, at Mangan, and his eyes swept in an arc over the others who had come up, marking them for vengeance. But tonight was no longer a propitious time for confrontation.

'Go ahead, have the bitches,' he said as he turned away. 'And happy St. Patrick's Day!'

CHAPTER EIGHT

By now, even the most inept of the men's leaders accepted that there were no rebels between Warrenton and Centerville. Indeed, that there were no rebels north of the Rappahanock river. They'd retreated, leaving nothing behind but the smell of sizzling bacon from the stores they'd burned and tree trunks shaped like cannons that had fooled the Yankees for over eight months. Their general, Joe Johnson, having decided they were too exposed north of the river in their old positions around Manassas and Warrenton had ordered them to retreat across the Rappahannock – the better to defend their capital, Richmond. Fearing that the war would be over before they had the chance to fire a shot, the men who had joined since the Battle of Bull Run were bitterly disappointed. A previously unknown Northern Brigadier-General by the name of Grant was advancing down the Mississippi, Union soldiers had landed on the Carolina coast and now the rebels were retreating in Virginia – the Confederacy could not last long more. The unblooded men of the Brigade had missed their opportunity and the mood in camp was bluer than if they had been defeated in battle – at least then they would have demonstrated their bravery.

To make matters worse, they continued to march over and back in the mud. They had been ordered back to Warrenton, presumably to triply ensure the rebels had actually left, even though every jackanapes knew they had. Their worst experience occurred as they crossed the Bull Run battlefield and ghosts rose to confront them. The ground had been rock hard the previous July and even those bodies over which some care had been taken were not buried very deep. Now that it was a quagmire with another army tramping over it, they squelched back to the surface. The men grumbling that the war would be over before they got a chance to fire a shot went silent when they saw the skeletons of their predecessors squirming around in the mud beneath them - skulls grinning in ribald merriment at the naivety of the greenhorns who still walked the earth alone.

A survivor swore he recognised his brother's bones amidst the muck. 'We buried our Frankie over there,' he said indicating the spot where he claimed to have seen him, 'I'd know the shape of that head anywhere and sure isn't the miraculous medal that mother gave him still around his neck. Look, it's got his initials on the back.' He pushed a silver token dripping with mud towards the men who'd gathered to listen, but they recoiled in horror for fear it proved the man's story true.

The officers hurried them past this Golgotha and the Brigade camped in a dank, dripping wood. Seamus's mood sunk to its lowest ebb since joining the Union Army. Life with the Irish Brigade consisted of marching back and forth in freezing morasses of mud that you'd fence the livestock off from back home. A large portion of the Fenian army he'd hoped to unite with, was led by a pathological killer – a significant number of whose followers tolerated or actively participated in wanton acts of rape and murder; he himself topped the madman's list of potential victims and the Fenians he was friendly with seemed half-hearted in their commitment. They were more interested in singing songs, telling stories, and getting drunk than invading Ireland. It was no consolation that nothing further was said to him about stepping out of line to go to the aid of a slave family. It wouldn't have benefited the reputation of the Irish Brigade if the incident became widely known.

A couple of nights afterwards he sat almost on top of a damp log fire that fizzled and sparked without offering any real heat and squinted at a letter from Kathleen outlining the deteriorating situation in Kilgarry. Padraic was doing his best to hold things together but Nolan appeared to be regaining his resolve. If anyone so much as lifted a turnip from his land, they found themselves and their families evicted with nothing but death in a ditch or a workhouse to look forward to. Peadar Treacy was found freezing and starving among the rocks of Knockdrisna, arrested, given a trial by a jury rigged with cronies of Nolan and hanged in front of his family in the square outside Newcastle West Courthouse. Cormac, Kathleen's second brother, had been arrested after drinking too much porter in the village and calling all kinds of calumnies on Nolan and the authorities. He too was now in jail awaiting trial on sedition charges, which meant transportation or years of hard labour, either way he would never be allowed to have a life in Kilgarry again. Only secret threats of the severest reprisals from Padraic prevented Nolan from evicting Kathleen and the remainder of her family. They were hanging on by a thread. His mother still ranted and raved and called for him and his long dead brothers and sisters.

It wasn't a letter that warranted re-reading but he couldn't bring himself to destroy anything Kathleen had created, so he folded it and placed it in the inside pocket of his steaming overcoat. Despite the deteriorating situation in Ireland and the way army life had taken a turn for the worst, he couldn't see that he had any choice but to stay his course. A debilitating realisation that left him staring motionless into the weak fire, with only the irony of feeling trapped in a huge country for company.

Once again it was Jer Horan who came to his rescue. He had managed to almost fry some hard tack and bacon by putting his pan right into the weak fire and thrust a plate at Seamus. 'Here,' he said, 'get that down you: nothing better for curing the blues than the runs. After eating this you'll be so busy trying to get your trousers down before you shit all over yourself that you won't have time to be depressed. You think what you did the other night outside Centreville was brave, huh? Well you know what bravery really is soldier?'

'No, Corporal. Enlighten me.'

'A man with severe diarrhoea chancing a fart.'

He glared at Horan, annoyed at his flippancy. But something about the deadpan face staring stonily back sent Seamus over the edge. First he snorted, then, he giggled, which triggered laughter that came rolling out of him in a torrent that wouldn't stop. He had no more control over it than…well, than a man with severe diarrhoea. He fell back onto the damp grass, brought his knees up to his chest and still he laughed. A part of him knew he was being manic, but the greater part of him enjoyed the release it gave him and he stayed with it.

When he'd recovered and sat back up, Jer was still there with the plate in his hand. If he found Seamus's reaction out of the ordinary, he didn't let on. Maintaining his deadpan look, he said: 'It was a good job I didn't tell you the one about the blind beggar and his dog.' He raised one eyebrow and set Seamus off again. This second bout though was only an aftershock of the first and he regained control much quicker. He sat up once more, wiped his eyes and finally took the plate.

'If I thought I was going to get that reaction I would have said it a lot earlier. You obviously needed it.' Horan said.

'I don't think I've ever laughed like it before. Maybe when me and my cousin Padraic were young…we got up to all kinds of mischief. We thought nothing could keep us down then. We didn't recognise our poverty as the degrading, imprisoning thing it is.'

'Well, prisons are for breaking out of.'

'I seem to keep breaking through one wall only to find myself behind another.'

'No matter how many walls you break through, if you keep thinking depressing thoughts, you'll stay in prison. Let your thoughts soar.'

'You're right, of course. But do you think we'll ever get enough good men together to free Ireland?' Seamus asked, half dreading the response to the question that haunted his every moment.

Horan didn't give him false hope. 'I don't know.'

Seamus nodded, appreciating his friend's honesty. He took a forkful of food, forcing his stomach to accept its greasy texture.

Horan continued. 'Not every Fenian is as fanatical as O'Rorke you know. There are several good men around, inside and outside the

Brigade. There are thousands of Irishmen scattered around Union regiments who'd gladly lay down their lives for the cause of the old country. There's a whole regiment of them up in Ohio, there's another Irish brigade being organised out of Chicago by a fellow called Mulligan. Hell, I've even heard there are several regiments and a couple of brigades with the Rebs, whose officers and men are as Irish as you and me. When this shindy is all over, in a month or two, there's no reason why you cannot all get together and run the English out of town. Don't be put off by lunatics like O'Rorke.'

Horan offered him more of the congealed mess to eat. He didn't want it and he knew the talk about invading Ireland was mainly just to cheer him up, but it made him feel better, so he accepted a second helping.

The following night, bivouacked outside Warrenton, Seamus stole away from a music session in full flow. After the Brigade's recent exertions, they'd been given permission to be at ease until late. Pat Gorman was knocking a mixture of happy and sad songs out of his harmonica, The Flanagans – father and son from Illinois – sawed at their violins, Pa Bourke had an old, battered banjo, Jer Horan led the singing and everyone joined in. A few jugs of whiskey had been appropriated for the company, the *craic* was mighty and the cold and damp were retreating. Seamus marvelled at the men's resilience but, realising that the whiskey wasn't dissolving the streak of morbidity that had solidified within him, he decided to see if satisfying his curiosity would.

He picked his way towards the rear of the Second Corps encampment, passing the fires of other men who, like the Irish, were entertaining themselves with music and song, others played cards or held desultory conversations, some sat in solitary contemplation, still more read or wrote letters. There were myriad ways men passed camp-time when at ease, but they all emanated from one source: boredom. Even the lively sing-songs of the Irish were just another desperate effort to stave it off. It seemed that once the initial excitement had waned, boredom became the defining facet of war.

He was now in the backwash of the Army, amidst the cooks, the groomsmen, the form-fillers and the paper-filers. And the sutler wagons. They weren't popular with the men because they mostly sold shoddy goods at exorbitant prices; they were especially notorious for selling bad whiskey that could see a man go through his monthly wages in a few short trips leaving him with nothing but a thumping headache and a jumbled memory. Most decent delicacies, like pies or cakes, were snatched up by the officers. It was a source of wonder and irritation to the men how the sutler wagons multiplied around pay days and disappeared again once they'd appropriated the majority of it. The previous day, a large number of regiments had been mustered in for pay and sure enough the wagons had materialised out of the surrounding countryside like natives that had been skulking in the grass waiting for the opportune moment to strike. Consequently, there were now a goodly number for him to sift through.

But the wagon he sought was easy to find. Green shamrocks and yellow harps festooned its canvas. A sign in foot-high bold black letters, proclaimed: *'Erin go Bragh.'* It could only be that one, advertising its Meagher-like flamboyance. The general owned the wagon. Presumably, he paid for the goods and split the profits with the sutler. A fat, sweaty fellow, the sutler was a distant relation of Meagher's wife – a nephew of a second or third cousin. Now that young lad was on Meagher's staff: running errands, polishing the General's shoes, poaching his eggs. He'd become a sort of pageboy because Meagher had given the wagon over to the slavewoman and her daughter who been violated and mistreated and whose man had been murdered by O'Rorke and his gang. It was a cross between a blood money payment and the price of silence. It was for the honour of the Irish Brigade.

The image of them wailing and clawing in despair at the body of their dead father and husband would not let Seamus rest. Once he'd heard from Pat Mangan about the wagon, he had to see how they were.

But now as he approached and saw the woman sitting alongside the display of goods he couldn't think why he'd wanted to come. She looked up at him and he was certain she didn't recognise him. How could she? It had been dark and she couldn't have been very sensible of her surroundings. But, as he drew nearer, she nodded in a deferential manner that implied recognition.

'Hello,' he said, 'so, you've been set up alright?'

She shrugged.

He heard the stupidity in what he said but couldn't bring himself to speak directly about what had happened to her and her husband and didn't know what else to talk about. 'Nice layout,' he indicated the goods display. Mugs, bowls, pots, and pans hung around the opening. There were biscuits and other delicacies still left on shelves inside. On the ground near her was an opened sack of coffee beans, with a weighing scales next to it. 'Got any whiskey?' he asked, because he couldn't enquire how she felt as a result of being raped and seeing her husband murdered before her eyes.

'Charity!' she called, 'bring a jug.' The woman retained her deference, but she kept looking fixedly at him, like she wanted to see into his soul.

The young girl he'd glimpsed the other night came out from behind the wagon. She was tall and slim like her mother, with wide brown eyes. No more than twelve. The woman waved towards Seamus and the girl handed him a half-pint earthenware jug.

He wondered how much Meagher was making on the whiskey being sold through this sutler's wagon. He asked the woman how much the jug cost.

'Two dollars, sir,' she replied.

'How much do you get to keep for yourself?'

She shrugged again and broke her eye contact. 'The General said he would be generous.'

Seamus gave a dollar to the girl and two to her mother. The act loosened his tongue. 'I'm sorry about…you know…the other night and everything.'

She returned her gaze to him and he held it for a moment. He had become more used to black people, though their colouring and appearance still held an exotic fascination for him. This woman was beautiful, she had sorrowful brown eyes, high cheekbones and her skin shone like it had been polished with a soft cloth. A woman more different than Kathleen with her pale skin, flowing black hair and freckles was hard to imagine. Yet, he felt confusion and disloyalty.

She dropped her gaze without saying anything. The girl moved back to whatever she'd being doing behind the wagon.

Seamus suddenly knew why he'd come. Though he did have a genuine concern for their well-being and wanted to ensure that the story about them being set up with a sutler's wagon was true, the real, real, reason he'd come was because he'd sensed a bond – a bond of suffering and humiliation – with them and wanted to test its strength. The few seconds he'd held her gaze verified its existence and marked it as strong. He knew his eyes were engaged with a representative of a race that had suffered abundantly more pain and humiliation than the Irish. He couldn't tell if she felt anything in common with him. She didn't seem to; merely accepting his money and handing the whiskey over with lowered eyes.

'If you need anything, my name is Private James Farrell, Company L, 88th Regiment, Irish Brigade.' She nodded slightly in acknowledgement that she'd heard, whilst, at the same time, conveying that the personal information he'd imparted was not, and never would be, of consequence to her.

He left to carouse around the campfires with his comrades.

***

It was a night for celebrating and drinking. Discipline was relaxed. The men were relieved that the rain had eased off at last and that they had finally settled in an encampment. The Rebels had retreated and the banks of the Rappahannock and the spires of Fredericksburg would soon replace the Potomac and Alexandria.

Sergeant O'Rorke skipped the festivities and went to bed early. He didn't drink, needing a clear head for his plans of murder and revenge. He recognised his own viciousness, but had no desire to restrain himself, especially now that the war and the Fenians had given him an outlet for it.

He lay down and, while men like Crosby and Flaherty caroused and drank outside his tent, tried to focus his hatred. That interfering bastard from Limerick was as good a face to start with as any. He didn't really care about what the prick had or hadn't done on his way through Cork. But rules were rules. He had ensured that Flaherty was mustered into Co. F like the New York East Side Fenians had requested. The man had been sent to do one thing only – weed out a traitor: the Limerickman who'd murdered Daniel O'Leary back in Ireland. O'Rorke was capable of doing it himself, but it was equally as pleasurable to command others in acts of violence. A licence to implement death and destruction was the great thing about this war and the opportunity to do it with a Fenian stamp was even sweeter. He wasn't some madman without a cause - though he enjoyed inflicting chaos and death, he wanted to inflict them on those in authority in Ireland and on those who aided or abetted them in anyway, but he was willing to stand back and allow others do the dirty work if that was what was required. It didn't really matter whether it was Flaherty or himself who made an example of the Limerickman. But, as he drifted to sleep, it wasn't the Limerickman he saw or the slave bitch - he saw the face of his dear, departed mother.

'Hush *Alanna*, hush,' she whispered, 'don't be afraid.'

But he was afraid. He was so afraid his wee-wee was running down his six-year old legs and he was whimpering like a puppy, though his father had told him to be brave and not to let the soldiers see him cry. 'For that's what they want Mikey – it gives them great satisfaction to terrorise people, especially the weak and vulnerable.'

Little Mikey O'Rorke hadn't understood all these words at the time, but he knew enough to realise he was supposed to not let the bad English know he was scared of them. That wouldn't be good. He wasn't sure why, but his *Dadaí* said it, so it must be right. And he *had* tried. But the shouting and screaming, the smell of smoke, the gunshots, the swearing and the fear on the alien, set faces of his parents overwhelmed him with a speed and ferocity that his little mind hadn't a hope of containing.

'Please *a Dhadaí*, a *Mhamaí*, make them stop, please.' Men with redcoats, guns and swords were everywhere: walking, pointing, shooting, stabbing, shouting with tongues he couldn't understand, although it had to be English because he did get some of the curse words. There were other men without uniforms or guns, they were bad also, they ran around with flaming torches pushing and throwing them onto the roofs of the houses in the village. The thatch on their next-door neighbours' house, Moloney's, was set alight, Tadhg and Peig ran out, screeching at the soldiers and the other men. Mikey watched as a soldier smashed the butt of his rifle into Tadhg's face sending blood and teeth flying into the air. Another ripped the front of Peig's dress, and he could see her naked breasts. The soldier and his friends laughed. Mikey gasped for air. This was Peig who often gave him spuds; who made him kneel down and say the rosary with her family on the numerous occasions he was there when they started to recite it. This was the woman who loved and scolded him like his own mother. She lived next door and would be there forever. But now she was naked and the soldiers were laughing at her.

'A *Dhadaí*, please…' He knew his *Dadaí* or *Mamaí* could do nothing, but he couldn't stop asking.

They were at his house now. The roof was blazing. His *Dadaí* tried to push one of the soldiers and was knocked roughly to one side. Maybe if that was all…

The first soldier moved on. But there were more. And more. They were all around them. Pressing in on them. So close he could understand what they said.

'That's a pretty wench.'

'Probably riddled with the pox. All these Smelly Brigids are.'

They couldn't be talking about his mother.

'She'll do for Crompton's lot. They're not choosy.'

'Crompton! Over here. There's one here for you. Christ! I even have to get Irish whores for you – not capable of wiping your own arses you lot.'

More laughter.

Dadaí was in amongst them again. This time he lashed out with his full force and caught one of the redcoats with a meaty thump hard enough to knock his head back. Then one of the hard shiny blades on the ends of the guns was pushed into his stomach and shoved upwards. There was a squelching sound like bare feet sticking in mud.

Not his *Dadaí*. His *Dadaí* couldn't be killed - he was too strong, too powerful. So it was still alright. Thanks be to God.

But his *Dadaí* was dancing and it was not a jig on their earthen floor. His legs were off the ground. The blade had come out high behind him; there was blood everywhere. It spread all over his back and poured down his front; there were big sticky lumps of it on the end of the blade and now it ran out his mouth also. His *Dadaí* made a gurgling sound he'd never made before. Mikey didn't understand anything that was happening - so maybe, even now, it would still be alright.

It was the soldier who'd stuck the blade into his *Dadaí* who finally made him understand. He started name calling really bad stuff. 'You're a stupid Irish pig,' he said to his *Dadaí*. 'Look,' he called out, 'I've stuck a stupid Irish pig. I'm surprised it's blood and not poteen coming out of you.' And other things, worse things, things Mikey had never heard before but knew that God would strike him down if he'd said them. But why wouldn't He strike the soldier down? Thick lines stood out on the redcoat's neck, his face becoming as red as the back of his coat and his mouth snarled like Byrne's sheepdog when you threatened it with a stick. And from them all there was a smell like from his *Dadaí* when he came back from the shebeen. Though he always just wanted to sing or sleep then and the soldiers wanted to do these bad things. Mikey finally knew that there was nothing his *Dadaí* could do to stop this and God wasn't going to do anything either. A soldier who saw what was happening laughed and rammed his blade into *Dadaí's* side. His father gave a long, low groan. His mother screamed. The dark parts of his father's eyes rolled and the whites grew larger. Blood poured out his mouth. Soldiers ripped his mother's dress, like they'd ripped Mrs Moloney's, but they didn't seem to want to stop at that with his *Mhamaí*. More soldiers closed in and started ripping the rest of her clothes.

'To hell with the pox, this one's worth the risk,' he heard one of them say. The others laughed horribly.

His father stopped dancing and Mikey started running.

***

Seamus joined in the carousing for a while, but his participation was shallow, a thing undertaken by his outer shell. His inner self remained sunk in a morbidity constituted of disappointment and anger, anchored by the realisation that the way of the world, liberated or enslaved, was as encapsulated by the events of two nights before and that drinking, carousing and good cheer were thin coatings which failed to gloss over men's true nature. Eventually, he extracted himself once more from the lively fires, this time he sought out the solace of his writing materials and commenced a letter to Kathleen.

Poised on the edge of communicating his true feelings about the truths he'd uncovered in the New World he stepped back, like from an abyss, and following on from loving salutations, wrote:

...It feels good to be a soldier and to be making a positive contribution to the Union cause.

I'm told there are lots of Irish in the Southern side also. I suppose that's only natural given that thousands of our countrymen enter America through southern ports like Charleston and New Orleans. We develop a ferocious attachment to whatever bit of ground we end up on, urban or rural; one we are very willing to fight and die for. I'm glad I ended up in the North; I couldn't fight for the Southern slave aristocracy and I don't see how any Irishman could.

The Irish who fight for the Union do not fight for the slave – they fight for pride; to repay the North for the life it's given them; for the money, but, above all, they fight for the glory of Ireland. There are more than enough good, fighting, Irishmen around (in both armies), who are gaining in martial experience every day, to effect a successful invasion and if the people, as they surely will, and must, rally to the cause, liberation will come. I still have every hope of sweeping into Kilgarry with good men of the Irish Brigade and overseeing the hanging of Nolan, his lackey agent, Maguire and their ilk from the twisted oak at the village crossroads. So, stick in there my love, I'm coming for you.

As the boys here say: 'We will mend one Union so as to sunder another.' That's their way of saying we'll use the experience of fighting for the benevolent union of the North American states to break the perfidious union of England and Ireland.

Kathleen, *mó stór*, I think about you every day, nay every minute of every day, I worry about you and how things are faring back there in the glorious country of Kilgarry, benighted by strangers and traitors. I take relief that, despite the worsening situation, you are holding up well – brave and dignified as always. Tell Paidín Mór and the others I'm thinking of them and I'll be home soon to lend a hand of one kind or another. Also, assure Padraic I was asking for him and that I beg him to look out for you and yours as much as his own circumstances will allow.

It is with great sadness and concern I learned of my

mother and her tribulations, along with the abandonment of the place I call home. But I am glad you didn't seek to spare me the dire news. To know, no matter how bad, is to begin to cope, to wallow in ignorance is to multiply the future shock and to magnify the present uncertainty. Now that I know, though it disturbs my sleep and waking hours, I can plan to put it right and use the knowledge as another spur to the stead of desire bearing me to revenge.

Keep safe, stay brave,

Your ever-loving, Seamus.

When he'd finished, he stood and walked out of the tent he shared with Pat Mangan, leaving the words carelessly exposed, almost disowning them. It wasn't that he didn't mean them or that he didn't still love Kathleen, it was more like he'd composed them to fly as free spirits on a gay breeze that would never carry anything of significance. He didn't consider that they would ever be held in the solid, earthy, loving hands of his betrothed; he felt as if he was consigning them to a nebulous infinity. He looked at the fires scratching at the night, at the blurs of men; he listened to their music, their singing and raucousness and knew that, regardless of the similarities in physical geography, there could be no reconciling of emotions experienced here with emotions left rooted in Kilgarry.

Two nights later still of similar disposition, he returned to the sutler wagons and he took the woman in her bunk while her daughter slept nearby.

CHAPTER NINE
APRIL 1862

McClellan finally divulged his great plan for the Army of the Potomac. Now that it was certain the Confederates were all safely on the other side of the Rappahannock, he would pull his men from their positions in front of Washington and Alexandria, transport them down the Chesapeake to land them on the Peninsula between the York and James rivers, from where they could dash into Richmond through the backdoor, smash 'the vipers' nest' and end the war. This way 'Little Napoleon' intended using speed and surprise to spare his men the ravages of a frontal assault on the rebel capital.

After their meanderings around Northern Virginia, the Irish Brigade got to spend one last night at Camp California before marching to the wharf at Alexandria and being thrust aboard *The Ocean Queen* – a large, well adorned steamer - and a small, cramped river boat called, *Columbia,* on which Seamus and most of the other rank and file found themselves. The travails of the march to Alexandria were lightened by the serenading of the regiments of General Phil Kearney, an Irish American general, who ordered his men to escort the Irish Brigade and see them on their way to the tune of "Garryowen."

With high spirits and renewed optimism, the men of the 63rd, 69th, and 88th clambered aboard their transports and set sail for Fort Monroe, a union base on the tip of the Peninsula. Surely no puny rebellion would be able to resist the thousands of gay-spirited, well-drilled, superbly equipped men in their shiny uniforms and glittering bayonets that sailed for the Peninsula with purpose in their hearts and God on their side? Private James Farrell, née Seamus O'Farrell, didn't think so, nor seemingly did any of his comrades.

Ominously, their thirst for adventure was soon dampened by a churning nausea as the transports were tossed high and low on a rolling angry sea.

Seamus gripped a handrail with snow white knuckles. His stomach weaved and bobbed with the waves. They'd had a few rough days on the *Victoria Star* coming over. Although it dipped and rose and was buffeted by a number of storms, it felt solid as it swayed with the blows. This transport was at the mercy of a roiling sea – and his stomach was unable to cope.

'Boys! Ye should have stuck with picking stones and topping thistles and stayed away from the briny deep!' Barney Sullivan, a huge Connemara man with a ruddy complexion and a booming voice, scoffed at Seamus and the others. Sullivan led a group of appallingly cheerful

Connemara fishermen from the 63rd in teasing and jeering those unaccustomed to stormy seas.

'Easy for you to say, Sullivan, you great big lummox,' Tom Dillon replied between heaves over the side, that he had to stand on tiptoe to achieve. 'Sure you were reared on those bits of board and animal skin; what do you call 'em? Cornicles? Carbuncles?'

'Coracles,' Sullivan corrected happily. 'And beautiful vessels they are too. You should see them skim and glide over the water, not like this lumbering box.'

'Christ! We're going to war man, not trying to scoop up a few mackerel for dinner. Have a bit of sympathy.' Dillon turned and puked green bile over the side, making Seamus wish he could empty his stomach as well.

Sullivan laughed. 'A throw of Clifden poteen to settle that stomach is all ye need.'

Without being able to stretch over the side, Dillon threw up the remaining contents of his stomach. It splashed over Sullivan's army shoes, who once more laughed heartily. 'Come on boys, let's leave these potato-pickers to their puking and we'll try to find a lot with sea legs who'll share a drink and a song with us.'

'Mad bastards.' Dillon managed to mutter before dry retching, as the Connemara men walked away.

Eventually, after what seemed like interminable bobbing, weaving and bouts of nausea, the batteries around Fort Monroe wobbled into view and Seamus thanked God that his nautical ordeal was about to end.

Jer Horan, bearing up better than most of the landlubbers, though sporting a sickly green colour, quickly disabused him. 'Don't get too excited yet there, boyo,' he said to Seamus, 'I used to go out now and then with my uncle in his boat on Lough Derg and when it blew across the lake, the way it's blowing across the bay here now, we'd have awful difficulty making landfall. I don't think Uncle Sam will want any of his precious boats dashed on the rocks or washed down to Richmond. We may be some time yet.'

How right the Tipperaryman was. So right that Seamus scraped the nadir of his soldiering career. They lay off Fort Monroe for five days and four nights in such cramped conditions that they had to take it in turns to go below decks for shelter. They subsisted on short rations of salt pork, hardtack and coffee, the bobbing and weaving omnipresent, the nausea especially taxing while trying to keep down the hideous mixture of biscuit, meat, and coffee. It was a blessing in some ways that the rations were short.

Horan, Pa Bourke, Mangan and others tried to keep spirits lively with singsongs, music, stories, and cards. But every attempted diversion fizzled out. Even the Connemara men and a contingent of the 63rd, who'd served with the British Army in India and spent half their military careers on board ships, had a surfeit of bobbing and weaving and cramped conditions by the third day.

More than any time since he'd left, Seamus wanted to be back in Kilgarry; he'd have done anything and promised everything if only God would make it so. He knew it was impossible, but he couldn't stop the silent prayers. The hungriest, harshest times he'd experienced back home weren't worse than this. At least he could take a blunderbuss, a musket, a pike, any weapon, and fight back, and, if he failed or got wounded, there was a lover and friends to succour him. But here, there was no one to fight and nothing to fight with; not even Jer Horan could bring him out of his melancholy. He'd never felt further from achieving his dream of liberating Ireland.

His guilt at lying with Mercy compounded his misery. He couldn't rationalise it. Indeed, he tried not to think of it, as if by doing so, he might come to believe that it had never occurred. But with a traumatic sea threatening his physical existence, his mental processes sought a berth in reality. He couldn't decide whom he had betrayed most: Kathleen or Mercy. If they didn't know about each other's existence, did it matter? His thoughts took him to that night in Cork with O'Leary's wife and the tragic conclusion it brought about. There was no justification for any of it and he tried to shut out the memory of O'Leary's wife stood there, covered in her husband's blood. A poor excuse for a man O'Leary may have been – his aggressive, drunken habits were hinted at in the manner of the man's murderous associates within the Union Army – but had he deserved death?

Seamus tried to convince himself O'Leary wasn't worth thinking about – as if O'Rorke was capable of hearing the conflict playing over in his mind from far off. What did it matter if they could or not? Those men wanted Seamus dead whether they could prove he'd been involved or not.

He loved Kathleen, but he couldn't shake Mercy from his thoughts. Though he and Kathleen had played with fire several times, he'd never entered a woman before; never experienced the velvety smoothness of it. The excruciating pleasure, with an underlying hint of pain, generated by the friction. The mewling, moaning sounds she tried to stifle for her daughter's sake evidenced she was not repaying a debt.

Her husband was not two weeks dead, but these alien times drove trusting strangers to seek comfort with each other.

He could only cope by compartmentalising his Irish and American experiences as separate facets of his existence. It didn't bear scrutiny, but it enabled him carry on. Meanwhile, the *Columbia* swayed and rolled and his stomach turned cartwheels.

On the afternoon of the fifth day, the wind eased sufficiently for the transport to come close to shore, but a stubborn breeze continued to blow, preventing it from docking. Instead of the solace of planting shaky feet on solid ground, Seamus and his companions, with their muskets and packs held high above their heads, waded through the ice-cold water that lapped beneath their armpits. On finally, finally, making their soggy landfall, they discovered no preparations had been made for their arrival and they were forced to establish quarters for themselves in yet another dismal clump of dripping woods as darkness fell.

Soaked through, shivering and debilitated by despair, they were elated when Meagher's bonhomie prevailed on the neighbouring General Howard and the Irish Brigade were invited to share the fires, rations and rudely constructed huts of his men.

Day dawned grey and damp, but proper rations were issued and the Brigade were put to work corduroying local tracks to help move

McClellan's army along the seven miles of swampland that separated its current base from Yorktown – where the nearest enemy fortifications lay. The combination of half-decent food, very decent coffee and constructive manual labour instigated yet another resurrection of optimism and hope within Seamus. By midday, there was a pleasing sting in his hands and his heart beat active and strong. Sean Cregan, Pat Duignan, John Mulvaney and himself were pounding thick branches and trunks of trees into the Virginian mud with sledgehammers. When they were secured as solidly as possible, shorter, stouter branches were placed crossways and the interstices were filled in with stones and earth spread by pick and shovel. For once, the glutinous quality of Virginian mud proved useful as it helped bind and hold the structure together; it required far more sun than currently prevailed to bond properly, but it would suffice to get McClellan's army up the road to kill rebels.

Seamus felt once again that he was an integral unit in a common cause, united with decent human beings prepared to give their all to achieve a successful outcome. As if to celebrate his rejuvenation, for the first time in weeks the sun burst forth lifting everyone's spirits. Right on cue the men broke into song:

John Brown's body lies mouldering in the grave
John Brown's body lies mouldering in the grave
John Brown's body lies mouldering in the grave
As we go marching along.

We'll hang Jeff Davis on a sour apple tree
We'll hang Jeff Davis on a sour apple tree
We'll hang Jeff Davis on a sour apple tree
As we go marching along.

John Brown's knapsack strapped upon his back
John Brown's knapsack strapped upon his back
John Brown's knapsack strapped upon his back
As we go marching along.

Corporal Jer Horan, worked with a crew further along from Seamus and added to the merriment of the Irish-born, unconcerned with the fates of John Brown or Jeff Davis, by shouting out: *Sean Brown's granny is crying for a shave; We'll sing for Thomas Davis to make ould Ireland free* and *Sean Brown's cabbage patch is growing out the back* instead of the proper words. After a few verses, it was impossible to tell which carried loudest down the line: the official words or Horan's, as most Irishmen followed his lead. A competition between both sets of songsters developed and Seamus lustily joined in on the side of Horan's unofficial choir.

Suddenly, he realised there was a different timbre to the singing: it had melded into a raucous sort of cheering and he looked up to see a dozen or more officials approaching on horseback. For a second or two, he thought the stoutish, important-looking, man riding slightly ahead of the others, was Meagher. Then, he realised that the figure was too short and too stout to be the Irish Brigadier and even the charismatic Meagher was surely too familiar a figure to warrant the wild cheering and hat tossing that ensued as this man approached. It could only be General George McClellan – 'Little Napoleon' – Commander of the Army of the Potomac, indeed, despite a recent demotion, Chief of all the Eastern Armies between the mountains and the sea.

Seamus wondered how such a diminutive man could generate the worship and acclaim bestowed on him by the men his entourage passed. Yet, as the party drew near, he found himself being sucked into it. Before he gave thought to what he was doing he'd begun tossing his forage cap in the air and shouting: 'Hurrah for McClellan! Hurrah! Hurrah! Hurrah!'

McClellan raised an imperious hand and the horses halted. Up close, Seamus observed a short, stoutly built man with light brown hair, blue eyes, and a fresh complexion. But it wasn't his physical characteristics that made the greatest impression. It was his presence: a magnetism that, despite the man's diminutive stature, drew one's attention and focus on him to the detriment of anyone else present. With a graceful, feline movement, he stretched out a gloved hand towards Tim Sweeney, who had been crouching at the side of the newly corduroyed road with Pat Gorman and others from the 88th, nibbling on their rations and grabbing a well-earned rest.

McClellan scrutinised the piece of hardtack Tim handed to him as if he'd never seen dried army biscuit before.

'Are you boys building me a road to Yorktown?' he asked, never taking his eye off the hardtack.

'Yessir!'

McClellan stood up in his stirrups. 'I'm grateful boys, grateful. And ashamed. Greatly ashamed that what you receive for performing this noble labour for me and your country is this reconstituted offal!' And he tossed Sweeney's hardtack contemptuously from him.

The men, including Seamus, cheered their heads off and threw their hats in the air once more. McClellan reared his horse and lifted off his general's cap in acknowledgement before leading his group down the line to further acclaim.

It was a masterly performance. The Mighty General; the Young Napoleon; the Saviour of the Union, proving he was in touch with the common soldier.

Tim Sweeney cheered louder than anyone, though when the hullabaloo died down, Seamus overheard him say: 'Jaysus, I'm starving, can anyone spare a bit of hardtack?'

These were days of hard work and nights of hard play. By day, the Irish Brigade chopped down trees, laid roads, built mortar emplacements and bomb shelters and cleared rough ground to create approach lines for cavalry and infantry that the regular roads, log-jammed with heavy artillery, could not take. At night they sat around campfires beneath dwarf cedars, playing cards, singing songs, making music, but, most of all, passing around the whiskey jug and telling stories.

Most of the tales were similar to, or obvious variations on, the West Limerick folklore Seamus was familiar with the pooka, the fairies, the banshee, Fionn MacCumhaill and the Fianna. But he loved listening to the regional twists and even those he knew sounded exotic when sitting or lying next to a warm campfire dressed in his army gear, surrounded by his army comrades on the American continent.

However, the stories that really made the hairs on the napes of the men stand to attention, especially greenhorns like Private James Farrell from West Limerick, were those recounted about the Battle of Bull Run by veterans of that infamous day for the Union of the American States. Most of those surviving veterans resided over in the 69th, but some had been encouraged to enlist with the 63rd and 88th to season the experience of those regiments. Company L of the 88th had five such veterans – a high proportion: Corporals Jer Horan and Sean Cregan, Private Pat Gorman, Sergeants Martin Brosnihan and Richard Byers. And, despite the mention of Bull Run from any of these four normally eliciting groans, whistles, exaggerated yawns, and sarcastic remarks of all kinds, at night, around the campfire, they acquired a cloak of reality that made the heart of the most dismissive man in daylight hours beat higher and faster with dread.

Horan, in particular, could make the men turn their eyes down and away from the firelight to hide the dread that rose to occupy them. The Tipperaryman would slug whiskey from a stone flask and recount what happened on the banks of a pretty stream outside Manassas railway junction. Of how high hopes and dreams of valour disappeared in a tangle of blood, guts, panicked civilians and stupefied soldiers.

He was often talking to himself by the time he finished. Most of his audience sleeping or turned in on themselves; wondering if the roads they were building carried them towards the glory Meagher and McClellan promised or the gore that was the lot of their compatriots at Bull Run.

Seamus was no different. He tried not to let it show, but his blood chilled and his ears pricked up like a scared thoroughbred whenever Horan discussed O'Rorke's performance in the battle. 'A madman he was; possessed by battle fury, he cut and hacked his way through swards of rebels, slashing tendons and limbs, leaving a trail of blood and mutilated flesh but his insane brutality saved a lot of Union lives.'

Hearing this, Seamus worried about the enemy he had made and what the battles he'd have to participate in would be like. He had to fight especially hard not to slip away and take comfort in the arms of Mercy and further betray his betrothed back in Ireland.

He worried that his defences could not hold out much longer.

CHAPTER TEN

It soon became obvious that whatever else this move on the back door of the rebel capital was going to be, it wasn't going to be quick. McClellan was a great favourite with the men and in civilian life had been a gifted engineer and chairman of a major railway company. Thus, he displayed excellent attributes for motivation and organisation. However, when military tactics called for boldness and quick thinking, these same attributes left him open to accusations of slowness and timidity, arising from over cautious preparation and a desire to spare his men.

Southerners took full advantage of this fastidiousness.

More than 55,000 of McClellan's men approached Yorktown defences that were manned by less than 18,000 Confederates. Courtesy of a rebel commander endowed with a love of theatrical drama: General John Magruder - Prince John, as he was affectionately known - a precarious game of bluff ensued. By sending out spies primed with misinformation and by continuously marching the same bands of men around the embankment walls of Yorktown accompanied by incessant banging on drums and playing of bugles, he succeeded in persuading McClellan, whose advance on the historic town ground to a halt for unnecessary consolidation within firing distance of its wall, that he had tens of thousands more men than he actually had.

The Irish Brigade was held in reserve; destined to miss out on the glory for, slow though the advance was, there could be little doubt that McClellan's behemoth would soon grind the Confederate chipmunk to dust and the rebellion was likely to be over before the Irish got a decent run at it.

Though a part of Seamus was secretly relieved, he retained his ambition of liberating Ireland and became anxious that the men's desire to do so would grow fat and indolent amidst the dwarf cedars and good grass upon which they lolled.

He had avoided O'Rorke and his cronies as much as possible since that terrible St. Patrick's Eve – only coming into their ambit when there was brigade drill, which wasn't more than once a week. He avoided O'Rorke's Fenian Circle meetings and didn't attend the senior officers' ones either. Instead, he tried to gauge and influence the inclinations of those he trusted like Mangan, Mulvaney, Dillon and Horan. They were all amicable and agreeable, but he wondered how much their hearts were really in it. He would often lay awake after Tattoo wondering if it was only men of O'Rorke's ilk that had a real taste for the fighting and bloodletting that an invasion of Ireland would entail.

And if that was so, was he cut from the same cloth as O'Rorke? And if he wasn't, did he have the ingredients to do what was necessary? He would toss and turn until Pat Mangan would lose patience and throw something, usually a badly scuffed boot, at him.

'Jesus! O'Farrell lie still will you, how's a man supposed to sleep? You're floundering worse than a beached whale on Banna strand.'

***

A mile and a half further east, Sergeant Michael O'Rorke was often restless too. Tormented not by fears of the unknown future but by recurring nightmares about events that had already happened. In his sleep, he shed the ice cool hatred of his waking hours, tossing and turning feverishly, as if doing battle with demons of nefarious origin and not the familiar species that had haunted him this long while. The ones that would not let him be. The ones that would never let him be...

Mikey crept back to the village that evening while the light was fading. Tiptoeing, sufficient innocence remaining to believe that if he went silently and prayed he would find everything repaired. Soon he was disabused even of this remnant.

At first, everything did seem magically mended. He would say the ten decades of the rosary and twenty Our Fathers he had promised Jesus and his Blessed Mother while traipsing around the hills that afternoon. He'd fulfil his part of the bargain later on – after supper and the family rosary – then he'd go down to the holy well at the back of the village and fall on his knees.

Mahers' and Keoghs' stood, as always, like stout guardians at the east end of the village. No change there. But then came the bitter smell of the black smoke he'd seen rising from near his house while he'd tried to concentrate on checking the rabbit snares along the hillside tracks. The snares were empty: which a more mature instinct would have recognised as a more definitive omen than the vague hopes fluttering his heart as he made his prayerful promises.

As if coalesced from the clouds of smoke, huge black crows circulated overhead. He came around the bend beyond Mahers' and Keoghs'. A pig with a swollen belly nosed at a dead person in the middle of the street. From the oak tree that had stood at the crossroads, since what his *Dadaí* said was the beginning of time, a man hung. His purple face twisted sideways and a huge swollen tongue protruded, as if he was put up there to make rude, unwelcoming gestures at anyone coming into the east side of the village. But young Mikey knew that he had been strung up there by the soldiers. He stood and looked; his half-formed intellect trying to cope with this nightmare that had somehow seeped into reality. But a numbness filled his head and blocked out understanding while the crows cawed in derision at such an ineffectual scarecrow. The rope holding the man (who looked like Tom Shinrone, the blacksmith) to the thick branch creaked in the summer breeze and was the only other sound to disturb the late afternoon calm.

He knew then that everyone in his village was either dead, arrested or gone into hiding. Sadness and fear weighed him down so heavily that his little legs found it difficult to support him. Bodies lay scattered carelessly around the village in various poses contorted by violent death. He came upon his father lying in the street outside the charred remains of their house. His wide, open eyes staring intently, but lifelessly, at the sky of one of the finest summers the villagers could recall. Blood and flies were all over him. As Mikey watched, a fat, greasy bluebottle probed at the white of his father's left eye. When his *Dadaí* didn't blink, Mikey finally accepted he was dead like the others.

He found his mother behind what used to be the house. Naked and dead. The blood black on her white skin. He knew it was a sin to look, but he couldn't tear his eyes away. It was such an odd, incongruent view of his *Mamaí* that it was difficult to grasp its reality.

He was still puzzling over it when the rebels hiding out in the hills – whose activities had brought the massacre upon the village – came and took him away.

Twenty-five years later and three thousand miles away, Mikey O'Rorke moaned at the loss of his home and that final view of his parents.

***

The Confederates crept away from Yorktown and the Union Army crept after them, with the Irish Brigade part of a tail undertaking road repairs and rearguard picket duty. Seamus kept himself as occupied as possible, volunteering for every bit of labour going; jumping at the chance of drilling; cleaning his gun three times a day; seeking picket duty; taking the lead in dismantling and setting up the half-tents carried by Pat Mangan and himself.

But this activity was not enough, and he found himself slipping back to the sutler wagons and Mercy's bed. He worked to compartmentalise his feelings for Kathleen from his liaisons with Mercy, but he wasn't very successful. Try as he might, feelings and emotions emanating in Ireland flowed and melded with American feelings and emotions until they were inseparable. He knew he was betraying both women. But still, he couldn't stop.

Mercy filled a vacuum in his life and he liked to think that he filled a vacuum in hers. He prayed she wasn't repaying a debt, though all he knew for sure was that she needed the company.

In the beginning, it had been a near wordless transaction. Glances and touches sufficing to define their needs. Then, as his visits increased, they grew more expansive with each other. He told her about his life in Ireland, even about Kathleen, though the weak, cowardly part of him omitted their betrothal and his intention to return was converted into a vague nebulous hope, not the definite, irrevocable, determination it constituted.

She spoke to him of a bondage viler than landlordism. Of growing up in a cotton plantation on the banks of the Mississippi. For a while not unhappy, knowing no better. Ignorant of ownership she played barefoot and nearly naked with other slave children while her Moma and Poppa and older brothers and sisters worked in the fields from early morning to fall of night. Every now and then they were corralled into a storage shed while the white master's daughter, Miss Emily, gave them a desultory education, enabling the brighter children to recognise letters of the alphabet and to add and subtract to nearly a hundred. Mercy wasn't sure now if there was a purpose to any of this beyond the young Miss salving her conscience about the slave children running wild. Maybe a little learning would make a more productive slave, especially in domestic and overseeing tasks, so long as it was insufficient to make them uppity with ideas above their station.

When Mercy was ten, she was set to working around the yard more and more: mucking out stables, drawing wood and water, weeding the mistress's flower beds and an ever-increasing number of other tasks. When she was twelve she was sent to the fields with her family. That was when she began to learn real pain and hardship. At night, when she returned to the bunk beds in the communal log-house, she had trouble unbending sufficiently from a day of stooping and stretching at the tasks of the cotton fields. Often, she hadn't enough energy to eat the bowl of evening gruel allocated to each working slave for supper.

At first she was relieved when the big master told her she was being sold to a relative of his for housework in Virginia. But when she grasped how far Virginia was from Mississippi, and that it was extremely unlikely she would ever see her parents or siblings again, she was so overcome with loneliness and grief that she was shackled and carted off to Virginia six weeks sooner than originally planned – so as not to unduly affect the productivity of her family.

Having always lived and worked in the fields and around the outside of the house, she was confused and clumsy inside. She tripped over, dropped plates, spilt wine; all the things inexperienced domestic help is likely to do. Her new mistress complained frequently about how their rustic cousin down in Mississippi sold them a 'pig-in-a-poke.' And how maybe she should be sent back or sold off. But John – the main house servant – taking her in hand and with patience and fortitude set to turning her into an accomplished domestic help for her new master and mistress. She would be staying after all, which was just as well given the awful stories of hardship and torture she heard about from elsewhere – at least the sneering, sarcastic remarks would not physically hurt her.

Despite her rustic innocence, it didn't take her long to realise that not all John's touches and smiles were meant as tokens of instruction or encouragement. She noticed that his hand lingered over hers longer than required when showing her how to pour a glass of wine without spillage or that he never stopped smiling at her from his position at the doorway while she waited on the family table. Nor did she think it entirely necessary for him to come right up behind her, so close that she could feel his breath tickling her neck and reach around her waist to guide her hand while she polished and cleaned in the dining room.

Though she didn't find it unpleasant. Rather, she was flattered to be the focus of attention of such an important house slave as John. Her womanly instincts overcame her rustic innocence, and she returned his smiles – let her own hand rest on his and wiggled her butt ever so slightly into him when he came up behind her.

John might have been Head of Domestic Service and indispensable to the smooth running of the household's affairs – but the fact remained: he was property – to be tolerated or disposed of as his owner saw fit.

However, he and Mercy received permission to live together as man and wife. An alcoholic Baptist minister related to the family even performed a short ceremony in John's room for them. They proceeded to live in the narrow wooden adjunct to the outhouses, sleeping tight together in the one bunk. She learned that such tolerance on behalf of their master was not only due to John's talents but to his being the master's son – whelped off of some pretty housemaid in his carefree youth, who'd soon after been sold on to a planter in North Carolina.

To her bitter and profound grief, she discovered that such tolerance did not extend towards their children: one by one the first four were taken from her arms and sold as soon as they were weaned. Nothing should interfere with their work, especially John's. When she protested, she was threatened with being sold on herself – not being of much value to the master or mistress other than as a companion for John. She was allowed to keep Charity when her owners realised someone should be trained up to take John's place before he became too old and the best person to do so was himself. To the envy of the other field and house slaves, who were rarely allowed anything more than breeding babies for sale, the three of them settled down to something approximating family life.

But their happiness was a slave's happiness – a very relative emotion. They continued to live in the wooden adjunct, smaller than the hen house, in which John fashioned an extra bunk from a fallen tree he was given permission to use. There was barely room for a primitive stove to cook their essentials. In winter, the stove also served as the heating source. Luckily, they didn't spend too much time there as their duties at the house started before dawn and lasted until after dusk.

Though John seemed content enough, Mercy did not think it much of a life; especially as she was certain John's father was lining her up for sale once Charity became more adept and before she became too old and valueless. They let it be known they were glad to see the daughter had inherited the father's Virginian finesse and not the mother's Mississippian ham-fistedness. With the arrival of the Union army on Virginian soil, Mercy felt her dreams of an emancipated smallholding move closer to reality.

When Johnson's army retreated behind the Rappahannock, their owners closed up the house; piled as much belongings as they could on as many pack animals and carts as they hoped to keep from both armies and, with their slaves in tow, started towards the master's brother's place in deepest Georgia. Their land and all possessions left behind might be in their enemies' hands for a while, but with the deeds of ownership lodged in a vault in New York, the master was confident he could come back shortly and reclaim everything, regardless who won the war. His highly paid lawyers in Charleston and New York would ensure it.

Mercy had no idea where, or how far, was Georgia, except John assured her it was not as far as Mississippi, which was a shame - though she supposed that those of her family who weren't dead were sold by now, she would have loved to have had the opportunity of seeing if any of her parents or siblings were still there. It was only when they were trudging up the Blue Ridge and told that there was another valley and an even larger group of mountains to cross before reaching Georgia and that, even then, they would be a long way from the brother's place, that she really began to realise how distant and how arduous the trip was going to be.

Despite the overseers' attentions with shotguns and dogs, slaves slipped away in the night and in odd daylight moments of opportunity. Massa threatened to shackle them all in chains like the ungrateful wretches they were. Mercy, maybe still imbued with Mississippian naiveté, whispered of possible escape to John when they lay side by side on the ground at night looking at the bejewelled Blue Ridge sky.

Her husband's loyalty to the father, who'd acknowledged him by making him Head of Domestic Service, was deeply imbedded. However, the mountains were hard going for a family of house servants. John realised, even before Charity began to pine and weaken from the ardours of the journey, that maybe he should listen to his wife and cut loose before it was too late. One moonless night, while the overseers were focussed on making sure they had the field slaves corralled, John and his family slipped away. He, walking out on forty years of his life to give his wife and remaining child a slim chance of freedom.

They fled back the way they'd come. Towards the plantation. Towards the only life they'd known together. They moved by night and holed up by day; for now, avoiding both armies loose in the region.

John proved his resources were not limited to domestic duties. He kept them alive and nourished by appropriating vegetables supplemented by the odd chicken or slivers of cured bacon from isolated farms in the surrounding countryside. That they were moving across a land suffering from the devastation of nearly a year of war made his feats all the more remarkable. The shackles of pre-war life had come loose and there were lots of people on the move across Northern Virginia, but a black family, unaccompanied by white masters, would have led to immediate brutal recriminations: hanging or shooting – maiming or branding and shackling at best. Squeezed by a pressing crush of Yankees, Southerners were under few illusions about whose side the slaves would take. To try and deter them from siding against their former masters, they made brutal examples of any slaves caught in the act of 'deserting' to the despised Yankees. So, John and his family crept as noiselessly and as invisibly as possible down the Blue Ridge and across the panhandle of Northern Virginia towards official Yankee lines.

They almost made it.

One night as they skirted a village southwest of Warrenton, a Confederate night patrol materialised out of the bushes and apprehended them. They were devastated - not only were they close to home, but they were close to the Union lines and had heard rumours that freed slaves were allowed to live on parcels of land belonging to their former masters. By the time the master returned, if he were ever allowed to, they'd hoped to possess a piece of Northern paper establishing their claim to a smallholding on a piece of the land they had done so much to make profitable. Instead, they were roped to other recalcitrant slaves and herded south into bondage once more, only this time, as escapees, their bondage would be cruel and oppressive and not likely to involve housework.

Then one night, before they had gone very far, they got what seemed to be a lucky break. As they were having supper unbound, a Union patrol commenced an intensive shelling of the Confederate camp. Shells landed in the midst of men and beasts; slaves and soldiers alike. In the resultant confusion of smoke and death, the ever-resourceful John grabbed his wife and child, pushed them on to a wagon and rode away from the inferno like the devil was on his tail.

Two hours later, they deemed it safe to stop at a shaded watering-hole by a brook in a thick wood of plane trees. It was then they realised they'd absconded on an ammunition wagon and what a useful offering it would make to the Union army.

They rested in the shade until the following night and then continued their journey towards their old plantation where they hoped the lines of the main Union army would be. As they camped in a peaceful glade with the brook burbling nearby, they counted their blessings at not only being free again but having four-legged transport and a valuable gift for their benefactors. They little realised as they lay down to rest that evening that it would be their last one ever together. The following night, they would run into the Union Army but, to their great misfortune, their first encounter would be with O'Rorke and his men.

Seamus lay next to her over several nights while she traced this story out. The exotic overtones of the story set off by his lover's way of talking.

'I prayed we'd git free. 'Stead we got us captured and tied on the cold groun' til the sun git up.'

Though bondage and absence of liberty were not alien concepts to him, listening to Mercy was like being transported to a universe which had previously existed for him only in the vaguest of rumours.

He wanted to promise her, like he'd promised Kathleen, that he'd take care of her and ensure they would both one day be genuinely free. But his duplicity would not extend quite that far, for which he was grateful.

So they took their comfort and told their stories, skirting around each other, in the manner of two great armies feeling each other out.

CHAPTER ELEVEN
MAY 1862

'What do ya think of Gosson's nag?'

'All show and no substance, just like its owner I'd say.'

'But the horse he's riding in the race belongs to Col Nugent. I'd say he has a chance and is worth a few bob. Say what you like about Captain Jack but he can ride a horse.'

'Colonel Kelly's I like – *Faugh-a-Ballagh* – couldn't get a better name – the battle cry of the Irish, 'Clear the Way' is right. And it's ridden by himself; they'll be used to each other.'

'Nah! Major Cavanagh and his *Katie Darling* is the one for me.'

'Ye can blow yere wages if ye like, I'm only going to have a laugh at the mule race.'

'Christ, yeah, that should be a good laugh alright.'

At last an air of excitement fluttered about the camp. There was going to be a horse race. A full card, over fences, with a mule race on the flat to round off the *craic*.

Seamus had never seen a real horse race. There was a painting of a horse race in the kitchen of Nolan's house that he'd seen when he went to pay the rent, but now, he would have a real-life, close-up view of the action.

The racetrack had been laid out in a wide field next to dense woods on the banks of the Chickahominy river, near to where the Brigade had been transported a couple of weeks before. The May morning of the race dawned calm and bright, setting the hearts of even the most unsporting a-flutter.

Meagher was in his element: dashing hither and thither, ensuring that the invited guests, especially the officers and foreign observers, were looked after; that enough food and drink had been organised for the intervals, that the jumps were sufficiently sturdy and challenging and that proper cards including colours, riders and owners had been printed. Seamus was finally seeing how the man's passion and eloquence motivated men to follow him. At least on social occasions.

Most of the army was further south and west, where it was rumoured real fighting was beginning. But the Irish weren't involved so why couldn't they enjoy themselves before they atrophied from boredom?

First, there was a Gaelic football match. Now this was something Seamus did know about. A couple of times a year, if the men were feeling strong enough and there had been enough to eat, Kilgarry would play their neighbours - Castletown or Malletstown. It normally ended in a free-for-all with every healthy man, woman and child of each parish taking part, the game sweeping over and back across several miles, going on for hours. Often those taking part in the pushing, shoving and running didn't have a clue where the ball was and groups of men ducked into shebeens along the way to wet their whistles before carrying on with the ruckus hours later. One fifteenth of August, a game had started from Our Lady's Blessed Well in Castletown and didn't properly finish until two days later in the nearby parish of Ballybruff, by which time the ball was in smithereens and even the most energetic of the parishioners were exhausted. There had been a few games since the Famine ended, but it was difficult to be joyful with Nolan and his militia thugs tightening a vice of terror around the people, killing off any awakening frivolity in the post-Famine parish. However, Seamus had learned enough to hold his own in this organised game on a properly marked pitch.

'I didn't think muck savages from Limerick knew a football from the crack of their arses.' Jer Horan said, by way of a compliment as Seamus lashed the stuffed pig's bladder high between the tall poplar goalposts for the sixth or seventh time.

Seamus smirked. 'Nice pass,' he said, 'and I thought Tipperary men were only good for rutting with their sisters.'

'If you saw the puss on my sister, you'd practise football too.'

Seamus laughed. 'That'd be why the other Tipp men are so useless then: they've got the better-looking sisters.'

Their crude banter was interrupted by the ball bouncing in front of them. Seamus snatched it; swivelled sideways out of a shoulder charge from a corporal in the 69th and kicked it into the path of Horan, who set off on a solo run.

It was hard work dashing around on the soft surface, clods of earth and splatters of mud flying everywhere and he supposed they looked ridiculous to the growing crowd of spectators - running around in their vests with their trousers inside their socks, some of them in their long-johns despite the presence of officers' wives - but it felt so good to be exercising non-martially on such a fine day that he didn't care.

From a clash between the 88th's cook and the 69th's bugler, the ball squirted his way. He clasped it and prepared to give it a whack, but just as he dropped the ball and raised his leg, he received an almighty thud on his left shoulder numbing his entire side. Stunned, he watched as the ball bounced away from him.

O'Rorke.

Seamus hadn't noticed him or any of his cronies in the game before now. Must have just slipped in; there was better organisation here compared to the parish affairs at home, but there wasn't strict control; players joined and left the game continuously.

Joy leached from the day. O'Rorke grinned, tipping him a lascivious wink like they were co-conspirators in something only the two of them had any knowledge about. Something immoral and underhand, but something they were in together.

'Fuck you, Sergeant.'

His antagonist laughed: 'I could have you put in the stockade for weeks for that remark. But I won't because it will be more fun seeing you hang from a sour apple tree.'

'Hang?'

'That or a similar execution is likely to be your fate.'

Seamus shrugged.

'We have sent your description back to Cork, our peers should have confirmation any day now that you are the man who murdered Daniel O'Leary. I have no doubt about it, but I'm sure a man like yourself can understand we want things done right. As soon as we get word back, you're a dead man.'

'Don't I get a chance to defend myself? Who are these peers anyway? My peers are in the 88th Company L.'

'Your peers are those who suffered under an alien yolk and who have determined to do something about it. They are not a bunch of slave lovers and above all,' he stared contemptuously at Seamus,' they are not those who condone sleeping with slave whores. You,' he prodded a finger into Seamus's chest, 'and your kind will not stand in anyone's way this time. You will not be given a chance to defend yourself with weasel words. The sentence of the court of your peers will be carried out in a manner and time of my choosing. Maybe later today.' O'Rorke winked, then turned before Seamus could respond and chased after the ball-carrying John Shinnors with an intent that signalled if he had to pull his opponent's head off to get the ball he wouldn't hesitate.

Seamus retired from the match.

Katie Darling ridden by Major Cavanagh won the main race and Meagher, with typical flamboyance, presented the skin of a tiger he'd shot in Central America to the winner.

'Will you look at the langer on your man?' Pat Mangan nodded at a mule who appeared to have something other than racing on his mind.

'Lucky mine isn't quarter that size or the girls would never have allowed me leave Tipperary.' Horan said.

'Well, the girls might have been sorry, but 'twould have been a lucky day for the rest of us.' Mangan kept the banter going.

'Come on boys, last chance! Who's your money on? Place your bets now.' John Mulvaney came along, sniffling, offering odds and carrying a pouchful of dollars.

'Trust a Galwayman to be making the money, no matter what the situation. I'd say now you'd nearly open a book on the first one of us to get the bullet.' Mangan said.

'I already have and all my own money is on yourself. Knowing where you sleep, I'm guaranteed to collect.'

The other two guffawed. 'What are the odds on the fella that's displaying his bayonet to the world?' Horan asked.

Seamus drank in the everyday banter. It was refreshing to be reminded that most of his comrades were ordinary men, Irish and otherwise, just wanting to get by as best they could, to survive. Though most of them had seen hard, even desperate times, none were eaten up with the obsessive hatred of O'Rorke and his men.

It was great fun watching the drummer boys struggle with the mules. The animals were obstinate at the best of times but, sensing that they were expected to perform in some special way, they were especially obstreperous. They all faced in directions other than the course in front of them, except for one, who suddenly galloped down the field with his unfortunate rider only half on him. This led to a crescendo of hollering, whistling and smart comments, which aggravated not only that particular mule, but the others as well, who now bucked, bit and brayed their unwillingness. The more the beasts tormented the poor drummer boys, the more the men were amused.

'Sorry! What?' Seamus realised that John Mulvaney was speaking to him.

'Will you chance a dollar or two?' The Galwayman repeated.

'He's in love, his mind ain't on no mule racing' Pat Mangan responded to Mulvaney for him.

Seamus gave what he hoped was a careless laugh. 'I'll have two dollars on that beige one who just threw his rider into the crowd. I'd say he'll be game enough once he gets going.'

He chucked the dollars at Mulvaney, who stuffed them into the leather pouch he carried over his shoulder and gave Seamus a slip of paper in return. "Ballygobackwards" was the name of the mule he'd chosen.

An apt name as he thought it was time to go backwards himself. He would surely do more good hiding out at home than here in the Union army. Here, he had gotten on the wrong side of a very dangerous element in the Irish Brigade and gotten involved with another woman. However, he had refined some martial skills on the parade ground and acquired a rudimentary knowledge of military organisation, which he could use to help the Crew and to protect his mother and Kathleen. O'Rorke's threat convinced him he'd been fooling himself when he'd thought there was more good to be got from remaining here – where he was likely to be wastefully killed by elements in his own side – than returning home. In a country as large as America, he would surely be able to make his way back to Ireland, where he was truly needed, whilst managing to avoid being arrested for desertion. There would certainly be comrades in the Brigade who would take a dim view of him walking out, but he wouldn't ever see them again and didn't owe them, so he needn't worry too much. He felt relief at coming to this decision and at giving up on the pretence that everything was fine. He was due to be on picket duty tonight and it shouldn't be too difficult to slip away from the duty sergeant before dawn; for now, there was the mule race and the evening's entertainments, including a play, to look forward to. He was determined not to visit Mercy before he left. It was time to prove his loyalty to Kathleen.

A pistol fired and the mule race started. Only two of the six beasts went any distance down the slope; the others were still turning and twisting sideways or refusing to budge at all. One of those who had taken off looked likely to throw his rider at any minute, the poor lad hung on desperately with a leg and an arm, the rest of his body having slipped down the other side.

The spectators, including Seamus, were cheering, jeering and catcalling at the chaotic spectacle. Meagher was with other senior officers in a stand overlooking the course; red-faced and shouting: 'Bravo! Bravo!' He had obviously been entertaining Generals French, Richardson and the others in grand style. 'The dumbest of beasts illuminates the path to glory' he called out with a flourish and toasted the recalcitrant mules with a swig of champagne.

Ballygobackwards, suddenly decided to go forwards, while the leading mule had stopped halfway down the track to stick his head in the window of a ruined cottage flanking the course. Seamus began to think he might be in the money and shouted his head off at the prospect. The surreal encounter on the football pitch receded for the moment.

A cannon boomed. He assumed it was to signal the start of other events a few fields away. A tug-o-war, sack, and egg-and-spoon races, amongst other items, had also been arranged. Another boom. And another. Suddenly there was what he recognised from field exercises as an exchange of artillery fire. A furious one.

The calling and jeering died away; everyone turned their attention towards the officers' stand for reassurance. But they too had gone silent; their good cheer evaporated. Meagher was sombre and serious. A rider galloped up and passed an order to General Richardson. Meagher bellowed for his regimental commanders.

'Come on, let's see Brosnihan or Byers and find out what's happening,' Mulvaney said. The mule race and other festivities were forgotten. The men began to coalesce towards their sergeants, lieutenants and captains. The generals descended from their stand and mounted their horses.

Seamus watched, knowing his life-path was again taking an unanticipated twist.

It started with another weary, wandering, rain-soaked march. The hardest and worst of all. Less than two hours after cheering and jeering the mule race, the Irish Brigade found itself slashing and tramping miserably through the swamps and muddy lanes of the Chickahominy floodplain. Rain sheeted down - lowering the final curtain on their entertainment.

'Christ, this is a nice dose alright,' Tom Dillon, head down against the driving rain, muttered on behalf of everyone.

'Mulvaney, are you going to pay out on that mule race?' someone called.

From Seamus's left, the Galwayman replied. 'Lads, ye can have all the money ye bet and more if I ever see a dry campfire again.'

Seamus plodded along, intent only on surviving this march and arriving at whatever destination the powers that be had allocated for them. There was no way of breaking off on his own for now. Initially, he welcomed the mind-numbing physical ardour of the march as a means of diverting his attention from darker, deeper, mental concerns. But as night fell, with no end to the marching in sight and the rain running in rivulets inside his soaked uniform, he prayed for it to finish. His boot snagged on a creeping root and he stumbled headlong into a pool of stagnant, foul smelling water. Pat Mangan and Tom Dillon assisted him out to half-hearted jeers from others nearby.

He resumed with as much dignity as he could muster – saturated and coated in damp, evil smelling slime. He dug deep in an effort to dredge up happy memories to sustain him; no longer concerned with the moral implications of melding memories of Mercy and Kathleen. Anything he could mentally grasp to get him through would suffice.

Around midnight, they bivouacked. But as they didn't strike the pup tents, there was no opportunity to change out of wet clothes.

Nevertheless, it was a blessed relief to get the equipment they carried off their backs. Using fallen branches, a group eventually got a damp fire going under the shade of a stand of tall pines. Seamus threw some coffee and sugar into his enamel mug and, while he waited for the boiling pot of water to be passed around, he toasted a piece of dried pork on the end of a stick.

The accumulated bone weariness of the day's activities took control of his body and he barely prevented himself from falling headfirst into the fire. Whorls of fetid steam rose from those parts of clothing closest to the fire. The rest of him shivered with teeth-chattering cold.

'Alright men, that's it. Move out! Forward! March!' Byers came along, shouting.

'Whaat?'

Seamus laughed incredulously. This couldn't be true.

'For God's sake, Sergeant, where would we be going on such a godforsaken night in such a godforsaken country?' someone asked for him.

'We have orders to be on the left flank of the army, in line of battle, by dawn,' Byers replied, a martinet at the best of times, it seemed to the men that he was being deliberately obnoxious now.

'What bloody good will we be, exhausted and hungry?'

'Just get a move on, will you? Orders are orders; I'm only obeying them same as the rest of you'd better.'

'Come on lads, let's go.' Jer Horan came along, adding a soft voice of authority to the instructions and quashing any doubts regarding their reality.

Seamus repacked his utensils, shouldered his knapsack and musket and walked dreamily after the others.

In the small hours of the morning, they crossed the Grapevine Bridge over the Chickahominy to the southside. Seamus was woken from his walking reverie by a loud splash.

'Help! Help! I can't swim.' A voice cried from out of the night.

'Peter Mullins has fallen in!' someone shouted.

Mullins was an engineer, a likeable, learned fellow over six-foot tall with dark curly hair, Seamus didn't know what county he was from. Though they didn't mix closely, Mullins, who wasn't averse to a good time, had often joined their fire for a sing-along with Pat Gorman or Pa Bourke. Once, he'd told a story of such dry wit about a Cavan horse dealer, even Jer Horan was in stitches.

Seamus didn't question the incongruity of an engineer who couldn't swim but, along with others, grabbed hold of the rope that was thrown to Mullins. There was a drag on the line as the engineer held on and they started to haul him ashore. Too many men were trying to help, jostling and pushing each other; however this was not what caused the rescue to go wrong. The engineer did start to lift out of the water, but his face already bore the pale-green hue of the grave. Despite all the hands on the rope the power of the swollen river kept trying to pull Mullins away and when he thumped off a rock a few yards from safety, it succeeded. He lost his grip and slid screaming with arms wheeling down the rushing black waterway. Men fell over each other trying to race after him, but within moments he was gone.

The vision of his grave-pale face, bearing the certainty of his imminent death accompanied Seamus on the remainder of the march.

They began to pass through the wreckage of the previous day's fighting. Twisted and broken hulks of artillery pieces and smashed caissons shadowed their route like dark, deformed angels. Maybe he was cursed to march forever through the twisted landscape, trapped between sleep and consciousness, as a punishment for his transgressions. In anticipation of such an eternal walk his steps took on a slow, heavy rhythm. He no longer always knew who he was beside; he hadn't seen Horan, Mangan, Mulvaney or Dillon for hours; though it was possible Horan had been alongside him a few minutes before. His companions kept changing until each member of Company L must have stepped up to have their moment with him. Or was it him that kept dropping back?

It ceased raining, but a biting breeze swirled cold damp clothes around his skin. Then, when he was nearly dry, a train of horses and artillery galloped past splashing and splattering, drenching him anew.

Shortly afterwards, on ground that appeared no different from what they had been marching through, word came back that they were in position to stack arms and rest. With a final, superhuman, effort Seamus found a clear patch and threw himself onto the damp grass. A horizon of ghostly, dawn-light dominated his line of sight.

He closed his eyes and willed his brain to shut down.

For in a short few hours, he would finally see the Elephant.

CHAPTER TWELVE

He woke in hell. Dead and dying men and horses were strewn in illogical contortions amidst the wreckage of ruined artillery and shattered trees. The body he'd slept beside stared lifelessly at him; mangled, stringy flesh hung where a left arm and leg should be. A horse with its bowels strewn about lay further down the gentle slope. What he'd thought were the murmurs of stirring men were the groans and cries of yesterday's maimed still lying on the field.

He'd slept in a charnel house.

He dragged his aching, chilled body up from the ground far quicker than he thought possible and hurried away to find healthy companionship.

Some Company L men were in a hollow near the brow of a hill roasting coffee. 'The dead arose and appeared to many,' Jer Horan exclaimed when he saw him approaching.

'If the dead arose here, there would be many of them and few of us,' John Mulvaney added.

Seamus threw a fist of green coffee beans onto the roast. All actions, even conversation, were conducted with a solemnity appropriate to the pall cast by the carnage around them; they recognised they should have been grateful when the Irish Brigade was kept in reserve and detailed for fatigue-duty only.

Before long, the aroma of brewing coffee reminded them they were still amongst the living and they should make the most of any comforts, however small. When it brewed, Seamus drank it unsweetened, hoping the bitter taste would shock his system into life.

Byers galloped up on a sorrel horse. 'Get ready to move on in five minutes.'

'But we haven't…'

Horan, grasping the seriousness of the situation, stood up and kicked over the flames. 'Right, boys, this is it,' he said and tossed his coffee away, intimating they should follow him and avoid an unnecessary conflagration with Byers.

A banshee screech proclaiming imminent death shook Seamus out of his lethargy. A shell thudded into the side of the hill and knocked him off his feet. Hot coffee scalded his thigh. When he scrambled back up, the world wobbled and men shouted but no words came out. He widened his jaws with the intention of shouting himself. The pressure on his eardrums released itself and he was hit by a cacophony of sound.

What seemed like the remainder of the Irish Brigade came pouring over the brow of the hill; Meagher, Gosson and other mounted staff officers, led the way. Green and gold harps with sunbursts colouring the morning; Meagher proclaiming Irish valour and glory. A shell burst not thirty yards in front of him. He jerked his horse back into line. His coolness and bravery under fire could not be faulted and Seamus watched in admiration. Then he realised his own men were about to come marching over him and he dashed off after Horan and Mulvaney.

The Irish Brigade was going into battle. By God, they had tried doing without the Paddies but it hadn't worked. All the horror of last night's march was forgotten. Men kept too long on the leash were striding towards glory. The hair-raising stories of Jer Horan and other Bull Run veterans were put to one side. The 69th and 88th had been chosen while the losers in the 63rd had been sent to pull artillery from the previous day's battle out of the swamp and to guard a bridge. The men chosen to fight were determined to make the most of their opportunity. No longer were they going to be teased and treated as greenhorns; from today onwards that was only for the 63rd.

Imagine! General Sumner himself sent for them. The excitement, the rumours, the bravado buoyed Seamus with a sense of purpose that gallons of bitter coffee could never even approach. He strode towards his destiny alongside Dinny Clarke, not one of his regular coterie; but as sound an Irish American that ever lived. As if he was his only brother, Seamus's feelings swelled with a love of this dark-haired man of barely legal height. He would kill to ensure Dinny Clarke lived.

The colours of the 69th and 88th fluttered in the early morning breeze. The spoiling whine of a shell rent the air once more and landed in amongst men over on the right. Probably as far over as the 69th where O'Rorke and his cronies were. Men and mud flew skyward. He didn't have time to feel anything. Colonels, captains, lieutenants, sergeants, and corporals were shouting at them to spread out, spread out. A thin line of hungry-looking Confederates was strung along the bottom of the field in front of a railway track. It was they who'd created the carnage he woke up to this morning. They didn't look like much, but, by God, they were going to get it anyhow.

'Get ready! Shoulder Arms! Steady! Steady! Wait! Aim low! Aim low! Fire!'

He had no memory of priming his musket or of bringing it to his shoulder. But suddenly he had a scrawny rebel in his sights. He would never, ever, dare tell anyone, but it was certain he fired high into the trees about his target's head. Smoke blanked out the line of Confederates; borne away with elation at firing his first shot in anger on the American continent, Seamus went roaring and sprinting down the field.

A shower of lead spewed out of the smoke; most of it went over their heads, but enough stayed low to make the charging Irish falter and hesitate. Men fell wounded and dead along several points of the attack. The lead shower brought a strong whiff of reality in its wake.

Seamus felt a swell of rage and disappointment at the thoughts of the charge stalling and reversing; at bloodlust being denied.

Meagher came to his rescue. With a characteristic flourish he galloped in front of the line. 'Up boys and charge for Ireland!' He reared his horse on its back legs for dramatic effect. 'Remember, the world is watching you. Don't let yourselves down now.'

More lead came whistling through the air. It seemed certain to hit Meagher, but he didn't flinch and it flew past. Even if the Brigadier-General had been swigging from his silver hip flask, Seamus no longer doubted his bravery. The bullets missed him. Two or three men fell but the enemy was still mostly aiming high.

A regimental captain screamed: 'Charge!' And the 88th took off again. Within seconds they were once more roaring their war cries and surging pell-mell down the field. Seamus felt a resurgence of euphoria.

Irish bayonets were going to taste blood and his own would not be deprived.

'*Faugh- a-Ballagh! Faugh-a-Ballagh!*' Another volley came flying out of the woods and fell with greater accuracy and effect upon its target. A lad called Mason, nicknamed 'Stones,' staggered in front of Seamus and fell back; he could see one side of the young fellow's face and at first couldn't see anything wrong. Then, as Stones twisted further, Seamus saw that his right eye was a bloody pulp with red and clear liquids bearing stringy dark substances, like bits of brain, running from it. The boy toppled face down; the bullet had exited the back of his head leaving jagged bone, gristle and blood in its wake.

Seamus registered numbness but was only prevented from carrying on with his charge by Byers's raised arm. At first, he assumed the sergeant wanted them to fire a retaliatory volley. But then he saw that other Union soldiers had been brought across in front of them and sent into the woods to rout the rebels. The image of Stones's pulped head diluted his anger with these soldiers for infringing on his glory.

They closed up the gaps where their dead and injured had fallen and watched other brigades in their division go to work. It seemed that the Irish had been held back again – not trusted to do the important stuff.

Seamus sensed the 88th tighten and contract; cloaked in steam and vapours. Meagher and his staff held their horses steady before them.

Dinny Clarke took a well chewed plug of tobacco from his mouth and offered it silently to Seamus. He shook his head. Clarke spat with venom onto the field, replaced the plug and proceeded to work it vigorously.

The chewing, sniffing, shuffling and coughing noises transcended into something greater than the compulsive movements of anxious men held at a standstill, though what they portended could not be foretold. The flags drooped in the early morning dew – their power having dissipated as suddenly as it had been bestowed.

The battle in the woods sounded like the snarling of rabid dogs, clawing and biting each other. It was soon apparent one was gaining the upper hand: there was sustained musketry crackling and shouts from the same line. Smoke belched out of the woods. Union blue spilt out; at first in dribs and drabs and then in one big skedaddle. Men ran; in dread of the slavering beasts that had accosted them in the woods. Here came Confederate grey hurrying them along; soon both predators and quarry would be upon the Irish Brigade.

Then General Sumner himself was riding in front of their line. 'Boys, I am your General. I know the Irish Brigade will not retreat. I stake my position on you.'

They knew themselves what they were. They were the last line standing between victory and defeat. The backend called upon to stem a rout and save the United States of America. The Irish Brigade.

They were charging again, with a ferocity reinforced by the pent-up tension and frustration of the previous minutes. Seamus wasn't screaming, *'Faugh-a-Ballagh,'* anymore. He was just screaming. There were the Confederates, before him at last. Out in the open, in bright daylight. No more half glimpses or grappling in the dark. There was the enemy and here was his bayonet. He bore down on a ragged piece of scum, a retreating Union soldier crossed his line of vision, Seamus cast him contemptuously aside.

His nerve endings were pre-emptively savouring the sensation of pushing his bayonet into the sinewy flesh before him when his target sprung catlike to one side; Seamus felt the butt of the man's musket slash across his back, but already there was another scrawny face in front of him and he lashed out at it, without considering pain or missed opportunities, then punched another rebel in the face with the fist of his free hand and readied his bayonet for a stab at yet another.

His life to date: its hopes, loves, humiliations, tragedies and petty triumphs distilled into the outcome of this mad stabbing, punching, kicking, caterwaul on the edge of these Virginian woods. It wasn't just his own life that depended on the outcome, it was Kathleen; his mother; Padraic; Mercy; Kilgarry; Ireland. He fought and screeched like a golden eagle defending her chicks from a merciless predator. Prior to this his opportunities to lash out were confined to drunken inter-parish brawls, maiming defenceless animals, burning hayricks and firing shots over houses. But now he had real opportunity against a real enemy. The hardened, drawn, face before him was not that of a backwoods Mississippian farmer scrabbling a living and protecting his homeland, but the face of an omnipotent, uncaring authority determined to keep peasants like him in his place; it was the face of the enemy within: Catholic militia men back in Kilgarry, and O'Rorke and Flaherty here in America. He lashed out with a viciousness that busted the despised visage into a satisfying mush of blood and broken bone. That was the stuff for 'em.

He lashed out all around. Generations of anguish demanded satisfaction.

Slowly, he grew aware that the primal forces surrounding him were shifting. The grey line was giving way and the blue moved forward with less resistance. The bastards were starting to give away. But they would not escape his vengeance. He increased his violence. He was a Celtic Beserker. No mercy to his children's enemies. He hacked, slashed, and punched, and when he saw their backs, he fired his musket, reloaded, and fired again. But this required too much patience so he dashed after the fleeing rebels, determined to dole out speedier vengeance with his bayonet.

The Brigade drove the Confederates back over the railway line and into the woods. The cover was dark and dense in there, but Seamus was not going to be deterred, he had waited all his life for this opportunity to lash out and he was far from sated.

'Stop! Halt! Regroup, 88th!' Regimental Captain McMahon shouted orders came to Seamus like whisperings in a dream and as such he chose to ignore them. He hurried after a dirty, grey back, determined to maim it but was grabbed by the collar and hauled backwards. He tried to shake off the restraining hold. Martin Brosnihan's authoritative voice brought him to his senses.

'Private Farrell, you will rejoin your company as commanded by your superior officer!' Seamus slowly returned from the hate-filled reverie he had slid into. The glaze cleared from his eyes and, almost to his surprise, he grew aware of the other members of Company L, still facing frontward but dropping back in line with the rest of the 88th. Brosnihan and himself were several yards ahead of the rest. He realised he'd started on a suicidal one man charge after the rebels – slavering like a maniac. The shock of what he had been doing hit him and it took great effort to disguise the shaking in his limbs as he fell into line.

As the Brigade dropped back, it gathered its dead and wounded. Father Corby moved amongst them praying, offering consolation to the stricken.

Meagher was there too, on foot. 'Well done, lads! Glorious work! Glorious work!'

Dinny Clarke was hit in the leg, just above the knee. Seamus and Tom Dillon half lifted, half dragged, him across to a battered little barn near the railway line and laid him down on the straw next to other moaning, groaning comrades. Clarke's wound was bloody, though it didn't seem too serious. But as they lowered him, he begged.

'Boys, don't leave me, please! They'll take the leg. Stay! Ye'll stop them. I know ye will. I want my leg, I do, I really do. I need it!'

'Don't worry, Dinny, it's only a flesh wound. No bone has been hit. They won't take the leg. A good clean dressing is all it needs.' Dillon said.

'Boys, please don't leave me.' Clarke begged once more.

'See you tomorrow, Dinny,' Dillon insisted and they walked away.

They had no choice. Though Seamus didn't think they would remove the leg, he wouldn't have swapped places with Dinny for the world. Already the rasping of saws on bones and accompanying screams emanated from the rear of the barn.

Sumner was with Meagher and his staff when they returned to their company. 'You've done the name of Irishman proud today, boys,' the general said to everyone within earshot, 'and you've performed a great service for your country. In fact, I do not exaggerate when I say you have saved the Union, for if that rebel charge had broken through and turned my flank, there was nothing between here and the Chickahominy to hinder their progress.' Bowing to the men and saluting Meagher, the old gentleman sauntered off, trotting his horse. Meagher's chest puffed out from the praise he and his men had received.

The rebels had been driven back that day; but for how long and how far? The pickets of the Irish Brigade were alert that night and there was an extra cautiousness around the fires. Yet, there was also a pride that would not be denied. They sat around asking of each other, wondering about the injured and recounting stories of those who'd died.

Their wearying march to the battleground and the ferocity of the skirmishing had been cathartic of the need to drink, sing or boast.

After doing his turn on picket duty, Seamus returned to the fire with Jer Horan and Pat Mangan. He didn't speak much. No one mentioned his earlier ferocity; maybe it wasn't noticed in the melee of the charge; maybe it was no different from how they all behaved. But he couldn't get what he'd done and felt to fit any pattern of previous experience. The intensity of his lust for blood and vengeance had been unique. He had fought and hated many times before, but nowhere near that scale. He tried not to recognise its similarity to the intensities driving O'Rorke and he desperately tried to block out the feelings of pleasure, even joy, he had experienced at letting go; at being so bestial. He availed of the earliest opportunity to crawl into a dry groundsheet under a warm canvas, marvelling at the great changes the previous twenty fours had wrought in him.

Outside, two armies settled uncomfortably in front of each other; restless and wary. The cries of the wounded made dark music while the surgeons sawed.

The rabid dogs of North and South were sated for now. The Battle of Fair Oaks was over and the Confederates had failed to break out from their defensive positions in front of Richmond and overrun the Northerners.

    The Irish Brigade had indeed saved the Union.

CHAPTER THIRTEEN
JUNE 1862

Their reward was a return to the tedium of camp life. At least this time, they remained at the front line within earshot of the enemy. But, after a few days, even this novelty lost its lustre and once more the Irish Brigade felt condemned to stasis while the war was fought elsewhere.

When they'd cleared the bodies from the field and barn and buried their dead, tents were set up, pickets shook out and streets marked. Meagher exuberantly christened the site: 'Camp Victory' and they settled down within sight of the spires of Richmond, and within earshot of bells that surely tolled the Confederacy's final hours.

Seamus tried to keep himself busy by volunteering for extra picket and fatigue duty. He continued to recall, rather too vividly, his lust for battle and blood; driven by an uncontrollable urge to take out every slight and humiliation he had suffered on a people he didn't know, on land that was far more theirs than his. A sneaky pride birthed alongside the shame. He tried to disown it, but it whispered seductively of courage undaunted and battle honour attained. He couldn't recall killing anyone. He had discharged his musket, lashed out several times with his bayonet and struck many blows with his fist as he rampaged. But, despite this frenzied activity, he couldn't say for sure if he'd done any damage beyond busting a nose or two. Still, it felt sufficient to have entered battle and retained his courage intact; next time, he would strive to be more controlled in his actions for he recognised that only then would he be a soldier of real worth. Only then would he be any good to those at home he would one day return to.

A large part of him longed to return to the killing fields. There was death and danger out there, even madness, but also relief from anxiety about Kathleen and his mother; escape from humiliation at the hands of O'Rorke and his cronies and absence of guilt about his liaisons with Mercy. On the battlefield there was only the moment. And though he'd suffered from a form of insanity and all around was injury and death, he'd never felt more alive. Not even when he was raiding with the Kilgarry Crew as Captain Rock.

Dinny Clarke didn't return. Some said infection set in, that he had lost his leg and was mustered out to become another crippled beggar in the streets of New York or Washington. More said he had died from fever and loss of blood and was spared this humiliation. Seamus pushed away images of Dinny's pleading face as they'd left him on the straw of the dilapidated barn.

He began to feel lethargic and listless, no matter how much drilling, fatiguing, and picketing he engaged in. An outbreak of gambling beyond the usual poker games swept through Camp Victory. A simple game, but a sure-fire way to lose money, called Chuck-Luck took hold in the Brigade. On the reverse side of a gum blanket six squares, numbered 1 to 6, were painted. The Better placed his money on a favoured number and the Banker rolled the dice. If the Better's number came up, he collected his money plus the Banker's matching stake, if it didn't, the Banker collected both stakes.

Seamus had never gambled with dice or cards before - he was familiar with the rules of poker and forty-five, but he'd played neither for money. Around the campfires of the army, he had been content to watch others play, relieved that he didn't have to go through the tension of staking his hard-earned money on the flick of a card or two. He never knew for sure what attracted him to Chuck-Luck, maybe it was the mesmeric quality of the bone dice rattling in the empty salt and pepper pots followed by heart stopping silence as the players waited to see where it would fall after it was finally tossed into space. He began to place money on numbers just to experience the rawness of that moment which followed the tantalising rattle of the shake.

And began to lose. Not heavily and not all at once. But, despite little triumphs here and there, and despite being careful not to stake too much at any one time, the trend of his Chuck-Luck experience was distinctly downwards. And while he laughed his losses off and would never admit them to Jer Horan, John Shinnors, Pat Mangan or any of his mates in Company L, they rapidly became another chain around his neck. While he had suffered many setbacks in life, the day he realised he would be unable to send any of his monthly pay home to his mother and Kathleen stood out then, and later, as one of the blackest and lowest of his life.

Martin Brosnihan swept Seamus's last five dollars off the ground with a flourish. 'Coffee and caviar for me, coffee and hardtack for you.'

Seamus made a thin grin which he hoped hid the bleak truth behind the sergeant's teasing. As soon as common decency allowed, he slipped away from the game and the banter of his companions. Dusk was falling and with Company L not on the roster for picket duty there would be no other military tasks until morning, which was unfortunate as he desperately needed something productive to occupy his time between now and then. Another evening of picking lice from his hair and clothes would not diminish the loathsome vermin one iota; sleep wouldn't come, though undoubtedly thoughts of failure and feelings of humiliation would.

It was unlikely that the money he sent home made any immediate difference to Kathleen or his mother. Kathleen and her family had cobbled together the second annual rent payment to Nolan back in September when the harvests were finished, in theory that should save them from eviction for now - at least for non-payment. They would both be surviving off the potatoes, cabbage, and turnips – the harvests in 1860 had been good around Limerick – there was sufficient food until at least the end of the Summer. There was little else available for them to buy, except the odd sack of flour or meal. His mother was evicted and living with Padraic, who could be counted on to provide the little it would take to keep her. He didn't get to send money home every month anyway as the Army was not so well organised that it paid out every month, yet *he* knew that he had blown this month's pay on Chuck-Luck and failed in the obligation he had placed on himself to take care of his dependents in Ireland. He couldn't bear the thoughts of lying on his blanket feeling that failure eat away at him even more voraciously than the lice.

He went looking for the only comfort he was currently certain of in the Army of the Potomac.

Mercy neither reproached him for staying away nor welcomed him back him with open arms. She took him to her bed and made love to him with only slight detachment. Afterwards she spoke specifically of her dreams for the future.

'I need a little more money and then I'm taking Charity up North,' she said matter-of-factly.

His breathing had yet to settle back into a steady rhythm. 'To New York?' he gasped.

'No, further North. Probably Chicago. As far away from here and Mississippi as possible.'

'What will you do?'

'A rich man's accounts in a big house, where Charity and I can stay and be accepted as free people; maybe change our names. Though, as that's what I most want, it's unlikely to happen. I'll be a seamstress, a washer-woman, a nanny, anything that will mean a better chance in life for Charity than I had.'

Briefly, he wondered if she expected him to offer help, to take her North and look after the girl and herself. Then he realised this was a selfish thought, based on a need to boost his own esteem. She wanted nothing from him except to be someone to hold and make sporadic love to as she and her daughter passed through this empty, tragic phase of their lives. Thankfully, he found enough dignity not to patronise her fatalism.

'Do you think people like us will ever get what we most want?' he asked instead.

'I don't know, it sometimes feels as if we're to be given little pieces. Just enough to tantalise us, then God slams the door and says: "Sorry, that's not for you!"'

'We need to get a foot in the door before he slams it.'

She laughed. Neither bitter nor sardonic. 'I guess that's it,' she said.

Suddenly he wanted her to ask him, to beg him, to go with her and look after herself and her daughter. He saw how good life would be with this feisty, determined woman. Immediately, he also saw it would be impossible. A penniless Irish emigrant and an ex-slave with a child. He'd seen enough of America already to know that society wouldn't tolerate this combination – North or South. Maybe around the Five Points where 'society' didn't encroach, and its rules didn't apply – but neither of them wanted that.

Anyway, Ireland was where his obligations lay, this was merely a brief escape from them.

'We won't see each other again after I go North,' she said.

It was no more than common sense. No more than the next logical step and not more than what had been in his own mind. Yet, its very reasonableness pushed him onto the defensive.

'You don't need me anymore, is that it?' he asked.

'I would if I let myself. I want us to stop before I become reliant. You should too.'

'And if I don't?'

'I'll be here for you until I leave, which will be soon. That's all.'

He looked at her. It had only been a few short months, but they had been through too much individually and together to worry unduly about modesty, though his Catholic mores made him more circumspect. She lay on her back, cherry-dark nipples protruding from small, perfectly formed breasts. Sheen from the flickering candlelight made her skin luminous. He choked back despair at the thoughts of not seeing her again and reached out, determined to live for the moment. Nearby, from behind a threadbare curtain, her daughter's deep breathing filled the stillness until their passion rose once more.

***

O'Rorke was moaning in his sleep again. The men outside glanced at each other and shuffled silently away. He held mesmerising power over them during the day; it was a power they obeyed out of fear rather than respect. Yet his night-time mumblings and moans bore a Stygian quality that scared them far more than his daylight looks and commands. They drew closer to their own fires or wrapped themselves tightly in their blankets, desperate not to think about the dark demons stalking their captain.

The leader of the rebels who took him from the devastated village and its inhabitants was a kind, tall man called Dáithi O'Laoire – whose people came from just outside the village, though their cottage was now a tumbled heap of stones and its occupants, apart from Dáithi, in their graves or scattered to the four winds. He tried to get Mikey's aunt in the next village to take the youngster in. But she refused adamantly, citing her enormous difficulty in putting food into the mouths of her own brood and parading before them, as evidence, the emaciated sticks that were Mikey O'Rorke's cousins.

'But living in the mountains with us is no life for a small boy,' Dáithi argued.

'Well, it would be a better life than starving to death down here in the valley with me,' Mikey's aunt retorted.

'You're the only blood he's got left,' Dáithi tried desperately.

'And I suppose you're going to say next that blood is thicker than water. But the blood in these thin veins,' she indicated his emaciated cousins, 'is thicker for me than his, so I've made my choice.'

Dáithi saw he was beaten and, to Mikey's relief, took him into the hills, where he had several months of running wild and free. The men adopted him as a son. Some had children of their own in houses in the valley, others had children that they'd lost to hunger or the emigrant ship, others didn't yet have any offspring, but all gave him affection and attention.

There were sixteen of them. And Mikey hero-worshipped them all. They were local men – most were the male remnants of family units that had lived in the locality, tilling its soil, for centuries. Sometimes they went on raids: attacking property and livestock belonging to the gentry or taking revenge on the militia for some atrocity or other. Mostly, they just got on with eking out an existence; attacks in the valley inevitably led to further atrocities on the locals, especially any surviving relatives and, sometimes, treks into the mountain to try and round them up, though mostly the militia had given up on that.

Locals aided them as much as possible, but they had to be careful not to attract unwarranted attention towards themselves, so as not to suffer the fate of Mikey's village. When Lord Dunshaughlin commenced wholesale clearing of tenants from his land, throwing families onto the road, not caring whether they lived or died, his most heartless agent was found beaten to death outside Mikey's village. As he was a brother of a sergeant in the barracks at Sligo town, the village was put to the sword. Neither the law nor Mikey ever found out who'd murdered him – O'Laoire denied all knowledge. It could have been a host of people. The only thing Mikey ever knew for certain was that he'd lost his family and his home as a result of the 'justice' that ensued.

But for a while he had a new family. Apart from O'Laoire, those who gave him most affection were: Francey Boyle, a squat carpenter with a booming laugh; Billy Madigan, the last surviving member of a family of fourteen, not long out of boyhood himself, his affection towards Mikey somewhat cloying now that his parents and siblings were either dead or exiled; Patrick Maher, an evicted tenant farmer, rough and ready by nature, his wife and two daughters, victims of fever, lay buried in the small graveyard outside the village, he'd lost the will to meet the rent after they died; Seanie Fitzsimons, an emaciated hedge-school master, who had to go on the run when the landlord ordered him hanged or transported for spreading papist notions amongst his tenants, tried to take Mikey in hand and give him a rudimentary grounding in Latin, Maths and Classical History.

None showed hesitation in sharing their scraps of food and tattered clothing with him. He loved them all, feeling safe and secure in their company. It was many years later before he understood they had merely been a band of hungry men with no futures.

When the soldiers came, he was checking snares that he'd helped Pakie Byrnes, at sixteen the next youngest in the group, set the previous week. They were in an area called the Blindy – a particularly rough patch of stony heather and bog where a wandering creature was liable to be careless in its haste to reach better ground. And sure enough, behind a rock that teetered on the edge of a boghole, a rabbit with bulging eyes and a broken leg hung on the strip of cloth that Pakie had securely staked into the thin margin of solid ground beneath the rock. The rabbit's head hung forlornly down the hole, but it was past caring about earthly woes and Mikey was too pleased with this addition to the meagre supper pot to feel any sympathy. He was untying the dead animal when he heard the shots.

It didn't take long to realise it wasn't just Dáithi and a couple of the lads firing at cousins of the fellow he held. There were too many shots and they just did not have the ammunition to waste even if that much game miraculously appeared. Something was wrong, like that day in the village, and he began to creep back towards the hideout with his heart alternating between leaping in his chest and plummeting to the pit of his stomach.

There were soldiers all over the mountain; their red and green uniforms bestowing a murderous gaiety on the bleak landscape. As Mikey watched, Patrick Maher was cut down while he scrambled for cover. A shower of musket balls hit him and he danced like his *Dadaí* had done, his soul dispatched to join his wife's and daughter's in the village graveyard below.

Pakie was running around between them, feinting this way and that, leading a bunch of redcoats a merry dance. To pass the time and keep active the men had invented a game called Duck-the-Bullock which entailed a runner trying to avoid getting hit by a thrown bundle of knotted rags while zig-zagging between rocks laid out in crooked lines. Pakie was the champion at this, nearly always getting 'home' to the jeers and catcalls of the older men, who claimed it was only because he had youth on his side that he was any good. But the redcoats were fitter and more numerous than Dáithí's men and when one of them succeeded in tripping Pakie, the others fell on him like a pack of wolves, sticking him with their bayonets. Even at the distance Mikey maintained jets of red were visibly spurting into the air.

Seanie Fitzsimmons and a tall dark-haired fellow called Corbett, wanted for several crimes around the locality, stepped out from behind a large boulder with their hands in the air. And were immediately shot.

Mikey continued to watch while the others were hunted and killed or shot while offering to surrender. Finally, the soldiers approached the main cave and, though initially driven back by the gunfire coming from inside, succeeded in gaining entry. After more shots and shouting they emerged with Dáithi gripped between three of them and a fourth prodding him in the back with a bayonet. A soldier in a different uniform, seemingly in charge, went up to him and hit him viciously across the face with the back of his hand. The crack flew sharper to where Mikey lay than any of the gunshots.

Dáithi was carried off, presumably to dance at the end of a rope. The others were left where they fell. Then the soldier in charge walked up to the ones carrying Dáithi and started shouting; it wasn't clear if it was at Dáithi or his captors. Suddenly, the rebel leader was spread-eagled on the ground, his head face downwards over a rock. The soldier in charge raised a large, broad sword skywards before chopping full force down on Dáithi's neck. The older Mikey O'Rorke knew the nauseating swish and thud of that sword as it entered the flesh could not have carried to where he lay, yet those noises haunted his dreams. The soldiers took Dáithi's dripping head with them as a trophy and proof of their triumph, leaving his torso to rot with the other bodies.

Mikey waited until the mountain was clear of soldiers then he crept out of his hiding place and went to walk amongst the remains of his protectors. They were all dead. Dáithi, Francis, Billy, Patrick, Seanie, Pakie, Corbett, Noeleen…all his friends…all his protectors.

He lit a fire in the cave and had a troubled sleep filled with crimson sprays and squelching bayonets. He spent all the next day battling bluebottles and flies while he dragged their bodies into a pile, covered them in dry heather and branches from a grove further down the mountain and set them ablaze. The bodies smouldered and smoked for a while but once the fire had bored through the clothes onto body fat, they blazed bright in the darkening sky. He wondered if anyone in the valley below would recognise his bonfire for the memorial it was.

Exhausted, he slept better that night, though dreams of flies, blood and swishing swords had come to stay. He thought about letting himself drown in them, but after a few days of scurrying, scavenging, and sleeping the sleep of a dullard he chose to live and started down the mountain to find his bitch of an aunt. A hate-filled life had come to seem better than none and he realised that power lay with whoever swam in the most blood and brought the hungriest bluebottles to feast on their victims' eyes.

A realisation that became his sustenance.

***

Pat Mangan handed Seamus a letter. 'There was a late mail drop last night,' his tent- mate said discreetly, strengthening the guilt that stirred within Seamus. It was from Kathleen. At first, he resisted opening it, this time not so much out of fear or a desire for privacy, but because it felt like a sordid thing to do after been with Mercy.

'Well, aren't you going to read it?' Mangan wanted to know. 'I'd love to have mail. If I had someone writing to me I wouldn't delay seeing what they had to say.' Mangan always spoke so guilelessly that it was not possible to tell if this was an admonishment or not.

Seamus ripped open the envelope and squatted by the bubbling coffee pot to read its contents, sipping from a hot mug. A brightening dawn cast fire shadows across the pages.

April 16th, 1862

Darling Seamus,

I do not know if you will receive this, as I haven't had an answer to my last letters. I fear not, but I am compelled to write and live in hope. I have very bad news, my darling.

Padraic didn't want me to tell you, but I feel you should know, need to know even. Your mother passed away on the 19th of March. We thought that having come through the winter, she was going to be alright. But, summer or winter, there is no easy life here. *Beannacht Dé lena anam.* I know this will not be of much consolation to you but it was a release from her suffering. Her mind never properly recovered from the eviction and, though Padraic and his family were very good to her, she was not living any life worth the name. She spoke to herself a lot of the time and called for you and all her children long dead. She is released now from the harsh realities of this life and I think it's she who is the lucky one; the rest of us are left to carry on for another while.

She is buried in the small graveyard behind Kilgarry Church and hopefully it will not be long now until you can visit it and say goodbye in person. She'll be looking forward to that, I'm sure.

We're all looking forward to seeing you my darling and praying for the day that you'll return safely to us. But we know you have a job to do that has the blessing of Jesus and his Holy

Mother, so that when you return life will be better for us all and we can look forward to a long
one together.

Things are quiet here at the moment. The spuds have gone in and we pray for a good crop. In the meantime, we have to get through the rest of spring and summer as best we can. With the help of God we will be alright, though last year's store is running down after the hard winter.

Nolan and Maguire are lying low. Many are saying they are drawing up plans to turn the whole area into sheep and cattle grazing land and evict us all after we've paid the Autumn rents. Padraic says their henchmen have been going around bribing the local ne'er do wells with porter and money to help with the dirty work of throwing their neighbours onto the road and tumbling down their cottages when the time comes. Don't suppose it will cost too much to win them over. Nolan has been working on other magistrates in the locality and on the colonel in Askeaton barracks to ensure they provide the legal and military might when the time comes. A lot of bottles of claret and roast beef being consumed in that cause, I've been told.

Buíochás le Dhia, you will be home by then with help and we will be able to meet these challenges head on, might with might if that's what it takes, as it undoubtedly will.

Love, I hope, that this letter reaches you though I am desperately sorry for the bad news it contains. But God is good for granting her release and her blessings from heaven will help those of us still here to find a way through.

My undying love always,

Kathleen.

He refused to give way to tears. That was not the way through, his mother would not have wanted it – herself having being long since been wrung dry. Nevertheless, the burden of her death and the juxtaposition of Kathleen's declarations with his night of passion with Mercy weighed so heavily on him that he was almost bent into the fire.

'Are you alright?' Mangan asked. 'Bad news?'

'My mother died.'

'Ah! I'm sorry for your trouble. I thought the woman had ditched you.'

'No, Kathleen still loves me.' Right then the strength of that love weighed like the heaviest burden of all.

'Go with Horan to see Byers and ask for sympathetic leave. Not even that bastard can refuse a man time to grieve for his mother.'

'No!' He hadn't meant to shout.

'Alright, didn't mean to cause further upset. What do you want to do?'

He stared at the guttering fire. 'I want to fight. I want to fight and I want to kill,' he finally said.

CHAPTER FOURTEEN

But the waiting went on. Skirmishing and picket fights constantly broke out along the narrow front, but, back where the Irish Brigade was sent, lethargy and boredom became as entrenched as the army itself. Having reached the gates of Richmond it seemed that McClellan, the brilliant engineer, hadn't the wherewithal to unlock them. Life, once again, took on the forms and shapes endemic to sedentary army life.

Tent structures became elaborate. Most, whether dog tents, Sibleys or Combination-Halves, were raised a few feet off the ground to improve circulation; when it wasn't raining, the atmosphere was heavy and sultry, though this far back from the swamps there were far fewer invasive mosquitoes or other biting insects, and the miasma was healthier. The sutler wagons became more permanent, many of the owners constructing log dwellings. Ladies of the night from Richmond frequented the camps – neutral as to which side of the American quilt generated their income. Father Corby had the men erect a chapel of logwood and pine branches. Many soldiers availed of both services without undue strain on their consciences.

Seamus eased off on the Chuck-Luck, picked lice from his clothes and ever-increasing body hair, rarely overdid it when swigging out of the campfire jugs and prayed for his mother's soul in Father Corby's chapel. He easily avoided the wares on offer from the Richmond 'ladies' but could not desist from visiting Mercy's wagon, which, though more damning to his soul than the gambling, was at least financially less self-destructive. He didn't think he loved Mercy; he accepted he was dependent on her. Maybe for the sex; definitely for the intimate human bonding. In some way that he didn't completely understand, he felt free from any obligations towards her, in a way that his love for Kathleen wasn't. His betrothed was also a feisty, independent woman but his love for her was bound up with Ireland, land rights, evictions and hunger, and his feelings for Mercy weren't.

He was pondering these issues one morning, not long after he'd learnt of his mother's death, when the Brigade musicians came marching past playing trumpets, flutes and banging on drums while a bunch of serious, dour-looking officers on horseback and a regiment of men as pinched and miserable looking as their leaders followed. Meagher and his staff came trotting alongside.

'Boys! Let's have a great big *céad míle fáilte* for the 29th Massachusetts! A very welcome addition to our glorious Irish Brigade.'

This time not even Meagher's ebullience roused much of a response. Maybe it was too early, but, more likely, Jer Horan put his finger on it. 'Sour-faced New England Puritans without even a droplet of Celtic blood in their veins. Why in the hell are they being assigned to the Irish Brigade?'

Despite his agreeing with Jer Horan in criticism of the decisions of those in power, Mangan acquired a jug and suggested a few men should call on their new neighbours that afternoon. Jer Horan admitted it wouldn't be very Irish of them to do otherwise.

'Not sure them Puritans appreciate *úsice béatha*,' Mangan said on the way, 'but my old mother would turn in her grave if she thought I wasn't being neighbourly.'

'We don't want to give it to say to them that we didn't make the effort, do we?' Mulvaney asked.

They came to a group of soldiers lolling outside the first street of newly raised tents. Seamus noticed there was no gambling or semi-concealed drinking going on. The lanky bluebloods were most likely too busy debating the finer points of Old Testament slewing and smiting. The Irishmen were prepared for a cool reception, but the deep enmity took them aback.

'Howdy, boys,' Horan started in, 'thought you'd like to crack a jug with us, help you settle in with the Irish Brigade, like.'

The nearest men of the 29th, who had to have seen them walk over, looked up with feigned surprise and ill-concealed contempt. One of them, a pock-marked fellow with sergeant's stripes, addressed Mangan. 'Paddy, take your popish firewater back to your hovel and don't bother us again.'

Seamus felt Dillon stiffen with resentment and he placed a restraining hand across him. Though a good four inches shorter than the tall, dark Kerryman, Dillon had far more aggression, pound for pound, packed into his being.

Mangan held his own, verbally. 'Ah, it's no skin off our noses if you don't remove the blueblood pokers from your arses. We were just trying to be neighbourly, should have known better of a bunch of Boston brahmans.'

'That's right, you should have known that we don't want to be contaminated by Irish muck savages. Go back where you came from and leave us in peace.' A companion of the youth's, with piercing blue eyes to match his blood colour, spoke up.

Dillon could no longer be restrained, and Seamus no longer tried. The two sets of men started aggressively towards each other. Men materialised out of thin air. As if on cue, they poured out of the tents of the 29th, and men of the Brigade came up behind their three comrades.

Like moths to a flame, both sides had been attracted by the putative violent breaking of the tension that had been building all day.

'Stop! What is going on here?' The colonel of the 29th came striding up, accompanied by a coterie of staff – a tall, grey-haired man with a sour twist to his face, name of Ebenezer Pierce. The three Irishmen in front of the Brigade saluted.

'Beg your pardon, Sir,' Mangan replied, 'we meant only to pay a social call on your men and make them welcome.'

Colonel Pierce stared at him and at the other Irish in turn. It occurred to Seamus that the intensity of his stare saw him well named.

'Well, Private, I would be grateful if you would allow my men settle into this uncomfortable assignment at their own leisure. You will appreciate that they are not used to mixing with your sort of person. No offence of course. Now turn around and go back to your own diversions and let my men to theirs.' Pierce turned away without waiting for a response. Mulvaney merely shrugged and turned away himself; the rest of the Brigade started back to what they had been doing before the situation with the 29th had arisen.

Uncomfortable assignment. Your sort of person. No offence of course. How Seamus hated the supercilious shit that he and his *sort* had been forced to swallow all their lives. It was well past time that the tables were turned. He contained his smouldering resentment by reminding himself of the delicious irony inherent in fighting alongside Pierce and his *sort* so as to use the experience gained against them as soon as possible afterwards.

He prayed to his mother that those days would not be long in coming.

Mercy had even more reasons to resent Pierce and his ilk, but she refused to let it poison her determination to make a success for herself and her daughter up North. She always deflected the conversation whenever Seamus talked about getting even.

'Make somethin' of yourself and forget about those who want to do you down. Tryin' to get even only fills you with the hate that's within them.'

He thought of his mother; he thought of Kathleen and he thought of the fertile land around Kilgarry and knew he couldn't forget about 'them.' Only when he had gotten even could he make something of himself.

That night, after his visit with Mercy, he made his way back to camp imbued with the usual mix of glowing pleasure and nagging guilt. As he passed through a line of trees behind the main camp a shadow detached itself from a gnarled oak and punched him in the throat knocking him winded to the ground.

Before Seamus could collect himself or get his breath back a knife whose blade glistened in the moonlight was at his throat. 'Not so brave without your lily-livered friends or slave-whore to support you, are you?' A voice, whose breath stank of cheap whiskey, growled.

Flaherty.

He'd chosen a bad time to attack Seamus O'Farrell. The groundswell of grief, uncertainty and anger that demanded release at Fair Oaks, had built up again, exacerbated by the death of his mother and the sneers of the 29th Massachusetts, making him a very dangerous animal just then. He clasped the wrist of his assailant's knife hand with an iron grip, stalling him from cutting his throat.

He was certain it had been Flaherty he'd seen raping Mercy that night in the clearing. Hatred churned Seamus's emotions. The man was a murderer and a rapist and undoubtedly a shirker, only in the Army to kill, rape and steal from his own side. A bully, whose kind would never be where the lead was flying in a real battle, content, like he'd been on the pier that day, to goad and egg others onto acts of violence, unless circumstances overwhelmingly favoured the execution of these deeds by himself.

Flaherty still imagined he had the upper hand in this encounter. 'Going a bit soft is O'Rorke, waiting to hear back from Cork on what to do next. Ordered us to leave you be for now. Well, I ain't prepared to let it be. Not going to take shit from any snivelling Limerickman, despite having enjoyed his whore first.'

Seamus busted Flaherty's nose with a head-butt. Coming up from underneath meant he didn't get as much leverage as he would have liked; but he got enough to crush gristle and push the knife hand off him at the same time. The look of wide-eyed, pained surprise on Flaherty's face was alone worth the effort, not to mention saving his own life.

'Hou bastard – my hose!' Flaherty seemed to have forgotten about the knife and held his nose with the other hand.

Seamus gave him a lick of his fist in the side of the jaw. Again, because he was underneath, he didn't get as much power in as he'd have liked. But, as Flaherty was off-balance already, it was enough to tumble him sideways. Seamus saw his opportunity. He swivelled his hips as powerfully as he could and turned him over with his right knee and thigh. Now he was on top. And he pounded the foolish soldier with a primal rage. He might be shouting. He didn't care. He grew breathless.

He sat on his opponent, gasping in the humid night air. Realising he had the knife in his hand, he looked at it in surprise. Flaherty was conscious: he exuded a stench of stale breath, cheap whiskey and blood; right then, he epitomised everything and everyone that had made life a hardship for Seamus and his loved ones. He considered finishing him off but didn't want to lower himself to such plumb bottom depths; besides, he had expended a sizeable amount of his pent-up angst in the beating he had administered. It wasn't completely dissipated - he was aware that a hard knot of it gripped his insides like a vice, but at least it had been distilled down to a manageable core.

Flaherty's eyes flickered and he stared at Seamus with an all too conscious glare. His broken jaw gave his twisted smile an even more prurient sneer. 'She was good: your slave bitch.'

The Kilgarry man plunged the knife into his tormentor's chest. A dollop of blood pumped onto him from a severed cardiac artery, but his victim's heart stopped immediately and the blood fell back again. Flaherty's eyes rolled in his head showing their whites. With a strangled 'ungh!' he fell silent.

Seamus O'Farrell, alias Captain Rock of Kilgarry, had, for the first time, definitively killed.

He felt no immediate remorse or even that he had crossed a significant boundary in his lifecycle. He needed to get rid of the body and get cleaned up. He thought of sneaking back to camp and enlisting Jer Horan's help – he alone amongst his comrades was likely to have the worldly wisdom and compassion to accept what had happened without judgement. But, though he'd trust Horan with his life, it would introduce too many variables.

Flaherty's attack appeared to be a whiskey inspired personal vendetta; highly unlikely to have been sanctioned by O'Rorke – who, though bloodthirsty, would have wanted trappings of legitimacy to bestow upon his death. O'Rorke and his cabal would of course have their suspicions once they discovered Flaherty had disappeared, which would make them all the more determined to get him – but what else was new? The only chance he had of sowing doubt about what happened to his attacker lay in disposing of the body immediately. Leaving aside O'Rorke and his men, no pleadings of self-defence were likely to save him from a firing squad if such a frenzied counterattack was ever pinned on him. He had to get rid of the body himself. And he had to do it now.

There was no one else around. Flaherty had chosen a good spot to jump him: a secluded stand of trees between the sutler wagons and the main camps. There were a lot of high jinks, music, and laughter around the fires, which should have drowned out the noise of their brawling. Provost-Guards were thin on the ground and the pickets were stationed a good half mile away. If he could get rid of the body without being discovered, he wouldn't need to fear the evidence of any witnesses; of course, there would be plenty of suspicion, but there was nothing he could do about that.

He grabbed the body beneath the armpits and started to drag it towards the swamps. Flaherty had been in full uniform, including boots, that now snagged on every root and rock along the way. He thought about removing them, but he couldn't, even temporarily, leave evidence like that lying around and tying them around his own neck or the body's was likely to be more of an encumbrance than a help. So, he persevered, sweating profusely in the warm air. He'd had enough exertion that night to last a lifetime and he was on fatigue duty at seven-thirty; it was now well after three. Flaherty was the dead one, but he would be the living dead. He almost laughed, before recollecting the horror of what he was doing. A piece of blue uniform tore in a patch of briars and he had to stop to ensure he'd left nothing incriminating showing.

Eventually, panting and sweating, he reached a muddy quagmire from where he had seen six men struggle to pull out a mule two days before. He found some heavy stones and stuffed them inside Flaherty's uniform, then he tipped the body into the murk. Instantly, it made greedy sucking sounds and the dead man began to sink. After, he'd washed the blood and mud from his exposed skin and rubbed the stains on his uniform until they became indeterminable damp patches Seamus sat for a while. In the eyes of his Church and his upbringing, he had committed a grievous sin. *Thou shalt not kill.* He had adhered to this commandment throughout his life, even during his most active nights with the Kilgarry Crew; he had sanctioned and committed many acts of violence against property and animals; had even threatened violence and murder against humans, but he had never carried it out and never intended to, except in a situation of war. In the army he had a duty to kill in the line of battle and, though he hadn't succeeded, he'd tried hard to do so at Fair Oaks. And, apart from his embarrassment at being overcome by battle lust, he was satisfied that he'd tried to fulfil his duty. But now his first taking of life had been in a brawl, and, though he'd been attacked first, he knew his response was frenzied and he hadn't had to murder to survive.

He waited for guilt to assail him. But it wouldn't come. Though he tried denying it, a grim satisfaction at taking out such a hateful, sneering enemy was what he mainly felt. He recognised a vague, underlying unease, nothing more. He thought of a little black boy prone in his father arms on a New York dockside and wondered if he rested easier. He thought of his mother still warm in her grave and how, even in the quiet desperation of her later years, she would have shunned and disavowed such an act of vengeance, and still guilt wouldn't override his satisfaction. Finally, he gathered himself and began heading back to his tent. He should be able to avoid the Provost Guards and sneak in without attracting undue attention; his companions in the 88th were used to his comings and goings in the small hours.

The morning would be time enough to worry about what kind of person he was turning into.

Now, he needed sleep.

CHAPTER FIFTEEN

McClellan's army was changing base. Switching south of the Peninsula to a place called Harrison's Landing on the James River.

'You mean we're retreating?' Willie Jones, one of the more cynical members of the 88th, asked when Byers outlined the principles of the envisaged move.

'*Private* Jones you would be best holding your tongue if don't want to be going to the James manacled in a guard wagon. But for your information: a change of base before a superior enemy is one of the trickiest manoeuvres in the manuals of warfare and, as he has to rely on dolts like you to carry it through, I'd say General McClellan is one of the bravest commanders in history to even attempt it. So, if you would care to strike camp, please?'

'Yes, Sergeant!'

Jones had said what was on everyone's mind. They had chased the Confederates to within sight and sound of the spires of Richmond and won a battle; the rebels were dug into thin defensive positions before them and *they* were the side retreating! Nothing was more dispiriting than a retreat, especially an unnecessary one. But, soldiers obey, besides, most still had faith that Little Napoleon knew what he was doing. So, they secured their rolled-up beds and struck their camps; at least they were moving – escaping for a while from the interminable boredom of camp life.

Right on cue, a waspish firing sounded from the north-western flank.

'The Rebs know we are retreating and they're onto us like wolves onto a wounded deer.' Dillon remarked.

'A wounded animal has a habit of turning around and attacking its tormentor,' someone quipped.

'I'd back the wolf every time,' Dillon responded.

The firing increased. Artillery boomed. A full-scale battle had commenced up near the Chickahominy. Word came that the Brigade was to remain at the ready and the expectant buzz of battle electrified the air around the half-lowered camp site.

Seamus checked his musket. There was a residue of powder halfway down the inside of the barrel that, if left unattended, would help to clog up the weapon and cause a misfire that could be fatal on the battlefield. He tied a rag to the ramrod and pushed it through, then he used the clean side of the rag to polish the outside. He also gave the buttons of his uniform a shine and stood ready for war.

But there was more waiting. A whole day of it. The Irish Brigade first stood around, then lounged around and eventually napped while the rest of the Army of the Potomac filed past. There was no doubt they were retreating: drivers, quartermasters, cooks, corporals, sergeants, captains, lieutenants, majors, colonels, generals, and ordinary privates pushed themselves and each other frantically along in a rush south away from the Chickahominy and towards the James. Thousands of wagons, horses and men dashed past; at first it was engaging to watch such an army on the move, but it soon grew monotonous and even the sounds of battle on the northern flanks melded into background music that rose and fell with the rhythm of an unpolished chamber orchestra.

Byers either lost interest or received orders to let the Brigade stand at ease for they were allowed to brew their coffee, fry their bacon and slouch around. The early morning tension seeped out of the men and they resigned themselves to being left behind again while the rest of the Army went on to glory.

Seamus was able to ignore the Chuck-Luck games that started up, lying down next to a game with his head on his rucksack, concentrating on sleeping. Though his unease had grown, the guilt remained low key: an uncomfortable burn at the base of his stomach –

nothing more. Even if his response was disproportionate, Flaherty had attacked him first.

He dozed. And dreamt he was being rough handled by O'Rorke, his cronies and the militia. He tried to fight them off, but there were too many.

'No, no, let me go, you bastards...'

'For God's sake man wake up, unless you want Byers to place you under arrest.' Pat Mangan was trying to shake him awake.

He assumed he'd only dozed for a short while. But as he struggled back to consciousness, he realised the sun was way around behind him – it was late afternoon. He had slept for hours.

'We're moving out,' Mangan clarified for him.

He was not any the better for his sleep. The night's activities had caught up with him: he ached all over. It was agony to lift his neck and twist it in the slightest direction; the inside of his head felt as if it was about to explode, worst than if he'd gorged himself with the cheapest whiskey. He rose unsteadily and blinked in the weak sunlight.

'If your old Ma could only see you now,' Jer Horan grinned at him.

Seamus tried to grin back. He had sworn Mangan not to tell anyone about his mother's death. He didn't know why for sure, but it had something to do with shame at her dying half-mad in his cousin's house because he couldn't protect her. He was surprised to find that he had no intention of telling even Horan or Mangan the truth about Flaherty either.

He began to understand that not all the buzzing in his head was due to over-tiredness. The decibels of the firing to the north had increased in intensity and now reverberated like close, angry thunder. The men of Company L were milling into line with the rest of the 88th - Byers and the other officers, commissioned and non-commissioned, barked orders and sarcasm to harry everyone along – Mangan had woken him just in time to be rescued from what at best would have been a vicious tongue-lashing.

Whilst attempting to line up, he sipped at his canteen, the water tasted sour and metallic after lying in the sun for so long.

'Here, just filled cold from the stream over there,' Mangan, who'd seen his grimace, thrust his own canteen at him.

Seamus came closer to tears at this act of kindness than he had at anytime in the recent past. 'Thank you,' he managed to say as he put it to his lips. The cold nip of fresh water sharpened his senses, and the world came into better focus. The Irish Brigade was mustering. They were going to fight again, after all. Meagher would be along in a minute with entreaties to preserve the glories of the Irish martial tradition.

'You'll never guess,' Horan came up and spoke in a low voice as they began filing into place.

'What?'

'Peter Flaherty has deserted.'

'What!'

'Peter Flaherty has deserted. Your old enemy. O'Rorke's latest lapdog. Did a moonlit flit. Or else fell into a swamp pissed as a fart.'

Seamus slowed his thumping heart and tried to conceal his shallow breaths. Looking at the tips of his boots he asked: 'How do you know? That's just another stupid camp rumour.'

'No, he's gone alright. There was a right hue and cry over at the 69th earlier. Search parties all morning – no sign. The Provost Guard have been combing the countryside all around. Already holed up in a whorehouse in Washington I'd say, if not at the bottom of a swamp. By all accounts, he'd had a skinfull when last seen. Some fellows in the 63rd saw him, apparently heading towards the rear where the sutlers are. Undoubtedly looking for cheap whiskey.'

Seamus remained silent.

'You didn't see him did you?' Horan looked at him and nodded towards where the sutler wagons had been last night and smirked conspiratorially.

He knew his friend was only teasing but it was a struggle to hide his shock. He forced himself to respond. 'What d'ya mean? Of course, I didn't.'

Horan gave a low guffaw. 'Pity, I was hoping you had the chance to push him into a swamp-hole where he belongs.'

Seamus said nothing.

'Naw! There's some real fighting coming up and fellows like him are all mouth and no trousers – did a flit before he wet himself.' Horan continued.

He should have been relieved his sergeant so obviously assumed he had nothing to do with it. But he knew O'Rorke and his remaining cabal wouldn't be so dismissive of their friend's whereabouts.

Then Byers started shouting nearby and all thoughts, apart from self-preservation, flew from him. 'Leave everything, apart from your weapons, behind. We can pick them up on the way back. Our presence is requested up near Gaines's Mill, the Rebs are threatening to break through there and if they do, they'll overwhelm us. We'll all be dead or prisoners by nightfall. Move out on my mark. Forward! March!'

Seamus went off to fight once more; primed to legitimately kill his fellow man. They marched in a late afternoon sunlight, which lit and warmed them on their way. In step behind Horan, Brosnihan and Byers, Seamus felt his spirits rise and his muscles unwind; though he understood what he was going towards could be fatal, he felt what he always felt when he had an immediate purpose. Alive.

Despite the heat of recent days the ground remained damp - even where it curved away from the swamps and lagoons, the red mud of Northern Virginia sucked their steps downwards. Though conditions in the fading, but warm, sunlight were very different from the horrific night march of a few weeks previous, the suffering started again. Most had heeded Byers's advice and left all the non-essential stuff behind, but after a couple of miles of hard marching on soft ground their woollen uniforms became oppressive; discarded jackets, overcoats and the odd cap soon littered the route. Not even Byers, red in the face himself, was cruel enough to enforce regulation wear. By the time the Chickahominy glittered on the horizon, Seamus was gulping his metallic tasting water like it was the coolest, freshest, spring water he'd ever had the privilege to imbibe.

The landscape changed as they approached the river and the sounds of battle intensified, knotting the stomachs of even the most stoic of the men. The low-hanging sun was an ominous appearance, reminding Seamus of a cannonball packed with canister and grape aglow in the microseconds before explosion. It seemed it was no longer a life-giving force, but an object to be feared and cowered before, and they had no choice except to continue marching towards it. He was relieved, when at the bank of the Chickahominy, they wheeled more directly north, and it was no longer in their main line of sight, though Seamus remained conscious of its portentous presence on his left shoulder.

He was soon distracted by the columns of smoke and clouds of dust washing down towards the river from the battlefield two miles beyond. Squinting ahead, it was difficult to see what men or objects were swirling about in the fog of war.

As Union soldiers spilled out of the murk, jeers rose from the men around him. Men from New York, Ohio, Chicago, Cavan, Galway, Germany; men with blackened faces and eyes bulging out of their heads, sweat running in rivulets of fear down their foreheads and cheeks.

'Betrayed! Betrayed!'

'It's a big skedaddle!'

'Sold down the river!'

Suchlike they cried as they ran or stumbled along.

'Poor devils,' Horan said. 'It was the same at Bull Run. Is there anything as upsetting as the sight of broken men?'

'The sight of the poor saps who are being sent into the line to replace them?' Tom Dillon suggested.

No one laughed.

Company L and the rest of the Brigade came to a standstill – a jam formed while the men waited for their leaders to clear a way along the bridge leading to the battlefront on the north side. Officers waded into the defeated men streaking across the bridge; shoving them roughly to one side, occasionally whacking them with the flat sides of their swords or jabbing them with their bayonets. Like panicked sheep they appeared not to notice, though they did begin to move mutely aside to let the Brigade through.

John Mulvaney came up to Seamus and passed him a folded piece of paper. 'It's for you – been sent along the line from the lads over in the 69th I think,' he sniffled.

'How did you get it?' Seamus asked.

'Sean Cregan passed it to me, damned if I know who passed it to him though.'

Seamus looked at the paper. It was a folded envelope. At first, he thought it was a message from Mercy, telling him of her plans. She had surely moved out that morning with the rest of the wagons. Maybe it was goodbye because she had gone North. Then he saw the handwriting and knew it wasn't hers – wasn't any woman's. *Private James Farrell – Company L, 88th regiment. Private and Confidential* it read in bold writing. A man's hand. He ripped it open and straightened the paper inside. Someone had written: *Captain Rock – Kilgarry Crew* and drawn a crude figure of a grinning skull with a dagger running through it. He knew instantly what it was and whom it had come from. He had sent one himself to Paul Nolan last Summer. It was a death threat, and it came not from the Confederates across the way but from his fellow Irishmen up the line in the 69th. Specifically, from O'Rorke. As he had feared: regardless what anyone else thought, O'Rorke and his remaining men were holding him personally responsible for Flaherty's disappearance. The aliveness that the march to battle had instilled in him dissipated. He couldn't drag his eyes from the leering skull with the dagger in it.

'No need to thank me,' Mulvaney huffed.

Seamus had forgotten he was still standing there, respecting his privacy by not coming too close. No one had seen what the note contained. He put it in his pocket.

'Thanks,' he said to Mulvaney.

The Galwayman smirked. 'Don't mention it. Bet she ain't worth it though,' he gave a final sniffle and turned to go back to his place in the line.

Seamus stood next to Horan, trying to ignore the note and its threat to his life. After all, there was a more immediate one waiting at the other side of the bridge.

Eventually they were able to follow Byers across. When they got to the other side, they fanned out towards the North-East. Artillery booms, musketry crackles and men's cries rose to a crescendo on the far side. It was impossible to discern anything comprehensible through the evening murk of smoke and the scrubby forest land they now found themselves in. Though it was apparent that the men retreating over the bridge were no isolated file of shirkers – defeated and wounded men swarmed all around. The Union regiments were taking a pasting and in flight. And, for the second time in a month, the Irish were being asked to stem the tide.

They attempted to cut a positive swathe through the chaos of defeat and grubby scrubland. The green flags were out in front once more: symbols of hope and encouragement. Meagher rode around like a man possessed, attempting to rally and harry every man he came across.

Seamus winced as the Brigadier-General rode his horse into the midst of a group of forlorn 12th Indiana men and whacked one of the poor bastards on the head with the flat side of his sword, knocking him to the ground. As the man struggled back up again, Seamus saw a gaping red wound soaking the side of his shirt: there was one man who had an obvious reason to leave the battlefield and didn't deserve Meagher's punishment.

Meagher looked pissed; whether he was drunk on the excitement of battle or the contents of his whiskey collection, or a combination of both, wasn't entirely clear. He rode around in circles with a flushed face and hair askew, his usual swagger and poise absent. Jack Gosson and other staff rode nearby looking embarrassed.

Sumner and his staff rode up to Meagher and pointed into the distance. Meagher dashed off with the alacrity of a man who'd been told his house was on fire. The Brigade started after him as best and as organised as they could in the circumstances.

'Wouldn't mind a swig myself,' Horan said, nodding at the departing Meagher.

'Company L! To me, on the double!' Byers yelled and they set off through the smoke and retreating men. Using the sergeant, who'd stuck his forage cap on the end of a bayonet, as a focal point, Seamus and his comrades made their way across a solid clearing that rose steeply out of the bottomlands into a prominent hill.

They were passing through what had earlier been the rear of the battle. Now with the large numbers of panic stricken, wounded Union men and horses and artillery that continued to stream across, it was ground on the verge of being overrun.

They came to a large hospital tent, erected against an abandoned log-house. Thousands of men with multifarious wounds and broken limbs lay writhing or prostrate outside like an apocalyptic vision of agonised souls – the stark, black, five-foot letter 'H' on the flag swirling above the tent surely designated entry to the lower chambers of Hell and not 'Hospital.' Others – upright men – were being pushed and bayonet jabbed away from the entrances by provost guards. From inside came screams and shrill cries of agony as the surgeons sawed and sewed on the 'lucky' ones deemed sufficiently injured to be permitted entry. Seamus and the others lowered their heads and, marching as quickly past as the counter current of retreating men allowed, prayed they wouldn't soon be back begging for help at this entrance for the damned.

They pushed up the hill, following Byers' cap; in the distance they could see Meagher still prancing along followed by his staff – the brigade and regimental colours out ahead of the advancing units were the only definite points of reference in a nebulous field of smoke, galloping horses, bogged-down artillery and panicking men. This panorama of chaos was overlain by the din of cannon and musket fire and the cries of men. The Irish Brigade moved deeper into the tumult.

A general on a white horse galloped up to Meagher forcing him to stop for orders.

'That's ould FitzJohn Porter. Looks like we're going to be thrown into the lost cause once more.' Mangan explained to Seamus. He spat a wad of tobacco onto the ground. 'Sure 'tis nothing new to us.'

Meagher turned towards the Brigade and, holding his sword aloft, indicated that the men were to rally to and around him. As Porter rode off again, Meagher tried to control his rearing horse, he ducked now and then as the lead flew around him but didn't ride out of range. Whether or not it came from the inside of a bottle, Seamus had to admire such courage. He wondered if Mangan had a flask secreted somewhere, he normally had contacts for every stash and hidden supply. But, looking around at the grim, determined faces nearby, he knew it wasn't the time to ask. They were picking up speed as they hurried towards the rallying point; he would seem weak if he stopped and asked for a nip.

So, he hurried on. And even if every man was hurrying because he was afraid that the man next to him would find out he was a coward

– it was no consolation to him. Every step was agony. He didn't know if it was suppressed guilt over killing Flaherty, the subsequent death threat from O'Rorke, the scenes of defeat and mayhem they had passed through, or a combination of all these, but this time he felt no elation, no pent-up tension that could only be released by fighting and killing. He desperately, desperately, did not want to reach that plateau at the top where the lead flew around Meagher. What he wanted was to burrow into the leeside of the hill and curl up until the fighting was finished. He had sated his need to fight, had sated his need to kill. Now he just wanted to rest.

'Good man, Limerick. That's the spirit!' Horan yelled at him above the battle din.

He was shocked that there was anything about his demeanour indicating a desire to fight, certain his unwillingness, cowardice even, must be evident for all to see.

He said nothing but trotted with the others towards the top where balls of lead swarmed like angry bees. *God please take this cup from me.* He realised he hadn't prayed for some time and vowed he'd attend to them a lot more in future, if only God would take him out of this. By praying to and respecting God, he'd get back on a righteous path. Surely then, everything else would come alright for him?

Such thoughts imbued him with hope for a future, though his desire not to reach the top of that hill was more desperate than ever.

He reached it.

Company L piled onto the plateau on the heels of Byers. Finding himself at the top, Seamus felt no less fearful, however an air of unreality washed over him and it was as if the fear did not belong to him, but to someone whose emotions he had been given the privilege of experiencing. Thus, when a fly smacked into Byers's forehead and blood and gore arced into the air from the resultant hole, he didn't immediately realise his sergeant had been killed and laughed at the absurdity of what he'd witnessed. Someone else nearby groaned and fell over in a crumpled heap. Here and there along the line, others did the same. In those moments after reaching the hill, he continued to laugh aloud while his comrades comically crumpled into bizarre contortions with looks of shocked surprise on their faces.

'Men of the Irish Brigade! We must hold here at all costs,' Meagher called.

A bullet whizzed past Seamus, its passage stinging his face and unravelling his thoughts so that he saw the reality of the battlefield with a petrifying celerity.

The men who'd previously tried to hold this line had made rudimentary efforts to entrench, but, apart from some shallow scrapings and a forlorn abatis, there was no cover worth the name on the summit. The slope in front of him was so thickly carpeted with discarded artillery pieces and the bodies of men and horses that this flotsam and jetsam of war had become the Union's most effective line of defence against total collapse as the Confederate charge slowed on the gory encumbrances.

Seamus never knew fear like what he now experienced atop this Calvary. To the deepening gloom, the swirls of smoke and the din of cries, shouts, artillery, and musket fire was added the ululating, banshee screaming of the rebel yell. A thousand she-foxes mating on a winter's night would not have made the hair stand on the back of his neck as straight nor caused his knees to quake as much.

The rebels' progress was slowed on the nightmare hillside, but not stemmed. They were coming to kill Yanks, Irishmen, or whoever stood in their way. They'd made their breakthrough, now all that remained between them and the annihilation of McClellan's army was this hilltop and the thin line of men formed on the summit. And they celebrated with their trademark yells. It had been a long, bloody day for them also. But the prize was now in their grasp.

Seamus was shocked to notice his hands didn't tremble as he aimed at a rebel with a large slouch hat. A peacock feather quivered on its side; he aimed at a spot just below where it started to curve, right where the man's brains pulsed inside the skull. But he didn't fire. Yet. The man skipped over fallen bodies and discarded equipment as he came up the hill. Seamus spat his hatred of him onto the ground.

'Steady boys, let them come halfway, then aim low and give them all you've got, but not before. Don't waste ammunition.' Regimental Captain McMahon paced in front of them. 'Companies in rows with rolling fire.' McMahon exuded calm and it spread to the men. 'Fire!' He shouted.

Seamus lowered his aim slightly and fired. He saw his man go down. All around him other Confederates fell, further encumbering the passage of those still coming. He fell back as the line behind stepped up and poured another withering volley into the rebels.

Five seconds later he was up front again, a salty taste in his mouth and a ring of black powder around his lips from biting off the head of his cartridge. He fired again into the advancing rebels. Their foremost buckled. They came on more desultorily now, not as sure of themselves, the rebel yells more like puppy yaps than banshee ululations. The alternate line delivered their volley. Officers urging the men on whilst exhorting them to aim low, use the ammunition wisely and pick out specific targets, brought a pocket of order to the field of chaos.

Seamus lost count of the amount of times he loaded, stepped up, fired, dropped back, loaded, stepped up, fired, dropped back. He became an automaton, responding to his leaders' shouts and the rhythm of the men around him. He lost his fear. Even when Confederate artillery found their range and began to gouge large holes out of the hilltop, he didn't feel concern for his well-being. He was an indestructible cog in a terrifying machine, intent on grinding hordes of grey beings into red meat on the hill slope before it. He never noticed that other units were rallying around the Irish Brigade as their determined stand became apparent or that Union artillery was being hauled back up the hill to cancel the Confederate guns across the way. The grey victory charge was halted; their broken and bloodied bodies girthed the hillside. The sun finally set and darkness cloaked the awful sights, but Seamus O'Farrell and his comrades fired into the night as if intent on puncturing the blackness and exposing the grey horde behind.

Eventually their commanders ordered a halt and the men collapsed where they stood. They had done their duty. The rebels wouldn't reach the top of the hill this evening. Green fingers had helped plug the blue dyke.

For a while they lay there. Gasping. Unable to speak, apart from prayers, curses, and exclamations. Their weapons too hot to handle. A detail came amongst them with lanterns hauling out the dead and injured. Canteens were passed along to ease parched throats.

As he had done earlier that afternoon - less than four hours ago by the clock - Seamus lay directly on the ground with his knapsack for a pillow. But despite his bone-deep weariness, he couldn't sleep. There was too much activity: relief parties moved around searching for the dead and wounded, offering coffee and hardtack to those fit enough to accept; officers went around dispensing encouragement and orders; a few hardy souls looked for brothers, cousins, and friends. All the time: movement and noise.

When eventually it settled down, long after midnight, Seamus grew aware of another sound. A low murmuring susurration. At first, he feared that a Confederate raiding party was sneaking up on them, whispering to each other as they came. Then as he became more alert, his ears tuned into the sound. They were Confederates alright, but not a raiding party. They were the wounded left to vie for themselves on the field.

'Water,' they called in weak voices. 'Help me.' 'Shoot me.' 'Mother...?'

'Poor bastards,' Mangan said. 'I'm tempted to go down there and start putting them out of their misery. But I'm too bloody tired and I'd probably get myself shot, by one side or the other, in the dark.'

Seamus's blood chilled. He had heard a lot of unnerving sounds and cries in Ireland and America, but nothing had prepared him for the pathetic calls of these abandoned men. Forgetting all his earlier piety and promises he cursed God for his non-existence. Then he spent the rest of the night turning and fidgeting: his body too tired to get up and move about, his mind too active and disturbed to sleep, other than fitfully. To the south and east, he heard the cries of the Union wounded, fainter because they were further away. There was also in the distance the rumblings of wagons and the pounding of hooves as McClellan's huge army continued to retreat or 'Change Base.'

Later, it rained. The men lying on their arms hunkered deeper into whatever cover they had – which was very little as they had left their belongings behind at the Fair Oaks camp and discarded their jackets along the way.

The falling rain eased the cries for water. For most of those abandoned on the hillside, it eased their cries for ever.

CHAPTER SIXTEEN

Towards dawn, Seamus slept less fitfully. But still woke shivering, damp, and more bone weary than when he'd laid down. He struggled into a sitting position. Hot coffee was distributed and he snatched a mug with alacrity from an orderly's grasp, spilling half of it in his shivering haste.

There were immediate calls to stand to arms. A few more streaks of light on the eastern horizon and the Confederates would come again. After so nearly overrunning McClellan's army the previous dusk, they would move quickly to ensure they succeeded in the early morning. Damp clothes clung to Seamus as he stood up, making him shiver all over. *Christ this is unbearable!* How much could a man endure?

Later, he realised he was lucky not knowing the answer then.

With the rebels stirring below, Seamus picked up the musket which he'd lain next to all night and the cartridge box which he'd endeavoured to keep dry. For a while, the heat from the overused musket had kept him warm, afterwards, it became one more impediment to a good sleep.

He hastily cleaned his clogged-up barrel and wiped the damp from where it had settled on the musket and fell cold, hungry, and sleepily into line once more. The debilitating fear prior to the battle of yesterevening was replaced by a numbing fatalism. He had forgotten patriotism and the desire to gain martial experience; thoughts of Kathleen, Mercy, Flaherty and O'Rorke, even his mother, had faded to a background buzz. What was to the forefront of his mind right then was a hot meal, dry clothes, and a decent, nightmare-free sleep.

'Here they come!' A cry went up.

Seamus hunkered down on one knee and prepared to face the renewed onslaught.

Seven days of fighting, retreating and fighting followed. Always fighting. Snatched sleep, gulps of coffee, fistfuls of crushed hardtack and dried bacon. Always retreating. Always fighting. Seamus's thoughts and actions, though punctuated by vivid incidents, occurred in a feverish blur in which notions of a future or a past were subsumed in a primeval instinct for survival.

Somewhere, amidst the blur, he became a soldier.

That first morning, the Irish Brigade fought a holding action long enough to allow the remaining wounded Union men and equipment to be removed from the field and taken across the bridges of the Chickahominy, though the majority of those screaming and moaning in the 'Hell-Hospital' had to be abandoned to the mercy of their enemy. Then, with a more subdued Meagher coordinating, they pulled back themselves in an early morning drizzle, abandoning the hill to the rebels. Hoping they had bought enough time for McClellan's army to be saved.

Coming down from the hill Seamus realised, with a clarifying shock, how completely enclosed by enmity he'd been. While fighting the rebels to his front, the 88th had been sandwiched between the 69th, which included, amongst its mostly brave and decent men, O'Rorke and his cabal to his right and the unfriendly Anglos of the 29th Massachusetts to his left.

The Irish stood and fought many times as they sought to re-cross the Chickahominy. The Confederates snapped at their heels with the tenacity of crazed terriers. The heaviest fight on the way back occurred at the wooden bridge they had crossed over the previous evening. It had taken a lot of punishment from Southern artillery since then and Company L, amongst other units, were requisitioned to buy time for the engineers to repair it and then destroy it again after the Northern units had crossed. They took what cover they could in front of the bridge. Seamus, crouched between Pat Mangan and Jer Horan, plugged away at the rebels from behind some bushes. The morning's cold and stiffness had worked its way out of his bones, helped by surreptitious offerings from Mangan's hip flask. When the big Kerryman slumped over on top of him his first thought was that his friend had imbibed too much of his own stash. Maybe he was just exhausted. Then Seamus felt the stickiness and saw the blood. The Kerryman's eyes rolled until only the whites were visible; his head and limbs flopped lifelessly across Seamus.

Pat Mangan was dead.

A bullet from a sharpshooter's rifle had drilled a hole just above his right ear shattering the back of his skull as it exited. No chance. No last succinct words. No final wishes.

Horan saw what had happened. 'Let's get out of here before that sharpshooter draws a bead on us.'

Seamus, numb with shock, managed to say: 'We have to take Pat with us.'

'Impossible!' Horan barked. He reached across and started to go through the dead man's pockets.

'What are you doing?' Seamus demanded.

'Taking any personal effects for his loved ones. That's all we can do now. Leave him on the field, we might get back for him later. If we don't, sure what does it matter to the poor devil? If there's such a thing as a soul, it has taken flight from here. And, knowing Pat Mangan, the direction it took could only have been upwards.'

All he found, or at least all he removed from the body, was the hip flask, which he shook and, on hearing its contents swish he took a long swig before handing it to Seamus, who marvelled at the corporal's coolness. A spattering of lead rattled the branches above their heads, sending a shower of green and brown leaves cascading onto them and providing a skimpy funeral bower for his tentmate. Horan was right: they had to get out of there. Their position was becoming increasingly isolated and that sharpshooter would already be sighting them from one of the trees out in front.

He laid the body on the ground and rolled its large, lifeless bulk underneath the bushes. A dogwood, its petals strewn on the ground by rebel lead, would have to serve as a grave marker. Seamus would instruct an orderly to direct any burial details here. More balls peppered the bushes, cascading further leaves onto their friend's body and at least bestowing greater colour upon his transitory funeral bower.

He covered Pat's face with the coat the Kerryman had discarded moments before being shot. When Horan tugged at his sleeve and started moving off, he followed. Crouching low, they scampered back nearer the bridge where more comrades from Company L, other companies of the 88th and units from the 63rd, 69th, and 29th Mass. were spread out in varying degrees of cover ranging from bushes and rocks to depressions in the ground.

Seamus told an orderly where his friend's body lay; but he never discovered if it received a proper burial. Such was the speed of retreat, it most certainly never did and Pat Mangan would lay there until whatever was left by the rebels, vultures and wild boars leached into the red Virginian soil.

They swept past their Fair Oaks base and saw all their supplies and equipment ablaze. There was no time to retrieve any of it and rather than leave anything that might be of use to the rebels it was all torched. Seamus thought with regret of his letters from Kathleen and of the personal effects Pat Mangan had left behind.

Father Corby rode up. 'Shame about the chapel, Father,' a private in the 63rd remarked. The chapel tent, which had been purchased from the proceeds of a generous collection amongst the men and erected with an elaborate ceremony, was on fire.

'It is, boys,' Father Corby replied, 'but it is only canvas and can be replaced. What's a greater pity is the Bibles, prayer books and sermons that were in the tent. Those I can never properly replace.'

Seamus noted the sadness in the priest's face. It seemed not even good and celibate men would be spared from loss in this war.

Large numbers of wounded and dying lay in the fields around Fair Oaks. Realising they were being abandoned, they started up a pathetic wailing, hobbling, crawling, and limping after their abler comrades, pleading not to be deserted.

Seamus's leg was grabbed by a man whose right ankle hung from his own leg by the slimmest of tendons. 'Please, please mister give us a pull up. Let me lean on your shoulder. Sure, I'm light as a feather. I'll be no trouble. Only don't leave me here for my throat to be slit. The rebs will have no value on me apart from me boots. I have a wife. I have children. Two little girls. They need a father. Don't leave me. Please, mister.'

Seamus's instincts screamed out to help the man and he leant down towards him.

'Private Farrell! Re-join your company now!' Captain McMahon was harrying the able-bodied, hurrying them so as escape the clutches of the rebels breathing down their necks. Nothing could be done for the dead or the crippled, but the able-bodied were to be harvested to fight another day.

Seamus looked into the pleading, watery eyes of his beseecher and with a slight shake of his head turned to lose himself in the hazy, inchoate, chaotic world of war.

Three days of mayhem later the Irish Brigade turned and fought again at a small railway village called Savage Station. There was no sign of Meagher. Rumour had it he'd been arrested for drunkenness. General Bull Sumner rode across and led the Irish into battle himself. Major Quinlan, a regimental officer, was at the head of the 88th. Jer Horan had been promoted to sergeant in the re-shuffling which followed the death of Byers. Seamus and the others double-timed across swampy fields to charge Confederate artillery sited on an incline outside the village that had been harassing the retreating troops with severe effect.

'*Faugh-a-Ballagh! Faugh-a-Ballagh!*' They screamed as they charged. Canisters screeched through the air and blew ragged bloody holes in the charging Irish ranks, before splitting and tossing mini black balls of death and destruction amongst them.

'Close up! Close up!' Horan and the other leaders shouted after each deadly swipe. 'The sooner we get there, the sooner we can stop them.'

Seamus fixed on his friend's back as an indestructible guide amidst the bloody chaos around him and charged screaming with the others. Men went down all around, but he led a charmed life. Out of the corner of his eye he saw Sean Cregan fly backwards from a hail of lead whose passage had merely ruffled his own hair. Exultant at his immortality he laughed uproariously as he closed with the rebels. It was Fair Oaks all over again. A caterwauling melee. But, as if in deference to its name, Savage Station, was an even more vicious, hard-edged, brutal fight.

There could be no doubt he killed and maimed here. With flesh-ripping violence, he slammed his bayonet time and again into rebel bodies, using fist, claw, and head to ward off attention while he went about his killing business.

He cut a path to the top of the hill. Men from various units of the Brigade swarmed over the Confederate artillery. Colonel Pierce, *Ebenezer* Pierce was directing his men to spike a cannon with a bayonet blade. A practical idea, except Seamus O'Farrell was not sacrificing his precious bayonet blade to spike any cannon. He needed it to make more blood flow.

He was squinting through the battle smoke for more rebels to kill when a canon being dragged down the reverse slope exploded amongst the 29th and tumbled him backwards, knocking the wind out of him. When he dragged himself to his feet, there was carnage where the triumphant, spiking 29th had been moments before. Pierce lay moaning softly a short distance from the others. The hand that had been directing men with an officer's sword, a mere bloody stump.

The tumble that Seamus had taken knocked the battle lust out of him and before he'd thought about it, he'd rushed to the colonel's aid.

'My men, my men,' Pierce was calling, 'my poor men.'

'Your men will be fine, Colonel,' Seamus said, not knowing whether they would or not. Pierce held his bleeding stump aloft as if he would direct proceedings despite his injury. Seamus stripped off the man's jacket and tied the sleeves tightly together around the limb, hoping it would suffice as a tourniquet long enough to get proper treatment to the colonel.

Pierce was flushed and slightly demented, hanging onto consciousness. His dour, Puritan, New England features transformed into lines of pain. Seamus wondered if he realised an Irish papist had come to his aid and, if he had, would he allow him to help or would he prefer to bleed to an untarnished death?

He half-dragged and half-carried the Colonel down the hill until he came across a couple of stretcher bearers. Handing his burden over, he informed the orderlies of their patient's identity and bid them take care with him. As he turned to go back to the fight Pierce called to him in a croaky voice: 'I'll pray for your black papist soul.'

'Thanks, Colonel, and I'll pray that you'll live to thump a good many Bibles with your remaining fist.' Pierce might have laughed or it might have been a painful wheeze.

Seamus faced the hill.

'You're a man of many talents.' O'Rorke was standing there on his own, looking hard at him.

'I need to rejoin my Company.'

'Ah, it's all over – another glorious rearguard action by the Irish. One for the annals. Pity Meagher was too drunk to see it – for himself anyway, maybe not for the rest of us. We might be spared some rhetorical bullshit. Although it's doubtful, he'll come up with something, even though he wasn't near the field.'

'Over or not, I still must rejoin my Company.'

'Wherever your Company is, I outrank you and I command you to stay here. Stand to attention!'

'Yes, Sergeant.' The lack of enthusiasm obvious.

O'Rorke gave a harsh, humourless laugh. 'You're a piece of work, Limerick.'

'Sergeant, my company needs me.'

O'Rorke made a dismissive fly-swatting movement with his hand. 'Not right now they don't. I, though, need to know what you did with Flaherty's body. I know you threw him into a swamp-hole. But which one? His poor old wife should have a marker to grieve over. He wasn't up to much, old Flaherty, but he deserves a known grave all the same.'

Seamus knew O'Rorke didn't care about Flaherty's grave, not to mention his wife, who would surely never leave her Five Points hovel to visit the site anyway. He was trying to catch Seamus out, see if he gave anything away to confirm his suspicions.

'I know nothing about Private Flaherty, though I heard he'd deserted and was probably in a whorehouse in Washington.'

O'Rorke gave his harsh laugh again. Then his voice went cold, so cold that Seamus, though still in the hot flush of battle, felt a chill grip his guts. 'Don't act smart with me, Limerick. You got away with Dan O'Leary's murder, but you won't get away with this one. You see, Flaherty told me that some night on the way back from your slave-whore he was going to jump you. I know you visited her that night and I know he had enough drink taken to have a go. You're not the innocent country bumpkin you act, Limerick. I've seen you fight and I know you've enough to overcome Flaherty, who was all mouth. Thing is though: he was loyal. You're not. The likes of you need wiping out before we get to the English. And I'm the man to do it.'

Seamus thought O'Rorke was going to go for him right then and there. He knew O'Rorke was in a different class to him when it came to fighting and killing and he wouldn't have a chance at the best of times. Now, after the exertions of this evening's fight and after dragging Pierce down the mountain, he knew he had no chance at all. O'Rorke looked as he'd been through some hard times himself recently. He was more bedraggled than Seamus had ever seen him: his uniform tatty and torn in places, his beard and face flecked with other people's blood. But he looked in control; ready for more. A savage hunger in his eyes suggested he was merely warming up. However, he was also far too clever to take on a fellow Union man in the open. More and more soldiers were swarming around them, the hilltop was regarded as secure enough to be left to the Artillery. Already Crosby, Donnelly, Jakes, and others from O'Rorke's coterie had gathered around their leader. Crosby had his smarmy grin on.

'I am loyal,' Seamus called across to O'Rorke.

'Not enough. Your type are the most dangerous. One minute you seem to be on the right side, the next you're rescuing the English, the blacks, and murdering your own. We will not succeed with the likes of you.'

Crosby's grin widened.

'Nice work!' Horan, John Mulvaney, Sergeant Brosnihan and others from his Company were coming by.

'The next time you go into a fight, watch both ways. Traitors deserve nothing better than a bullet in the back.' O'Rorke fired his parting shot, for now.

Though they had lost Sean Cregan and Pat Mangan, and other wounded, the men of Company L were in self-congratulatory mode.

'It's just a shame it wasn't for the ould Dart.' Mulvaney exclaimed about their successful charge. Time and again, Seamus had heard this exclamation from his comrades after a fight. And it was a pity indeed that the expenditure of all this blood and energy was not for their beloved Ireland.

Once again, McClellan's army, including the Irish Brigade, left their dead and wounded on the field. Once again, the Confederates snapped at their heels. The Northerners rushed towards Harrison's Landing on the James River, pushing through White Oak Swamp - an overspill of the Chickahominy and one of the marshiest, boggiest places on the

Peninsula. With Stonewall Jackson pressing from the north and A.P. Hill moving in on them from the west, it seemed inevitable that they would be caught in this pincer movement and destroyed in the swamps. All the time, the Irish Brigade fought in the rearguard; striving to ward off the rebels long enough for the main army to get through.

Seamus lost count of the number of engagements; the numerous men he fired at, who, in turn, fired at him and the midnight retreats long after the rest of the army had moved on. They seemed to fight every minute of the day and move every hour of darkness, with no time to eat or prepare food - apart from cramming down the ubiquitous hard tack. Sometimes they moved and fought at the same time. His brain occupied a feverish twilight zone where a bullet in the back from O'Rorke might not be unwelcome. Except for the ignominy and shame: only those running from a fight got shot in the back. Why should he allow O'Rorke the satisfaction of pinning that on him? Despite his feverishness, hunger, and exhaustion, he kept an eye on his enemies. Front and back.

One evening, after thwarting Stonewall Jackson to their front and turning to take on A. P. Hill on their left flank, black waves of exhaustion swam in his brain and it felt like the end. No further could he go; no further would he go. Suddenly, the survivor in him got to rejoice at the booming of shot and shell whistling over the Brigade's head and falling amidst Jackson's men in the swamps behind them. Union gunboats on the James had come to their aid. The support signalling that they were nearing sanctuary and hadn't been forgotten after all. He lifted his head and pulled himself up straighter.

Bull Sumner rode up to the Brigade and pointed towards a Union battery he wanted to protect, roaring: 'Boys, you're going to save another day!'

Seamus ran towards it with tears of pride in his eyes. Later, in the darkness, snatching a short rest on the putrid ground, he wondered who this person was. Then Horan came along telling them to fall back immediately.

There was no further time for wondering.

CHAPTER SEVENTEEN
JULY 1862

One final hill and safety; one last push and the great 'Change-of-Base' would be complete. One more incline. Malvern Hill. At its foot, on the other side, Harrison's Landing – an impregnable Union fortress, capable of being supplied indefinitely by vessels coming up the James, had been constructed.

One gently sloping farmed hillside, and then: sanctuary.

Except General Lee, the new commander of the Confederates, chose it as the site for a final, ferocious assault on the Northerners and Mikey O'Rorke chose it for the same on Seamus O'Farrell and so it became one more site of blood and gore.

In cold, drizzly, dawn-light the Irish Brigade stumbled over the top of Malvern Hill and fell into line between the fearsome Union artillery ringing the summit. Holding the defensive high ground, they turned to face the enemy. Their position would have given them cause for cheer if they weren't so exhausted. Men slept standing up or crouching in position. The smell of boiling coffee and broiling beef wafting from where Meagher and the other officers were stationed maddened the men with a ravenous, slavering hunger. At last, when a dawn assault didn't materialise, they were given permission to fall back to the leeward side and take what rest and sustenance they could find. Too tired to drink or eat, Seamus lay on the ground and fell into a deep, dreamless sleep.

He woke to the sound of battle raging on the other side of the hill, though the mouth-watering smell of cooking meat had a more compelling impact on his senses. Rising stiffly to his feet, wondering if he would ever again have normal body rhythms, he saw it was late afternoon. At least now he had sufficient energy to appease his appetite. He walked over to where a group of comrades from companies K and L were roasting a beast on a spit.

'Catch your own sheep,' Horan called to him when he saw him approaching. 'I heard ye're good at that down in Limerick and having seen ye're women I can see why.'

The others laughed.

'At least, unlike you, I've refrained from skinning, gutting, and roasting my girlfriend,' Seamus riposted.

'Won't stop you eating some of mine though, will it?' Horan said carelessly.

Seamus had to laugh. He had never met a more larger-than-life figure than this Tipperary man. He had one of the sharpest wits Seamus had ever come across, aligned with a gentleness that came from inner strength, yet he was ferocious in battle and Seamus would follow him anywhere.

'Find yourself a plate and you can have a bit of her left titty.' His friend was now saying. Brevet First Sergeant or not, off-duty he was still one of the men.

A cannonball whizzed through the air and landed with a thud on the other side of the hill, making the ground vibrate on their side. But even those who were not at Bull Run were battle-hardened veterans now and no one flinched. They had earned this rest, having fought almost continuously throughout the previous week – in the rearguard, which, in a retreating army is the frontline. Let others save the Union for a change.

'She's done,' one of the Company K men called out. 'She's no use to anyone except for ating.'

'It's a good job Father Corby can't hear youse,' someone else said.

'Sure, tell him it's the lamb of God we're talking about,' came a reply.

'Line up with your plates, will ye?' Horan ordered.

Seamus ambled over to some bushes beyond the campfire to relieve himself. It was a large sheep, there would be plenty remaining when he was finished. The smoke and cries from the battle on the other side of the hill were distant, dreamy sounds, compared to the sustaining earthiness of his comrades' humour. He was only sad that Pat Mangan wasn't around to participate.

The bushes were in a natural depression on the side of hill; down there, leisurely relieving himself, the noises of both camp and battle receded. A hawk hunted in the glowering sky. He yawned. It looked like the 88th was going to have a battle free day. He was keen to return before the sheep was devoured. God, he had almost forgotten what it was like to experience ordinary, everyday emotions like hunger.

He was buttoning himself up when they pounced. They had probably been watching him a long time, even while he was sleeping. Waiting for their chance. O'Rorke's face filled his vision, he had a side glimpse of Crosby, Donnelly, and Jakes. Others were obviously there because he was held tightly by at least three men. O'Rorke stepped right up to him. His breath smelt stale from the week of hard movement and fighting, or maybe it was just the badness inside him. The breathing of the others came to him like the panting of savage beasts. The moment had come for him to be assassinated.

'Count yourself lucky,' he said to Seamus, 'we decided to wait until you'd done up your flies. It's more dignity than you deserve and certainly more than you gave Dan O'Leary or probably, Peter Flaherty. Definitive word has come from Ireland. You're the man.'

Seamus opened his mouth to protest but all that came out was a self-pitying groan as O'Rorke plunged a blade into his kidneys. Instantly, he felt its heat in there, then, though the blade remained hot, tendrils of icy cold crept out along his insides so that he had the unbearable sensation of a piercing hot blade causing his innards to freeze. He was too shocked to call out. His eyes rolled – maybe he imagined it, but it seemed he saw the hawk swoop on an embankment and come up with a field mouse mangled in its beak.

'Finish him,' one of his captors said.

'Oh, I intend to,' O'Rorke replied.

Seamus wondered where he'd feel the burning-freezing sensation next. Would O'Rorke cut his throat or stab his heart, was the feeling different in different parts of the body?

'Die like all traitors must die,' O'Rorke pronounced with fetid breath as he stepped in close again. For the kill.

But instead of the anticipated increase in the awful burning-freezing sensation Seamus was hit by a terrific blow in the back that sent him plunging forward with a violence that carried O'Rorke before him.

A blackness welled up inside his body obliterating everything except for an enormous headache.

Shortly, that too faded.

Cold. Shivering. Looking up at the gloomy sky he tried to separate the darkness of dusk from the blackness that floated within his head. Where was he? The black inchoate forms flitting inside and outside of him refused to coalesce into anything coherent. Oh, yes! O'Rorke. The knife. The pain. Then something unforeseen had happened.

A shell! A shell had landed on or close to them as O'Rorke was about to finish him. Suddenly he was filled with a life-infusing euphoria. Despite the pain and the coldness, he was alive! Surely that meant the others were…dead? A rattling nerve-wracking sound filled the evening around him. It took him a little while to realise he had laughed aloud.

Amazingly, the hawk's ghostly shape still patrolled along the skyline above him. Didn't it know that the world had changed? He had been knocked forwards by the blast, but somehow had ended up lying on his back facing the other way. The sounds of battle and the cries of men filled his head, echoing from the other side of the hill and fighting it out with the headache for his full attention. But all he could see was the hawk crossing his eye line. With enormous effort, he rolled onto his side but a jolt of agony from the knife wound set him flat onto the ground again.

There was a right hullabaloo on the other side of the hill, even in the enclosed ravine where he lay, there could be no doubt that a major battle was being fought. The smell of roast mutton wafted on the smoke polluted evening air. He tried calling out, though the effort was almost too painful. There was no one there. If he was able to crawl, he would have a whole sheep for his supper. There was going to be a lot more of 'Horan's girlfriend' to go around than previously thought.

He had to get up. Had to see what happened to O'Rorke and his cronies. Had to see if he could fight. Had to know if he would live. Too many people were depending on him.

It couldn't end like this.

Ten minutes later, he'd made it to a half-standing, half-crouching position. Sweating with pain and weak from loss of blood, he nevertheless grasped the situation around him. Jakes was dead: lacerated by splinters from the exploding shell. Another man whose name he didn't know but who he'd often seen hanging around with O'Rorke was mumbling incoherently nearby; bubbles of red pulsing out of his mouth. Of O'Rorke and the others there was no sign. Coppery blood was smeared all over the grass; it could have been his own or it might be his tormentor's. There was no way of knowing. But if O'Rorke lived, Seamus knew where he'd be. After the blast it was certain that men would have come clambering over here, advancing to gain revenge for the attack, disturbing O'Rorke and taking him along with them.

Seamus staggered out of the enlarged depression and stumbled past the smouldering fire and blackening sheep to where his stuff lay. Having neither the energy nor the time to do a proper tourniquet he improvised, like he had done with Pierce, this time by binding the sleeves of his jacket as tightly as possible around himself. It didn't help much but it enabled him to straighten up a bit more once he'd picked his gun off the ground. He blinked in the late light and willed unconsciousness away. Praying he wouldn't collapse from loss of blood before doing his duty, he set off for the crest of the hill. On the other side two great armies were locked in a death grapple. However, the grand scale was not his concern now.

He fell and it took a supreme act of willpower to get up again. But his desperate desire overrode ordinary human agonies and strength. The artillery at the top of the hill loomed before him. He stumbled towards it. He needed to get beyond it, to the other side. Where the battle raged. To find O'Rorke. And kill him.

He paused at the top, next to an Indiana Battery Division.

'Soldier, you should be at a medical station back there,' a grizzled, bearded Hoosier corporal said to him, pointing to the tents down near the shore.

Panting for breath, Seamus flapped his hand dismissively to indicate he would be alright.

'The way them Rebs have their dander up they'll be up here soon enough. Why go looking for trouble when it's coming to you?'

Seamus blinked the sweat from his eyes and tried to make sense of the chaotic surging below him. But there was such a one-to-one melee going on that it was impossible.

'These tubes,' said the Hoosier indicating the Union artillery, 'aren't worth a piss in the wind now. We'd take out half our own side if we fired. Mind you if that's what it takes to stop them grey devils coming up here…'

Over on the right, where a wood girthed the hill, there was a flash of green and beneath it he thought he saw Meagher's white horse. He sidled in that direction.

'You're foolish. There's men with lesser wounds begging to be taken to a medical tent,' the Artillery Corporal called after him.

Seamus carried on. Shrieks of charging and counter-charging men, musket and artillery fire filled his head. A scarlet sun was dropping inexorably beneath the western woods, he knew that in the scant minutes before it disappeared two momentous events would have been decided. The outcome of the battle for Malvern Hill and whether it would be O'Rorke or himself that would survive it.

His legs gained momentum. With his musket held firmly out before him, he pushed Union and Confederate men aside as he cut a diagonal downwards path across the hill towards where the men of the Irish Brigade were surging once more. The tearing in his side and the blackness at the edges of his vision didn't exist. They couldn't exist.

He crossed the threshold separating calm from chaos. A wave of heat and sound washed over him signifying the death of civilisation. ''Tis yourself I see,' Horan called above the din. 'Did you give that sheep a turn before you came down? Don't want it burning while I'm away.' The Tipperary man turned and punched a grey scarecrow smack on the jaw to send him flying backwards like a rag doll.

Seamus summoned the effort to jab a charging rebel with his bayonet and continued moving across the charging Irish. Buoyed up by a day's rest and irritated at having it interrupted, their dander was up and they were performing in fine style. Despite his self-occupation, he felt a surge of pride at the sight of his fellow countrymen and their green flags writing another glorious chapter for themselves in this campaign.

'Come on, Erin's glory boys, drive them back!' He heard Meagher's cultured, but now frenzied, tone shout out. John Clifford, a cowhand from the 69th, who'd gambled with him on Chuck-Luck a number of times, was down. He went over to him.

'Are you alright, John?' The blond-haired private looked at him, his face sweating, but paler than his hair; he didn't look good.

'It's my chest. My chest. Oh God! Water, please. A small drink, please.' The brash, loquacious, cowboy part of him had already died.

Seamus handed him his nearly empty canteen. 'Where is the 69th?' he asked, feeling guilty because it felt like he was only giving the drink in exchange for information, which, if he was honest, was largely true.

Clifford grabbed the canteen. 'Over…right,' he gasped, before spilling most of its contents down his front. Seamus helped him get a decent sip. 'Stay with me, will you?' Clifford asked.

Seamus hesitated, but ungentle emotions overrode his compassion. 'I will send a stretcher to you.' He squeezed Clifford's hand then continued pushing perpendicularly to the main charge.

The Battle of Malvern Hill had reached those pivotal moments he'd learnt to sense over the previous days' fighting. Both sides were evenly poised; whoever broke next would lose the battle. Would the Union, with the Irish Brigade to the fore, allow the grey hordes to overwhelm them and storm over the hill to destroy the Army of the Potomac, or would the Confederates give ground and retreat towards the woods and swamps, allowing McClellan and his men to escape?

This consideration should have overridden his personal concerns, and normally, he told himself, they would, but not this evening. Instead of facing to the front where blue and grey were locked in mortal combat he continued sidling to the right.

A soldier, who regularly sang patriotic songs around the campfire, grabbed him. The man's eyes were demented; blood pumped from his neck: a mortal wound. Seamus pushed him off as gently as he could and carried on.

He saw O'Rorke.

Units of the 69th and 29th had driven a wedge into the rebel front-line and had pushed down the hill several yards. At that arc of the field there was no doubt who was winning. O'Rorke to the fore. The man's hatred was indefatigable. Always ahead of his Union colleagues he slashed, punched, head-butted, and stabbed his way forward, creating space for his comrades to push into. It was the spirit that won battles, that would free Ireland, that would get anyone in his way killed; that would see him – Seamus O'Farrell – killed. A spirit that had to be extinguished.

He was amidst the Irish Brigade, though far from the 88th. Amongst the 69th and 29th. He saw Corporal Coughlin, Sergeant Buckley, George Twoomey and many other familiar faces, along with the severe, scowling faces of the New Englanders. Reminiscent of an inter-parish football match, those who were not at the front-line were straining to reach it. Those behind fired out over the heads of their own men, while those at the very front leant out and stabbed with their bayonets at the grey line beyond. Meanwhile, all, even the poker-arsed New Englanders, screamed, shouted, swore, and spat as they tried to keep the enemy at bay. Pandemonium. He would get away with what he was about to do. Questions were sure to be asked afterwards about what he was doing in this part of the field, but in a melee like this it would be easily explained.

He began to swear at the rebels himself: pretending to jab and aim out over the heads of his comrades at the enemy beyond, though it was the enemy within he really aimed at. In his mounting excitement, he'd forgotten how weak he'd become; when he lifted his musket to his shoulder it felt like a lead weight, and in the blurry vision of his near faint, O'Rorke's head wavered like a tall reed in the wind. Oh God! Had he come this far to fail now? He remembered the cold, mad hatred in O'Rorke's eyes as he'd sunk in the knife and it steadied him. Just a few seconds more resolve.

He focussed on the back of his tormentor's head. There it was. It moved. Then it was there again. He squeezed. The back of O'Rorke's head exploded in a crimson shower; the battle line swayed forwards; Seamus fell – his last reserves of strength drained, unable to withstand the forward momentum. He sensed the tension of battle break as the Confederates gave way and the Irish Brigade chased them down the hill, whooping and hollering.

The fates had decided. Little Napoleon's army was saved. Seamus O'Farrell had survived.

But his soul was damned. And the black maw of hell opened to swallow him.

CHAPTER EIGHTEEN

Rain. Blessed rain. He teetered on the edge of the maw of hell, but a fine Irish rain fell in Virginia and its gentle caress held him.

But, like a mercurial lover, it grew rapidly unpleasant.

His existence was constricted to the pain in his side and the blackness that threatened his consciousness, though he was not unaware of the rhythms of the battlefield. The gladiators were deserting the arena. The vanquished Southerners scuttling downhill as fast as their defeated legs could take them; the victorious Northerners tramping back uphill, exhausted, but replete with the joy of victory – the more energetic survivors hollering and yelling their achievements or shouting insults after the departing rebels. One thing the able-bodied on both sides had in common was a desire to get off the killing ground as quickly as possible, to leave it to the crippled, maimed, and dead. To half-people like Seamus.

The rain grew in intensity, until it became a menacing sheet of moisture chilling him to the bone and making the ground beneath him so unstable it seemed likely to wash him downhill until he was entangled with the dead and dying heaped up at the foot of the slope.

He had to get off the battlefield.

Some of the not so critically wounded returned to offer succour. He heard voices calling friends and brothers. But on a field so vastly gory an individual was a mere droplet in the ocean. He would most likely be dead or washed away by the time someone got to him, but there was no possibility of rising to his feet. He had asked a lot of his limbs recently and they had responded, however this new requirement necessitated a resurrection no earthly body could execute.

He rotated on his good side and his face fell into the mud of Malvern Hill. He twisted it sideways to spit out as much muck as possible and to gasp at essential air. Then slowly, excruciatingly, he began to drag himself inch by inch, through pain, mud and wet towards the top of the slope. He passed out regularly. Many times he clawed at the ground only for his grip to come away with a fistful of grit, forcing him to feel around for a purchase that would enable him to hoist himself another inch up the slope; many times he slid back over ground that had taken him long, long, minutes to traverse.

He had to negotiate numerous obstacles in the shape of his fellow wounded, dying and dead until he was no longer sure he was even going uphill; it felt like he was scrabbling his way over and back the slope in a doomed Sisyphean attempt to reach sanctuary. But he couldn't stop, because aggravating as the physical obstacles of the stricken soldiers were, their moans and pleas for help, water and to be put out of their misery were unbearable. In moments of consciousness, this drove him to move upwards, sideways, backwards – any direction rather than remaining prone amidst such misery. So he passed the night.

Dawn saw him still scrabbling feebly around the slope with the summit nowhere in sight. He rolled onto his back and blinked against the rain: too exhausted to carry on. He would have to put his faith in the gathering light as an instrument to deliver him from the fires of damnation, hopefully someone from Company L, or anyone military or medical from the North, would come and find him in the daylight. He slept.

'There he is!'

It had seemed only seconds but he had to have slept longer: the light was brighter and the rain had eased. He shivered and shook, unable to say for definite whether he was exhausted, in pain, or even dead. But Jer Horan and Tom Dillon were coming towards him.

'Christ you're a sight for sore eyes,' Horan exclaimed.

'Get me out of here, please,' he begged in a half whisper.

'We most certainly will,' Horan replied. 'Most of Company L are combing the hillside for you. We're also missing John Mulvaney and

Martin Brosnihan; Sean Carroll I saw die at the point of a bayonet right next to me. James Lalor and Mick Duffy we brought back with us, but there isn't much hope for poor old Lalor; you can see the poor bastard's guts pulsing in and out.'

Seamus thought he saw a look come into Horan's eyes which said that he didn't hold out much hope for him either. But he was too much a friend and leader to say it aloud. 'Come on, John, let's stop blabbering and get this man out of here. See, I told you he'd be over this way somewhere, this is around where I last saw him; got himself mixed up with them 69th fellas – what were you doing? Trying to avoid the real fighting?'

Seamus was chagrined to discover that, despite his desperate movements during the night, he hadn't ended up that far from where he'd originally fallen. The futility of it all threatened to overwhelm him. Then he remembered that O'Rorke's body, with the back of its head shattered by his musket ball, would be nearby and he wanted to get out of there immediately.

'Please, get me out of here,' he pleaded once more.

'Right! Here we go,' Dillon said, and his two comrades bent, lifted him at either end and proceeded up the slope. Pain rippled through him, but he was being succoured, so he bore it.

Near the top they paused for a rest, laying his bottom half gently on the ground; Horan still propping up his top half. He heard both men draw in breath and swear on the expulsion. At first, he thought it was to do with the exertion of carrying him and he felt guilty, then his eyes took in what they were looking at and he exclaimed himself.

Malvern Hill was alive. Like giant slugs damp blue and grey shapes pulsated on the hillside as the wounded and the dying crawled for help and twisted hither and thither in their agony. Above it all, could be heard a low-level, nerve-jangling hum. Thousands wept, moaned, and pleaded; their agonies washed into one piteous groan on the purgatory of Malvern Hill. He retched.

'Christ! Let's go!' He heard Horan say.

Then his consciousness disintegrated into a series of vignettes.

Cold, efficient hands ministered him. 'Should be dead...' someone was saying. 'Do you hear me? You should be dead!'

'Thought I was,' he muttered.

'There's mud, grass and God-knows-what crammed into that wound,' the same voice said. 'Staunched the flood of blood; bound to pay for it later on though. Infection. The maggots will have a field day. Do you hear me? You're safe for now but you're likely to die of infection later on. You should start saying your prayers…'

CHAPTER NINETEEN
AUGUST 1862

Mikey O'Rorke had been running from the greasy fat bluebottle ever since he'd seen it feasting on his father's lifeless eyes; hiding from it; compelling it to feast on others – on anyone but him. He'd succeeded in evading it for many years, though he'd always known it was biding its time; awaiting its chance. Now its patience had been rewarded. For the first time since they had become familiars, he was vulnerable, unable to defend himself, and the wily scavenger had pounced. Making up for all the lean years, it gorged itself. And then invited myriad relations from the fly family to sip of him also; sip of the suppurating wound in his head seeking entry past the broken barrier of flesh to his brain where the really juicy bits were.

He ground his teeth in frustrated agony.

The nurse came and his tormentors scampered. But not far. As soon as she'd retreated to other duties, they re-emerged from hiding. First his own bold, triumphant bluebottle; then the braver subordinates; within seconds they were all back having a merry old time buzzing and feeding off him. Taking advantage while he was helpless. He thought about screaming again, but he had done it only moments before and it had brought no relief. He was able to drum his fingers so it seemed his hands were still attached to his body, though he was unable to lift them to his head or face. For all the power that was left in his muscles, the upper apart of his body might as well be located in the most unassailable corner of the world's most impossible peak.

His bluebottle sang. *'Got you now! Got you now!'*

He screamed. 'Mammy! Daddy!'

***

Seamus recalled continuous bumps shooting burning pain up through him and glimpses of other agonised faces; but until he awoke to see a swirl of dust motes riding on a sunbeam in a Washington warehouse masquerading as a hospital he recalled nothing else. His pain had subsided to a fuzzy, corporeal ache restrained by morphine. But neither medication nor time effected an adjustment to the horrors around him.

If he'd been a butcher by trade, like Mulvaney, perhaps he'd have been more acquainted with the multifarious ways that flesh could be hacked, split, and dissected. But surely not even an intimacy with the meat trade would have prepared him for the horrifying durability of the human body. Men who'd lost limbs were as common as white sheep, but the multiplicity of spilt skulls, gaping abdomens and mangled faces on those who *lived* was astounding. Men who should have been dead, men who would have been far better off dead – bore witness to the frequency that the supposedly frail human body insisted on carrying on against the wishes of its occupier.

The only certain killer in that hospital was disease – no matter how hard medical staff and volunteers worked to assist the body – dirt and filth languishing in the hot Washington summer could overwhelm weeks of laborious work in hours.

He grew close to a young Boston lad who, though the progeny of New England Puritans, neither objected to having an Irish Papist next to him nor to striking up friendly conversation with the heathen.

Jonathan Ludlow was his name, nineteen, a law student at a Boston college. His right arm had been shattered by a blast of grape and it had been amputated to above the elbow joint. Though melancholic about the loss of his arm and the resultant incapacity for ball games and horseplay, his natural optimism and profound belief in the will of God was winning through. He looked forward to being united with his parents and siblings and returning to college. After all, the loss of an arm wouldn't prevent him becoming a top-class lawyer or impact on his love of God and family.

He asked Seamus a lot of questions about Ireland and its problems, bemoaning the injustices that man had created in the world.

'Only by recreating ourselves in God's image can we right these wrongs, James,' the earnest young man would say to the cynical older one.

'And you obviously think this can only be done by spilling blood, else you wouldn't be down here fighting?' Seamus half wanted to know; half wanted to rile.

'Unfortunately, James, the sword is sometimes necessary to conquer evil and impose God's will. Though prayer is the most powerful weapon.' Jonathan would reply.

'And if the other side think God is on their side?'

'No matter what side *you* think you are on, God will ensure righteousness prevails.'

'After he has had his fill of blood,' Seamus thought, but he was too fond of the young Bostonian to goad him further or to remind him that the North wasn't winning the war, implying that righteousness was on the side of the South.

Without insulting or overtly pushing their respective views on each other, they parried back and forth throughout the day, keeping each other company, growing to respect each other.

Though he'd lost a limb, Jonathan was to be released from hospital before Seamus, whose wound still suppurated. Also, Jonathan was being discharged home while Seamus was being repaired for a battlefield return. Despite his chagrin at his inability to return to fight for God's righteous cause Jonathan had become noticeably more cheerful at the prospects of being reunited with his family.

'Gosh, I reckon my brother Paul will have grown some in the last eighteen months, bet I can still wrestle him to the ground in under five seconds though - only need one limb for that, thank God. And my sister – Natasha – wonder how many beaux she's got now – always was the pretty one, bet Father is more protective than ever.' Several times a day, he wondered aloud about his family, how they'd have changed, how they'd greet him: maybe the whole town would turn out to welcome the returning hero. Often Seamus closed his eyes and wondered about his own life while Jonathan wittered away, though he welcomed the background voice of his fellow patient; providing a pleasant ambience to his own darker musings, diluting a substantial portion of their bleakness.

Then one morning his friend was quiet. At first, it seemed nothing much was wrong. The nurse who visited their section regularly, a genteel lady from a local charity, didn't notice anything amiss. And Seamus, though he looked at Jonathan anxiously from time to time, had to admit she seemed to be right. He was sleeping a lot, but his colour and breathing seemed normal. No one got much rest in this charnel house that passed for a hospital and eventually it caught up with you. Jonathan needed to give his jawing about the righteous cause and his imminent family reunion a rest for a while.

But charnel houses harbour invisible agents bearing malignancies more powerful than visible mutilations. By nightfall, it was apparent his New England Puritan friend was afflicted with them. They burned him from his insides out to his finely chiselled, purebred face on which no amount of cool wet flannels could lower his raging temperature. But the invisible agents of infection didn't stop at dismantling his friend's body from the inside out, they also attacked and destroyed his high-minded personality before replacing it with that of the lowest foul-mouthed barfly. By the time the genteel nurse returned to bathe his forehead the following morning, Jonathan Ludlow was cursing and spitting like an emissary from Satan. He rocked from side and side under her touch, calling her a harlot and names that no refined son of a New England preacher could know. To her credit, she bit on her distaste and stoically nursed her favourite patient, who continued to rant and rave at her by way of gratitude.

Around midday he sat up straight in the bed and his eyes momentarily cleared. He looked from Seamus to her and said in his normal voice: 'The Elysian Fields beckon. I'll reserve you both a spot.'

Then he fell back onto the bed and Jonathan Ludlow's contribution to the Righteous Cause was consigned to Elysian Fields in a world yet unseen by Seamus or the Nurse. He was sure to be already fighting the good fight. In the world they occupied there was only silence, harshly and swiftly broken by the moans of a severely burnt soldier a few beds away.

After Jonathan's death what had been a difficult environment for Seamus became intolerable. Without his friend's positive company, the wounds, mutilations, moans, coughing, weeping and flies that had been ever present progressed from background nuisances to pervasive foreground horrors. He knew he had to get out or die. He willed his wound better, got out of bed before he was ready and made himself walk. He never complained to the doctors or nurses when it pained; mercifully and miraculously, he avoided major infection and succeeded in getting himself discharged weeks before he was ready, for he'd rather die a thousand times in the field than remain a day longer in that fly-infested, Jonathan-Ludlowless hellhole.

And so, six weeks after descending into the netherworld, a train ground to a halt in the Arlington suburb of Washington and he disembarked amidst a squeal of brakes; a screech of steam; a cacophony of shouts and a rumble of sliding doors. He disentangled himself from returning veterans and newly arrived recruits wondering with wide-eyed innocence where to go to find their regiments and struck off south-east in the direction of Fort Corcoran where the Irish Brigade was once again based, like they'd been just prior to First Bull Run.

Tramping along, he passed row after row of dilapidated warehouses that eventually gave way to seedy clapboard dwellings and, finally, smatterings of green grass and trees. Man-made structures or natural surroundings - he didn't care, he was elated to be out of that hospital and to be walking to rejoin his comrades; the familiar chill of anticipation he experienced at the outset of any venture pertaining to the Irish Brigade rippled through him. He'd had many bad experiences since joining the Union Army but he'd survived. Why were people like Pat Mangan and Jonathan Ludlow taken and a man like him spared? Maybe living in a dirt floor hovel in Ireland had armed him with immunity from infection? Maybe he was marked for something greater and maybe it was written that one day he would lead an army into West Limerick to liberate parishes like Kilgarry and fulfil the destiny of a people?

The ramparts of Fort Corcoran came into view and he quickened his step.

CHAPTER TWENTY

'Welcome back! I wasn't sure we would ever see you again.' Jer Horan broke into a huge grin when he caught sight of Seamus coming down the street towards the tents of Company L.

Seamus saluted his by now officially confirmed first-sergeant, and Horan returned in kind; both of them with grins as wide as the Shannon estuary.

'It's good to see you, James. Very good indeed.'

'It's good to be back, Sergeant.'

'Must have been some hole they've been keeping you in then if that's what you think.'

'It was pretty grim alright. But I'm here and alive. Thanks to you and Tom Dillon.'

'It was nothing more than what one soldier does for another; you'd have done the same for us.' Horan said, uncomfortable with the gratitude. 'Come on! Your old tent is made up and available.'

Pat Mangan wouldn't be there to share the other half and Seamus felt a sharp pang of sorrow at the recollection of the loss of his friend. There were many others gone too, not only in Company L, but, in all companies in the Irish Brigade.

Seamus pushed the thought that he was personally responsible for two of those absences to the back of his mind. After he'd reported to the Provost-Guard and commenced walking down by the 69th's streets, his old fear and uncertainty had returned. He'd killed Flaherty and he was almost certain he'd killed O'Rorke, but what if O'Rorke walked out from one of the tents and made an accusation that he'd shot him in the back of the head at Malvern Hill? How bad would that be? In front of all the others? Surely, there was no way O'Rorke could have survived such a wound?

But, someone else could have seen him do it.

These unsettling questions and thoughts preoccupied him once he'd entered Fort Corcoran and began walking, as per the Guard's instructions, towards Company L of the 88th. Despite his trepidation, no one bothered him; instead, he received greetings and nods from lots of men as he passed and it occurred to him again that, despite falling foul of O'Rorke and the tension with the Massachusetts 29th, he'd become part of an extended family since joining the Brigade – a family that he loved with less intensity than his extended family back in Kilgarry, but one which imbued him with confidence and reassurance. Hopefully, he could use one to rescue the other.

He didn't see O'Rorke or any of his men as he walked through. There were several new faces interspersed amidst the familiar ones he noticed on his journey across the fort. He'd heard Meagher was in New York trying to fill the gaps created by the Peninsula campaign. Scanning the fresh, clean-shaven faces he realised he was now a veteran who would have looked just as fresh to those who'd fought at Bull Run when he'd joined up in November.

Horan led him to his tent; a walk which became a procession as some of the old stalwarts like Pat Gorman, Tom Dillon and others still around turned out to welcome Seamus back. They included, to his delight, John Mulvaney, who miraculously walked off Malvern Hill the morning after the battle with a superficial leg wound.

'Welcome back, Limerick.'

'Did they feed you well?'

'Lap of luxury, I bet, while were tramping half naked around the countryside to end up in this godforsaken place.'

Seamus acknowledged their good-natured taunts with grins and nods. "Twas great lads, you should try it yourselves some time; but then you'd have to put yourselves in harm's way, so that's not going to happen, is it?'

'Harm's way? That's how you got hurt was it? We heard you stabbed yourself with your rusty bayonet to get out of the fight.' Tom Dillon retorted.

Seamus let it ride; he didn't want the discussion, even in jest, to stray too near how he got wounded.

'Mr Cranny! We've brought a real soldier to share your tent, maybe some of his good example will rub off on you. Though it's unlikely - Meagher must have combed the lowest back street dives for his latest batch of recruits.' Horan addressed this to a tall, thin, bored-looking young man who occupied what used to be Pat Mangan's tent-half.

Cranny grinned humourlessly. 'You must be the famous, James Farrell.'

'Famous, now is it? If you have to go through what I've gone through for this fame it ain't worth it. Don't do it son.'

Cranny gave that grin once more. 'I don't intend to,' he said.

'You'll do what you're told to do son,' Horan interjected.

Seamus disliked the newcomer; few could have replaced the affable Pat Mangan as a tentmate in his eyes, but he reckoned that this specimen wouldn't have replaced any of the Company L men killed or wounded in the Peninsula Campaign. There was something cold and sullen about him – he'd likely only joined for the enlistment bounty or was on the run from something in civilian life, or both. Horan was right: they must have run out of good men to fight for the Irish Brigade when they hired Cranny. However, everyone deserved a chance and it was not at all unlikely that they thought the same about him when he'd joined up first.

'Push up a small bit son; I don't need much space for what I've got,' he said as he dropped his rucksack on the ground. 'And don't worry we'll get along just fine. We're all on the same side and we were all wet around the ears to begin with. If you need any help or advice, just let me know.'

Cranny didn't seem worried; he pushed an oily slick of hair back from his face and looked sullenly at Seamus. At first, it seemed he wouldn't move, but then he gathered up his stuff and began rearranging it at the further end of the two half-tents.

'Well! I think a hooley is in order. I'll see what I can rustle up. See everyone outside my tent about half past eight?' Pat O'Gorman said.

'Only if you don't bring that bloody harmonica of yours,' John Mulvaney snorted. 'The thought of coming back to hear that thing nearly made me stay amongst the dead on Malvern Hill.

'Pity that blow you got didn't stem the flow of them snots,' O'Gorman retorted.

'When you're settled there, I need to take you to Meagher's quarters,' Horan, ignoring the others, said to Seamus, whose heart dropped immediately – did they know what he had really done, after all?

'I thought he was in New York.'

'He's back at the moment; keeps flitting to and fro. But he's anxious to greet as many returning men as possible himself and he specifically mentioned you to Colonel Kelly.'

'Me? Why? Christ!' Seamus felt a cold dread numb his blood; maybe it would be best to scamper, but he wasn't sure he'd make it past the guards and he didn't want to spend the rest of his life looking over his shoulder in fear of a court martial – he already had more than enough cause to be looking over his shoulder.

'I'll back for you in twenty minutes,' Horan said.

'Right,' he muttered.

It felt strange accepting Jer Horan as his First Sergeant; while he'd been a Corporal, Horan became his friend and confidant and Seamus still thought of him as that. But now as the Tipperary man, recently confirmed officially in his new rank, escorted him across the grounds towards Meagher's lavish tent Seamus became acutely conscious of the discrepancy in their respective ranks.

Sensing his unease, Horan spoke up, 'You know there is no need for any distance to lie between us because I'm now a First Sergeant. I know you well enough, James, to know you are a good and brave soldier and would not hesitate to carry out any order of mine. Outside of that we can be the same old friends as ever.'

'That's kind of you, Jer – I mean Sergeant! Sir! I can do with all the friends I can get, especially good ones like you.'

'You know O'Rorke has been missing, presumed dead, since Malvern Hill?

'Missing? There was no body found?'

'No, but sure half of the poor unfortunates who went down in that fight were never found, or, at least, identified. Both the rebels and ourselves pushed bodies from both sides into the same graves before the flies blew them up and burst them like stinking balloons. And what does it matter to the poor bastards now if they're sharing the same hole as the men they fought against above ground? O'Rorke, good riddance, may God forgive me, is surely rotting away on the side of that hill somewhere, and isn't it more than he deserves. More than Pat Mangan got?'

Seamus knew his friend said all this to make him feel better about his enemies, but the fact that no body was found made him uneasy.

'Maybe he's alive, injured, some place?' he ventured.

'Very unlikely, it's been a good few weeks now and no one has heard anything. Maybe he did a skedaddle like his mate Flaherty – though I doubt it, that wouldn't be O'Rorke's style. He was a maniac for fighting and would never have run from a scrap. No, a few of his men saw him go down in a melee with the Louisiana Irish Tigers. Wouldn't that be ironic: O'Rorke shot by a fellow Irishman?' Horan asked.

'Very.' Seamus, anxious to finish the conversation, was relieved when his senior companion changed the subject.

'I should warn you: Meagher is not in the best of moods.'

'What could possibly have happened to upset our ebullient leader?'

'His whiskey stash was stolen.'

Seamus guffawed. 'You're joking. Who dared?'

'Our gallant comrades in the 29th frowning on his Celtic insobriety; discovered he had a secret cellar in one of the outhouses over there and raided it one night while he was in New York.'

'The Yankee bastards,' Seamus said, then laughed. 'None of the Irish regiments would have dared.'

'Right. At first the boys were going to take them on over it but then everyone saw the funny side; especially when a couple of sergeants came over and gave out presents of bottles from the stash. Seems our New England friends have a sense of humour and a stirring of decency after all.'

Horan held up his hand to indicate silence as they approached Brigade headquarters and proclaimed their identities to an orderly who, a few moments later, ushered them inside.

Meagher sat behind a desk, piled high with papers; two officers – Colonel Kelly and Jack Gosson – lounged, gold-braided, on a padded bench against the right side of the tent smoking and talking in low voices. Kelly smiled thinly in acknowledgement of his men. There was silence as Seamus and Jer walked towards the desk; a chubby clerk, presumably Meagher's wife's relation who used to run Mercy's sutler wagon, worked on a bigger pile of paper at a smaller desk on Meagher's left side. There was no one else present.

'Gentlemen!' Meagher beamed when he saw them. 'What a pleasure; delighted, I should say. Delighted!' He came out from behind his desk and walked towards the sergeant and private from the 88th Company L. He looked more careworn than before - the smile creased his face like a rumpled jacket; his eyes had a slightly feverish look. The General was either feeling the pressure of command or had recently replaced his whiskey stash and over-indulged. There was no alcohol visibly present, but the whiff of malted barley permeated the tent.

Having seen Meagher out ahead of his troops dashing towards the enemy guns many occasions on the Peninsula, Seamus was no longer disposed to be negative towards him. He had to admire the bravery of anyone who led his troops like that – drunk or sober. He came stiffly to attention as Meagher came around in front of them.

'At ease men; at ease,' the General ordered and fixed them with his red-fringed blue eyes. Up close, eau-de-cologne and cigar smoke mixed with stale whiskey to give Meagher an odour that was not unappealing. 'Thank you, Sergeant Horan,' he nodded at Jer. 'I expected nothing less from a gallant Tipperaryman than prompt fulfilment of orders.'

'Thank you, General.' Horan saluted stiffly once more.

Meagher's intelligent blue eyes studied Seamus for a moment and he felt the full force of the general's personality. He stared at a spot over Meagher's shoulder but his feet shuffled around as he felt his leader's gaze bore into him, uncloaking the grim, dark secrets of his soul.

'Sergeant Horan, lock this man up!' Though Seamus had been half expecting it, he crumpled under the order. It was all over. They had found him out and they would shoot him like all murderers who killed people on their own side – it didn't matter if the victims weren't good people: murder was murder. He thought of his mother hunched over a three-quarters empty pot trying to eke out enough for him to survive just so he could be shot by a firing squad made up of his comrades.

It took a moment or two for the laughter to register. Meagher had lifted back his head and was chuckling throatily; Gosson and Colonel Kelly were laughing more raucously, Jer Horan had a grin from ear to ear. Meagher straightened up and, though maintaining a grin, he grew more serious.

'You see that's the problem with our race: we've been so downtrodden by the English that we've haven't a shred of confidence left and will believe the very worst about ourselves, no matter what evidence to the contrary.'

'Apologies, Private Farrell, but your face was a picture to behold,' said Gosson. 'You really believed you were going to be arrested then. I'm afraid I'm of too giddy a disposition not to get the giggles at that. Forgive me.'

Meagher spoke to him, while he was still trying to make sense of what was going on. 'The only reason you should be locked up, Private Farrell, is to keep the rebels safe. And those Southerners are one set of rebels we do not want to keep safe. You agree?'

Seamus nodded dumbly.

'Well, in that case, Private Farrell, it gives me great pleasure to promote you to Second Sergeant, L Company, 88th Regiment, 2nd Brigade, 1st Division, 2nd Corps, Army of the Potomac. Mr Johnson?' The clerk, beads of sweat on his pale skin, had stopped writing to take in the scene, now scurried out from behind his desk and officiously handed three white strips of cloth to Meagher on a silver platter.

Seamus presumed they were sergeant's stripes and Meagher confirmed this by handing them across and giving him a salute. He maintained enough outward composure to accept and return the salute, but inside, his stomach had dropped into his knees and it took a big effort to stop them from collapsing under its weight.

'James, I've noticed you in the field, I've seen the battle lust in your eyes. I've seen you stride forward foremost of your company, reckless of your own life and limb; intent on pushing back the enemy and gaining glory for your countrymen. Furthermore, I understand that at Malvern Hill you were seriously injured by a shell blast just prior to the main counterattack, but you rose like a latter-day Lazarus and was soon at the forefront of the fighting again. With a few hundred like you we could waltz into the old country tomorrow and drive the Saxons out. Alas, you are as yet too rare a commodity to facilitate this noble desire.' Meagher expounded in that English educated accent of his, which sat so incongruously with his fervent Irish patriotism.

Since making his personal acquaintance in the States, Seamus had been critical of Meagher, thinking a lot of his speech and attitude mere affected bombast. But the more he got to know the Brigadier – General the warmer he felt towards him and though Meagher was undoubtedly given to hyperbole and exaggerated mannerisms, often inspired by alcoholic over-indulgence, there could be no doubt that his bravery, patriotism and concern for his men were genuine.

Which made Seamus feel all the more fake himself. Sure, he had been reckless and had gone blundering off ahead of his company: but it was anger and stupidity that had caused this, not bravery. He had no thoughts for patriotism, country, or company at these times; he had no thoughts for anything much at all apart from inflicting pain and releasing pent up hatred. And, as for the incident with the 'shell' and his reasons for being on the frontline whilst seriously wounded: he didn't even want to think about those now, for fear his very thoughts would betray him.

'General Meagher, I'm very grateful, but I don't deserve these, really I don't,' he said as he took the stripes.

Meagher gave his full-throated laugh again. 'Now isn't that just the very problem with Irishmen that we were talking about? Self-effacing to a fault and no self-belief. There are painful gaps in the Brigade since last May. To get good men into the right positions we are prepared to override protocol. So, you are no longer a private, you are now a sergeant. First Sergeant Horan, you will see that Second Sergeant Farrell is issued with a new frock coat to carry those chevrons?'

Then he went silent and stared at Seamus with such intent that the latter was unnerved once more. Meagher spoke slowly and deliberately; wanting to be certain that the man before him garnered every word.

'I've been a failure myself; imprisoned, transported and belittled. I escaped and came to this great country and, despite floundering around in the law, the lecture circuit and adventuring in South America finally learned the great lessons of life that this wonderful *United* States has to offer: Confidence and Self-Belief. Those are the qualities it takes to succeed. Those are the qualities by which Irishmen, who have no end of other talents, martial and otherwise, will win back their country. And being blessed with leadership of the Irish Brigade in these *United* States I now consider myself in an ideal position to teach brave, patriotic Irishmen like yourself this lesson.'

Meagher paused for a moment and wiped a hand across his moustache, before continuing. 'Which is why I have asked officers, like Colonel Kelly here, to bring brave enlisted men to my attention; so that, whenever possible, I can personally pass on this advice and seek to instil some of this confidence and backbone that will be required to do glory to the name of Irishman in this war, but, more importantly, to have it applied for the liberation of our blessed homeland afterwards. People may call me a blabbering idiot, and they may well be right, but one thing they cannot deny me is experience in matters of martial success and failure. Would you agree, Sergeant Farrell?'

Seamus, despite feeling like a wayward son being lectured by a strict, but kindly, father, did understand and did agree with Meagher. Though, for him, between understanding these concepts and putting them into practice there still yawned an enormous chasm. But he also understood that these first steps towards seniority, however fraudulently based, could be steppingstones towards leading men to the liberation of Ireland under inspiring leaders like Meagher and he would say no more to jeopardise that glorious possibility.

'I agree, General, and I accept gratefully and I will do my utmost to ensure that neither the reputation of Irishmen nor these stripes will ever be tarnished. Thank you, Sir.'

Meagher leaned back and beamed; mission accomplished. 'A toast, gentlemen, a toast.' As if by magic, Jack Gosson appeared by Meagher's side with two flutes of a bubbly drink that was either champagne or sparkling wine – neither of which had ever before passed Seamus's lips. Colonel Kelly came across and shook his hand. 'Congratulations! Sergeant,' he beamed. Suddenly all five men present held glasses of the lively looking amber liquid.

Meagher held his up to the company and looked at Seamus. 'To brave sons of Erin everywhere,' he proposed. 'She does not forget those who bleed on foreign shores, but eagerly awaits the day of their return, when their exiled blood will be selflessly spilt on native soil dissolving the cruel bonds that currently bind her and prevent her from offering the secure happy refuge they and their families deserve.'

'Hear, hear,' the others said and knocked back their drinks. Seamus choked and spluttered worst than when he had his first gulp of poteen, stolen by Padraic from his father's secret stash, in Ballyallen Bog ten years before.

The others laughed good-naturedly.

'You've got to hand it to yer man,' Horan said about Meagher on the way back, 'he knows how to get you up for it. No offence intended, but how many other Brigadier-Generals would go to such rounds for a promotion to Second-Sergeant? Not alone would most of them not even know – they would not want to be bothered about it either.' Seamus wasn't sure what to say. He was aware of definite stirrings of pride amidst the whirlwind of confusion as his mind frantically sought to resolve conflicting emotions ranging from anxiety about the prospect of being court-martialled to the reality of being promoted to sergeant. He knew he was relieved to be out of the tent; he had found the atmosphere in there unreal, belonging to a world he had no hope of relating to. A world where gore and death were convoluted into glory and honour, where the likes of him could be propelled into the realms of Second Sergeant just by going insane and charging around screaming with a primed musket.

He saw the 63rd drilling by squares in companies and knew that was what he'd love to be doing right now. Being a soldier; working in organised groups of like-minded men to achieve a common goal. And even if real battle was not like that, anything was better than quaffing champagne with Brigadier-Generals in their tents.

'Jer…Sergeant – do you really think we will get to fight for Ireland?' he asked, so as to bring his thoughts back to where they really should be.

'You know, though I played along with the notion, I was never really bothered about that. When I left Ireland it was never with the intention of returning. As the fifth son of a modest-sized tenant farmer I never had much to look forward to, whether Ireland was free or not. I just wanted to have adventure and to make my fortune in America. This war seemed to give me the chance to do both.'

'Is that what you still want?'

'Yes, despite everything, I still want that. But I'd like to do my bit for Ireland now as well.'

'Why the change of heart?' Seamus asked and waited while Horan looked off in the distance, towards a point over the fort's back ramparts where smudges of reddish clouds floated; his normally open laughing features creased with what looked like pain; maybe sorrow.

'You missed the retreat from the Peninsula,' he said, speaking more slowly and staring more intensely than ever at the russet smudges of cloud. Seamus waited.

'A couple of weeks ago, we came back up through the Peninsula,' he continued, 'now I'm not saying the rebels didn't bring a lot of ill luck on themselves, but James, you should have seen the devastation we left in our wake during our advance in May. It was as if the worst afflictions of Black 47 in Ireland had been transported to Virginia. Ah, James! You should have seen the state of things: the houses falling down, the crops ruined, the children starving. *In America!* At one miserable hamlet outside Williamsburg, which I'd remembered as a pretty little place of whitewashed clapboard houses and flower gardens on the way down, a woman, a lot younger, but every bit as emaciated as ould ones I'd seen back home, crawled out on her hands and knees to us as we were passing and held out her stick of an arm. 'Food for my little one, food for my little one,' she pleaded. Well, she was so pathetic that a few of us went inside to see if we could help. The baby was dead several days, the poor little mite was blue – almost black; thrown lifeless in a wooden cradle wearing nothing but a stinking rag around its bottom. The woman screeched and bawled at us and called us all the names in the world, but we managed to take the baby out of the house and bury it in the back garden. Tom Dillon carved a simple wooden cross for it. We left her flung over the new mound of earth calling for the baby. Louise, I think was what she was saying, though it might have been Susie. The poor woman, sure we left her like that, but the kindest thing we could have done would have been to put her out of her misery with a ball in the head. She surely died shortly afterwards anyway.'

Horan paused again. Seamus heard the Sergeant over in the 63rd dismissing his company; the champagne bubbled sourly inside him, and he needed to use the privy very soon, but he waited patiently for his friend to finish.

'That had a bad effect on the boys. For Irishmen to think they were even remotely responsible for such suffering, after what our own poor old country has been through, was a very sobering experience I can tell you. Though we were medium-sized farmers ourselves and escaped the worst ravages of the famine back in Tipperary, for *me* to think that I had been even remotely responsible for causing suffering like what had been inflicted on our neighbours back home was devastating.' Horan's usually jocular demeanour was creased by frowns as his boot prodded absentmindedly at the ground.

'It got me thinking about how such deprivations could be prevented,' he finally continued, 'and the conclusion I came to was: that it can only be prevented when people are truly free. The Virginians aren't free because they've got the Northerners trampling all over them and they're trampling all over them because they enslaved the black people. The Irish aren't free because the English won't allow them to be. Maybe after this war is resolved we can resolve Ireland's problems by gaining her independence, if we can't, as I think most likely, I can say that at least I did my bit to prevent any more innocent people starving. I believe many others think the same. So, yes, I think we'll get to fight for Ireland.'

The two friends remained silent for a few moments.

'That's close to how I feel also,' Seamus finally spoke. Then, almost as an afterthought, he added, 'The people and the land that I love are in danger of disappearing.'

Horan looked at him and seemed about to say something serious, at the last moment he broke into his usual grin. 'Well, we can't do anything about it tonight, so let's have a hooley. We'll celebrate your return to the fold and toast Meagher with his own whiskey, I can tell you it's a lot better than that horse's piss he gave us in there. Poor bastard if that's all they left him with,' and he turned and marched off into the 88th's encampments at last.

The new Second Sergeant of Company L, followed.

CHAPTER TWENTY-ONE

The essential duties of a Sergeant, First, Second or Third, on campaign largely consist of seeing that the men don't straggle when they should be marching and don't hide when they should be fighting. A matter of logistics: ensuring one's charges reach a specific point at a specific time and perform a specific duty. These duties could be carried out by shouting, bullying, and coaxing. In camp, not being a simple matter of logistics, the duties were more complex. Seamus used this complexity as a balm to soothe his tortuous thoughts. Sensing this, Horan allowed Seamus leeway to undertake what were largely the duties of a First Sergeant.

Once reveille was sounded at five a.m., the men had fifteen minutes to wash and dress before assembly, then they formed up by sections and Seamus coordinated his section roll, ensuring each man was present or accounted for through leave – sick or otherwise. If he received any special orders from Horan, Brosnihan – who'd returned from Malvern Hill to be promoted to Second Lieutenant – or any of the other senior company or regimental officers, he would read them off and ensure that the relevant soldiers understood and followed through. After breakfast, he presented those assigned to guard, sentry or picket duty to Colonel Kelly, or his deputy. The remainder of the day, punctuated by lunch and a little free time which he filled by form filling and other administrative duties, was taken up with drilling and parading, sometimes just Company L on their own, sometimes with the other companies of the 88th and, once a week, with the entire Brigade. Every evening, he ensured that his men's apparel and equipment, from their jacket buttons to their bayonet tips, was shining bright for the inspection, formally known as the Retreat Ceremony. After supper, there was another roll call to ensure everyone was accounted for once again. At nine o'clock, 'Tattoo' was sounded and the men ordered to turn in for the night. It was then that Seamus's thoughts turned to Kilgarry and to those that depended on him there. The weight of those responsibilities shifted uneasily within him turning his stomach juices to acid when he wasn't preoccupied with his military responsibilities.

    Two letters of Kathleen's had arrived while he was in hospital; Horan had kept them for him rather than send them to a vague location in Washington where it was likely he would never receive them. He read and re-read them. She missed him and couldn't wait for his return, the list of daily humiliations she faced continued to grow. Paidín Óg, her eldest brother, had taken a wife, and Kathleen, though her workload increased, lost authority around the house. Paidín Mór, her father, was becoming ever more helpless and incapable of looking after himself; the burden of taking care of him fell on Kathleen, as well as the cooking, cleaning and tons of farm work. Paidín Óg had married one of the Tierneys who were always a bit too grand to bend their backs; though, as Kathleen wrote, in reality, they were no grander than any of them.

Nolan continued to fence off land and turn it over to pasture, there was less and less space for tenants, though the Murphys had not lost anything yet, they were increasingly surrounded by pasturage and she was certain it was only a matter of time before they were turfed out. Agitation had died down: most of the Crew, old and new, were dead, incapacitated or recognised the futility of action without hope of success. Padraic and herself prayed that he might return and provide the means. There was no hint that things were not as they always had been between them. Yet, he read and reread the familiar litany of grievances and avowals of love for evidence that this was so, seeking to rationalise his expanding jealousy of Padraic as the irrational fears of a soldier far from home.

He was grateful that Padraic kept an eye on Kathleen - after all, he'd made him promise to. Padraic was like a blood-brother to him and he would trust him with his life - which was what he'd had to do on many an occasion. He certainly had an eye for the girls, but it was a roving eye, one clearly signalling a love 'em and leave 'em type. Many a woman in the West Limerick region, though knowing this, still went for a roll in the hay with the handsome, dashing rogue that was Padraic O'Farrell. Kathleen had never been one of those girls. Aside from being his betrothed, she was a loyal, steadfast type who, having made a commitment, was unflinching in her devotion to seeing it through. In an uncertain world, where poverty and death stalked every step, she was a granite colossus reacting consistently and reliably to the world around her. Seamus could dismiss any thoughts of betrayal or disloyalty from that quarter and get on with being a soldier, preparing for the day when he would help liberate Kathleen, Padraic and other loved ones.

But.

Wouldn't it make sense for them to get together? Padraic, for all his devil-may-care handsomeness wasn't getting any younger and Kathleen, despite not being his type, was a beautiful woman in need of protection, not to mention a life of her own away from her family.

However, Padraic was his cousin and closest friend and Kathleen was his betrothed. They wouldn't do that to him. Would they? After all, what had he done himself? Cheated on Kathleen with Mercy.

The most striking effect of his jealousy was to dissolve any remnants of the imaginary wall he had constructed between his feelings for Kathleen and his feelings for Mercy. He had tried pretending it didn't matter that he was cheating on Kathleen because she was in a different world to Mercy. The hypocrisy of this thinking was exposed. *He* lived in both worlds forging a link smelted in lies and deceit. He had consciously linked martial prowess in America with Ireland but refused to contemplate any link in his love life – because it suited his selfish purposes not to.

He hadn't seen Mercy since he'd returned from hospital, and he hadn't expected to, she had gone North to pursue her dreams. With O'Rorke also out of the picture and his cronies reduced to skulking around like leaderless schoolyard bullies, he had concentrated on being a professional soldier. He had come back from hospital refreshed, renewed, and if the slate had not been wiped clean, it had at least been tidied up enough to allow him to complete his mission.

But now guilt and irrational jealousy were threatening to overwhelm him with a new destruction. Self-destruction. He suffered the heartache of contemplating Kathleen with Padraic through the sieve of his own selfish foibles. All that saved him from falling asunder was his duties as Sergeant and the company of Horan and the other officers of Company L.

There had never been any fear that he'd have to share a tent with the untrustworthy Cranny: it had just been another of Horan little jokes, he knew Seamus was about to be promoted and could therefore have his own tent close to the other officers. Horan himself had a log cabin that had been built into the fort's ramparts and comfortably equipped. Seamus, Martin Brosnihan, and John Mulvaney, who was now the next most senior sergeant to Seamus, had their own spacious tents nearby, Horan's hospitality and generosity meant they all had access to his quarters almost any hour of the day or night. It was by the light of a paraffin lamp on a large oak writing desk in Horan's cabin that Seamus read the letters from Kathleen. He read and reread them, looking for proof of his irrationality. It glared from her words. He reread them anyway because he couldn't blame her if she sought sanctuary in Padraic's arms. Though he would kill her. And Padraic. And himself.

He sat for several nights wondering what to write, not so much in reply to her letters, but to his own thoughts – thoughts she didn't know existed. While his comrades teased him about moping and urged him to join in their songs, stories, and Chuck-Luck games, he read, reread, wrote, and rewrote. Eventually, because he had to get something down before he shrivelled up and died inside, he wrote words. Words that spoke of battles and wounds; of recovery and promotion; of a great gathering of Union and Confederate Irishmen; of great hope and optimism.

And, of his undying love.

Then he went and got drunk, sang songs, told stories, and played Chuck-Luck.

***

When they've got you where they want you: at the bottom of the deepest, darkest hole where they can stamp on you, crawl on you and suck on you. When screaming doesn't help, there is only one thing left to do. Drag yourself up, climbing and stepping on them, for no one will help you. Only yourself. Always only yourself. Which makes triumph all the greater. And revenge all the sweeter. The doctors and nurses are jailers, holding you in place for the bluebottles and flies to feast on. They need to be made to see reason. Forced to understand that you knew their mewlings about irreparable damage and not long to live were fabrications to keep you in place while the bluebottles and flies feasted. You knew they were their agents.

But you had to be wily. Endure the crawling, scratching, and sipping for another while. Let them think you were as helpless as ever. Muster a little strength. Catch them off guard. When the fat nurse uses the scalpel to cut off the bandages that keep crusting onto your head, for example. She's not expecting anything. She's given up on you. You are soon to be dead; in the meantime your oozing, dribbling body needs perfunctory attention to keep those interfering busybodies from the medical board off her back. She squawks like a decapitated chicken when you grab her wrist and twist it so that the scalpel drops from her grip. And for a few moments there is a flurry in the ward as if indeed you had upset a roost of lazing hens. They settle again as they realise it is not any of them that's in danger, though they remain more alert and watchful.

'My clothes and my gun.' It's a thing of wonder to hear your own voice other than in a tormented scream. You are the most surprised of them all. But you hide it.

They are fetched, for what are you after all, but a deadman briefly resurrected?

You take them and move towards the door dragging the fat nurse with you, hoping the enormous strain isn't obvious. No one interferes. Why should they? If you don't drop dead, you'll return to the army or go on the run. Either way, it's one responsibility less for the overworked hospital. An unfit Provost-Guard, dewlaps swinging, tries to tell you to let her go and you can do what you like. But this way you are more certain of escaping from the bluebottle and of getting revenge. And only absolute certainty will do in both matters.

You make it to a treeline and there you do let her go. She seems more shocked at your endurance than her own ordeal. You imagine her throat slashed and blood pumping out while her fingers are clamped up there trying to hold her neck in place; the same shocked look on her face, but with her vitality draining away. With a simple movement of your wrist, it could be accomplished. But it would unnecessarily complicate things, invigorate the hunt and make it harder to do what had to be done.

You lie in the ripening corn, nibbling on ears losing their green, watching the clouds float westwards like wagon trains of emigrant cotton and listen to the perfunctory hunt for you. And plot and plan. And sleep.

The following day you get a lift on a wagon to Warrenton and learn that the Confederates have crossed over the Potomac to invade the North and McClellan is heading west to cut them off before they get to one of the major cities and cause a panic. People look and tell you to go to a hospital and leave the defence of the country to those who are able-bodied. And you *are* hurting, in agony even; it's as if the bluebottle had hatched a myriad little ones in your brain. But west is where you will get your revenge and you march with the stragglers and walking wounded at the rear of the army. They keep their distance; they do not think you will make it - the suppurating wound in your head will leak out your life before too long.

But, of course, they do not understand obsession. Or how sweet revenge against all odds.

***

There was going to be a battle. The decisive battle of the war. Seamus's focus began to shift from Kathleen, Padraic and Kilgarry to the coming fight. The Union government had turned to a hotshot general in the West called John Pope, who'd arrived from the Mississippi spitting fire and bombast and promising to teach Easterners how to fight. His lessons were self-salutary as he was ripped asunder by Jackson and Longstreet and made to look a complete ass. For a while, it was feared the Confederates would come tearing into Washington, eating up Fort Corcoran on the way, but Lee chose to invade Maryland in the hope of drawing the Union Army out into the open and defeating them in detail, rather than risk getting bogged down in siege warfare.

The Union government turned to the only man who could possibly save the day.

'McClellan!'

When he broke the news one evening at the end of August, the faces of the other officers present in Horan's cabin split into broad grins. 'By God he's the boyo for them alright,' Mulvaney exclaimed, sniffing loudly in celebration.

'If he's that good, how come we fell back from the gates of Richmond to here?' Seamus asked. 'And don't give me that 'Change-of-Base' nonsense.'

'Don't mind him, he's just anti-authority, doesn't even like our own sainted Meagher and he only liking holy water.' Horan said to others with the glint of devilment in his eyes. 'Say what you like about McClellan, he doesn't get men killed and, as far as I'm concerned, he can change his bases every day of the week as long as he spares my bacon.'

And despite the government's distrust of him, the men did love McClellan. He seemed to genuinely care for them and was mindful of their welfare. Though Seamus thought him a showman and a politician rather than a military leader, he had to admit that a general who cared about his welfare, genuinely or otherwise, was more appealing than one who would waste his life needlessly.

'This is a battle that must be won, whether it's McClellan or whoever, they cannot afford to spare lives; the existence of the nation is at stake and that's greater than a general's career or a soldier's life. A lot of blood is about to be spilt.' Martin Brosnihan said thoughtfully.

Even Horan became serious.

Seamus felt the familiar, almost comforting, stirrings of fear rise within him at the prospect of the coming battle. He intuited that, even if he survived, this coming fight would change his life for ever. For better or worse he couldn't say, but at least he should be able to push thoughts about Kathleen and Padraic to the further recesses of his mind while he concentrated on survival.

'Five dollars on six,' he called and waited for the dice to decide his Chuck-Luck fate.

While out in western Maryland, the storm clouds of war that would decide his greater fate gathered.

CHAPTER TWENTY-TWO
SEPT. 1862

On the trail of the Rebels, the Irish Brigade crossed the Potomac downriver of Fort Corcoran and began their march through Maryland, banners fluttering in the breeze of a Summer which seemed to be lingering so as to compensate for the incessant rain that washed out the beginning of the killing season.

This time, the further they went the better their mood became. They were marching through God's country and their spirits soared accordingly. There were no traces here of the hunger and devastation of war ravished Virginia and, though a few Confederate flags waved defiantly along the border, the people were overwhelmingly friendly and welcoming. As they marched in the warm sunshine, pretty girls and old maidens shuttled from houses and roadside crowds to press food, flowers, and homemade lemonade on the delighted soldiers, who ignored their sergeants and file-closers to grab what they could. Though not in need of provisions, they were greedy for tokens of human warmth and friendship. In Virginia they were the invaders, but here on Union territory, marching for the Union, the tables had turned. Now the Irish Brigade and the other units of the northern army were the liberators seeking to expel the slave owners and nation destroyers from sacred soil.

And, with this realisation, their confidence soared further: the only reason McClellan did not succeed on the Peninsula, or Pope along the Rappahannock, was the lack of support from the people and, correspondingly, the only reason the Confederates won was their receipt of such support. It was nothing to do with their fighting spirit or courage. All doubts and aspersions cast were erased cleaner and cleaner with each apple pie and garland of late summer roses pressed upon them. They now marched confidently to victory.

Seamus splashed his face with cold water from a gurgling hillside stream and stood to survey God's rolling country of green and saffron pastel fields, punctuated by white clapboard farmhouses and the low-lying timber steeples and red roofs of non-conformist churches. The landscape oozed a blue haze of prosperity and tranquillity.

'That is how it could be,' he said with a nod addressing Conor McCarthy, one of the few new privates to show dedication and enthusiasm for military life; a lad who wasn't in it for a bounty, lump sum payments, broken love vows or on the run from crimes or other failures in civilian life.

'How what could be, Sergeant?'

'Ireland, Private. Ireland. Given her freedom, there's land every bit as fertile back home, but it's either been turned into potato fields because there is nothing else for the people to eat, or into open pastureland and manicured lawns for the local landlord, who will likely never set foot in the place. There is no real variety, no real spirit about the landscape back home, though it's there, beneath the surface, waiting to be unearthed.' He nodded at the western Maryland farms again. 'That's what true freedom can bring. Beauty and Prosperity.'

McCarthy, a black-haired, fresh-faced youth, studied the landscape and whilst he nodded in agreement, he seemed nonplussed. 'It's beautiful alright, Sergeant, but if Jesus himself was given a parcel of land in West Mayo he wouldn't be able to turn it into that.'

'Why not?'

'Bog and rocks, Sarge. Nothing but bog and rocks. The landlords are bastards around there for evicting people and leaving them to die in the ditches, but even if the people were given their freedom in the morning, they'd want a plentiful supply of paint and brushes to make the landscape look that.'

Seamus did have a retort about individual freedom getting the most out of any land but couldn't help smiling at the serious demeanour of Conor McCarthy as he tried to figure how West Mayo could be made to look like West Maryland.

'Private?'

'Yessir?'

'Round up a few lads to forage for firewood, hot coffee would go down well.'

'Yessir!' The fresh-faced youth went off, relieved at having something practical and attainable to concentrate on.

The Brigade made camp that evening along the gentle sloping hillside. There were no songs; no carousing, for, though their spirits were buoyant and the pastoral scenery around them uplifting, there was a powerful realisation that they were going to war and getting closer with every mile. Further west, the soft rolling landscape crinkled into ragged mountains and from there the crackle of gunfire was clearly audible as the Brigade took supper.

'It will be a fine, hot day tomorrow,' Tom Dillon remarked as he toasted a piece of dried pork on the end of his bayonet. 'And I'm not talking about the weather.'

'Arra with any luck McClellan will have pushed them into the Potomac by then,' John Mulvaney responded hopefully. And, looking out across the pastoral scenes around them, it was hard to imagine their beauty stained with blood and gore. But the dull thud of an artillery shell from the mountain passes confirmed that men sought to kill each other wherever possible.

Tomorrow was indeed likely to be 'hot.' Notwithstanding the beauty of the landscape.

***

By the time he reached Frederick, the pain and dizziness had receded to a dull comfortless ache. He regarded it as another weapon; another tool to use as a means towards his ends.

He wandered into Frederick, fifty miles from Washington, on wobbly legs in tattered clothing with his wound still suppurating – the bandage had been changed two days previously by a compassionate farmer's wife in whose barn he'd spent the night. But now it was soaked through again and the spires of Frederick wavered before him.

There were Union men in town but they were the stragglers and the bureaucrats. No womenfolk rushed to meet him with flowers or tasty victuals. Instead, as he half-walked, half-stumbled, along a white picket fence glaring in the late afternoon sun a tall, thin Provost Guard detached himself from the shadows of a red-brick church and addressed him. 'Problems there, soldier?'

'Nothing I can't handle,' O'Rorke muttered in reply.

'Lost your unit, have you?' The Provost insisted with an edge to his voice. O'Rorke gathered his breath. 'They've lost me more like,' he replied.

'How did you get that wound?'

'I didn't shoot myself in the back of the head if that's what you mean.'

'I'm not saying you did, but you can't blame me for being suspicious when I see a soldier straggling up a street in the middle of the afternoon and his unit long gone. It's amazing what people will do to themselves to get out of a fight.'

The Provost Guard had a mid-western farm boy's drawl and O'Rorke resented this freckled faced son-of-a-bitch yokel quizzing him. 'What's the matter with yourself when it comes to fighting? Too full of chicken-shit to be a real soldier, so you have to go skulking around churches harassing wounded men trying to rejoin their company? How dare you interrogate me. I'll have you court-martialled.'

'Listen, soldier, I'm just doing my bit same as everybody else who cares for the Union. Anyone can put on a sergeant's uniform. My job is to believe nothing from stragglers without proof. And if you must know, I'm a bad asthmatic and was denied a frontline fighting role myself, so I applied for this Provost role instead. It's not frontline fighting, but I've discovered I'm just as likely to get my head shot off sweeping up the dregs of this army and keeping the peace between drunken soldiers as I am on any frontline. Though none of this is any of your business. So I'll ask you again, before placing you under arrest: how did you get that wound?'

'At Malvern Hill doin' real fighting.'

'A wound in the back of the head don't ordinarily indicate real fightin.'

O'Rorke had had enough. He shuffled closer to the Provost and growled. 'I run from nothing. Now it might be on a form somewhere that it's your asthma which is keeping you from the real Army, but I say it's your chicken-shit guts. Now are you going to help me rejoin my unit or are you going to continue to block me with your idiot questions?'

'Problem, Lou?' Another, older, Provost with a drooping grey moustache stepped out from the shadows around the church.

Lou from the Midwest looked at the pale, wounded, sergeant in tattered clothes before him and saw that the man, however he got his wound, was not fit to rejoin his unit. But something savage and hungry stirred behind the Irishman's eyes and the Midwesterner, though not, to the best of his knowledge, chicken-shit, felt a chill run up his spine that he wanted rid of and the only way he could see of doing so was to get this strange individual as far away from him as possible.

'No, no problem,' he said to his partner without taking his eyes off O'Rorke, 'this one is keen to rejoin his unit, show him to the wagon.'

'He doesn't look fit enough to rejoin his unit,' the older one said.

Before O'Rorke took up the challenge, Lou intervened. 'If he's keen enough he's fit enough, makes a change from fit ones with self-inflicted superficial wounds wanting out. Let him go.'

'He could do with a bath and a rest I'd say,' the older one persisted.

'He can have that when he rejoins his unit, can't be more than a day or two ahead, now take him out of here. Please.'

'Right O. Come on pardner, this way,' and the elder Provost led O'Rorke to a metal-sided wagon where, once he was helped up, he found a space amongst the drunks, the skulkers and the other dregs having to be escorted towards the fighting under armed guard.

Once the unsettling first-sergeant, if that was his real rank, was out of sight Lou breathed a sigh of relief and moved along to sweep up more of the flotsam and detritus that an army on the move leaves in its wake.

While Mikey O'Rorke got a ride towards revenge.

***

McClellan's men pushed the rebels through the passes of South Mountain into Western Maryland, to within a few miles of the Potomac; the Southerners would have to scamper back to Virginia with their tails between their legs or be annihilated astride the river.

While other units drove the rebels over the mountain, the Irish Brigade was held in reserve. Their contact with the fighting confined to the constant sound of rattling gunfire; dull boom of artillery and glimpses of wreathing clouds of battle-smoke in the inclines above them. Even when they were pushed to the front on the other side to chase the retreating rebels, they made only desultory contact, swiping across the rear of some of General A.P. Hill's men.

After their experiences on the Peninsula, they no longer felt regret at not being in the thick of the fighting and the Brigade, once they had crossed South Mountain, continued to enjoy the well-ordered, luxuriant landscape laid out before them. The new men, at least those with any interest in fighting, and the veterans gelled together as a cohesive unit on the trek through Maryland and up and over South Mountain. It was with confidence and hope for the future that Fenians amongst them attended a soiree organised by Surgeon Reynolds of the

63rd New York, who was now the Head Centre of the Fenian Circle of the Army of the Potomac.

Seamus, Horan, and others from Company L decided to attend. With Meagher off on one of his recruiting trips to New York, they listened to an inspirational speech from Captain John Rorty of the Artillery and Reynolds recited a long poem on the fighting qualities and victories of the Irish while homemade punch was doled out to the men from two large green barrels. Then he led the gathering in singing ballads and martial ditties. It was purely a social gathering with no tactical or strategic discussions. Seamus stood amidst his comrades accepting that tactics and strategy would have to wait until after this civil war was resolved, which would be soon. He was uplifted by the spirit around him and the light falling on ripening cornfields.

He was buoyed also by a tattered note that he'd folded into his pocket. Horan had passed it to him earlier in the evening while they were boiling coffee outside their tents. He claimed he'd forgotten about it but Seamus suspected he'd wanted to ensure there was no possibility of him heading off after its author before passing it over. It was from Mercy, on plain unlined blue paper but the writing, whilst scrawly, was perfectly legible.

My Irish hero,

Hope you achieve your dreams. I go now to pursue mine. It is not a road I wanted to travel but faith has opened it for me and I am determined to follow it to the end. I hope your on yours. I will think of you. Maybe I will write again.

Thanks and best wishes always,

Mercy (+Charity).

That was it. Short and simple, though bringing closure to something he thought ended messily and unknowable. The future, for both of them, was still a mystery, but he could at least be content they had helped each other and were now on their roads to separate destinies with good memories and no regrets of each other. That was a consolation to him and he could now concentrate on Kathleen, Ireland, and the coming fight. He lifted back his head and lustily joined in 'The Boys of Wexford.'

There was still a long road to travel but everything was going to be alright.

CHAPTER TWENTY-THREE

Then, two evenings later, in a restful camp on the banks of a lazy Potomac tributary, called Antietam, Seamus received the letter that had set his instincts screaming weeks before and his road took the nastiest twist imaginable. It began normally enough – even calling him 'My darling'- but soon moved beyond boundaries whose breaching had never previously been hinted at, though, once breached, the ultimate blow was delivered with a suddenness that dragged an almost merciful numbness in its slipstream.

...**My situation is impossible, no better than a slave in my own house. You are away fighting in a foreign war that looks as if it will drag on for years and, even if you succeed in bringing back help, the people here have become so lethargic and downtrodden I see no possibility of they ever rising up against their oppressors – in short, Seamus, I think you would be coming to your doom and bringing others to theirs if you were to return anytime soon with the intention of stirring Kilgarry to fight.**

Furthermore, I would feel responsible for you doing so, since your mother died, you have no reason, apart from me, to return, and in the current climate I could not be responsible for such an outcome. When we decided you should go to America it wasn't out of hope you went or were sent, but out of desperation. There was no possible alternative. It was with the longest of odds in the most difficult of circumstances. I fear that since then, nothing has occurred to shorten those odds or ease those circumstances. The opposite applies.

In the meantime, my own situation has deteriorated drastically. I am no better than a chattel in my own home and it's gone beyond what I can bear. Please, please, Seamus grant me the understanding to accept that this is a life someone like me cannot live. I would have borne almost anything for you. But to bear this and know that, even if you did return, it would be to no avail, is unendurable. I want both of us to live and I wanted more than anything for those lives to be lived together, but I've had to accept that this cannot happen. So, for both our sakes, I'm taking the only other option.

I'm releasing you from your vows of betrothal and I am asking you to do the same for me. I want you to stay in America and live a great life there. I am going to make a life with Padraic here. I know when you first read these lines you will to be angry and shocked. But please, please, remember what I said about current circumstances and the lack of alternatives. And remember also what a great friend Padraic has been to us both, I beg you to see this not as betrayal, but as two people coming together for mutual survival in a grim world.

I don't want to deepen or prolong your pain, but I've always believed in letting you know everything: Padraic and I are to be married next month. I will go to live with him and bring my father with me; I know Padraic will be as kind to him as he was to your mother, and indeed his own parents, there will be more space and tolerance for me there than in my own house. And I have no doubt whatsoever there will be more space and tolerance for you in America than back here in Kilgarry.

Dearest Seamus, I'm not going to say any more for now, I will write again soon. I know that despite my reasoning you will feel shocked and betrayed. I wish it were otherwise, with all my heart I do, but I want you now to get on with the rest of your life and to forget about impossible dreams of liberating Ireland and Kilgarry.

Believe me, when I say - you will always be close to me and prayers for your happiness and success will be the first to fall from my lips in the morning and the last at night.

        Kathleen.

He looked out at the weakening light and the shadows shifting across the rolling Maryland countryside, it seemed he wasn't seeing it first-hand, but at a remove, like a faded picture in a dusty old book, he saw, with shock, that its beauty hadn't waned.

It was early evening on the 16th of September 1862 and there would be a mighty battle tomorrow. Lee and his rebels hadn't cut and run across the Potomac back to Virginia after all but were standing in battle-line challenging McClellan and his army to come and force them across the river. There were conflicting rumours of who outnumbered who. But there was no doubting it would be bloody. Two large armies faced each other either side of Antietam creek. They would spill each other's blood and guts to decide the fate of America on the banks of what for millennia had been a restful farmland stream.

And here now, at last, would also be decided the fate of Seamus O'Farrell.

Crickets chattered in nearby trees; men sat around reading, smoking, brewing coffee, playing cards, chatting in low voices; the sun sank lower and the evening grew greyer. Smoke from bubbling coffee pots and tobacco pipes mingled with a rising damp to cloak the bivouacs in a muggy blanket. Nearby, the voices of some young recruits Meagher had brought from New York rose as they argued to be sent into battle on the morrow and not assigned to provost duty as Meagher and other senior Brigade officers intended for the greenhorns. Someone in the 29th was reading aloud from the Bible in a plum New England accent. Pat Gorman would have his harmonica out shortly. But, in general, the world paused for breath before unleashing slaughter.

Seamus wondered how it could carry on at all. He was stunned to realise he was breathing and continuing to live. How could that happen when his reason for living had ended?

But, there could be no doubt: the world was carrying on – the young recruits had nominated a delegation to go and appeal to Meagher to allow them to fight and they were setting off eagerly; the Bible reader was intoning; someone had started to sing 'Paddy's Lament' – the quivery strains of an Irish voice rose to compete with the plum Bible reading as if centuries of Celtic and Anglo-Saxon antagonism had been distilled to a vocal contest by a Maryland stream. Adding substance to martial thoughts, gunfire rattled beyond the creek where Joe Hooker's men were seeking to gain an advance foothold from which to launch the morning's battle.

His ribcage rose and fell in time to loud, strong heartbeats.

The world carried on and he lived.

Once the shock of survival wore off, he was hit by the thump of betrayal. Kathleen and Padraic. His betrothed and his 'blood-brother' cousin. He hated them for causing his irrational thoughts to be true. God damn them to hell. He hated them for it. And the logic of her reasoning did not soften the hatred.

Circumstances? Maybe her circumstances had grown more dire since he left. But what about himself? Yes, he enjoyed the camaraderie, the sense of belonging and purpose associated with being in the Irish Brigade. But these feelings were sporadic; ephemeral; seasoned with large dollops of doubt and antagonism. And the comforts of Mercy's bed. However, his transgressions were surely different. His circumstances had led him to America to attain vital support and experience so as to return and make their lives better. It had thrown him into the arms of Mercy but, though a passionate union, it was transitory. What Kathleen and Padraic were effecting was permanent and he was to be bid total exclusion. Banishment even. **Stay in America** she had written, banishing him from both her love and his country. The only two reasons he was here. The only two reasons he lived.

And, if staying in America was such a good idea, why did she not come out herself? There it was. The hollow core of her mendacious logic. Even if her circumstances were as bad as she said, she didn't have to marry Padraic – she could have come to America to him, if she truly loved him and if, as she implied, her marriage to Padraic was merely one of convenience.

His fists clenched and his teeth gritted and the angry pulsing of blood in his head blotted out the other evening sounds. He wanted to hurt, maim, kill. The feeling both energised and appalled him. His road was leading him down places he hadn't wanted to go and turning him into someone he didn't want to be.

He thought of writing to her, of explaining how well the Fenian movement was coming together out here, of his promotion, of all that he had learnt, of how close he was to returning in triumph, of how they were on the eve of what was surely the last great battle of this war and of begging her to wait a few months, weeks even, and he would be back with a liberating army. But he knew he wouldn't write that letter. Not now. Maybe never. She hadn't told him the whole truth; hadn't told him she'd lost her love for him and now loved Padraic. She hadn't told him, but the sense of it was there in her letter, pulsing beneath her written words like poison beneath the skin. He knew the truth of its existence, so he wasn't going to write.

He tried to absorb the pain of this truth, to clutch it to him like a tool, but it was greater than the pain of any of his fighting wounds and he didn't think he could bear it. He held his head in his hands.

Jer Horan, as ever sensing his distress, came to him. 'Sergeant,' he said, 'ensure your men's muskets and ammunition are clean, dry and replenished for tomorrow's fight.'

'Yessarge,' Seamus replied, wondering anew at how the world carried on.

CHAPTER TWENTY-FOUR

The killing on the bloodiest day in American history commenced in the misty first light of the 17th September, 1862, and did not cease until its final rays expired beyond the western horizon. The sun grew swollen and red before it set, reflective of the myriad wounds, mutilations and mortalities visited throughout the day on the tidy farms, shaded woods and fertile fields flanking the now blood-stained creek.

It started that morning on the far side of the Antietam when Joe Hooker's men came stomping out of the fog towards the rebel lines massed in the woods and fields before them. Between both armies lay a field of corn, ripe for the harvest – now a far grimmer crop would be sown there.

The Rebels, primed muskets at the ready, strained to watch the Federals come, in the early morning vapours their targets were no more than whirling blue imps, so they knelt down to peer beneath the mist and proceeded to shatter the distinct shinbones and knee joints visible under there. The Federals shrieked in shock and agony. The blue imps were checked.

But the blood had started to flow.

The world spun out of darkness into a dawn of grey pearls. It was a day of battle. A day for the present; a day when nothing could be done about the past and the future would have to take care of itself. And Seamus was glad. He wanted to live only in the present; to move from one moment to the next. Noting if those moments brought life or death, he was relieved to no longer care which.

After reveille, rollcall and kit inspection, the Irish Brigade breakfasted while Joe Hooker's men were slaughtered in The Cornfield.

'Some poor bastards are having a hot breakfast,' a Company K man quipped from one of the communal fires.

Another private held up a soggy strip of bacon: 'This looks and tastes like one of Dillon's socks after a day's marching over bad ground, but I'd rather be eating this than breakfasting on what they're getting on the other side of the creek.' The group gave a nervous snort of laughter.

The Brigade's equipment was primed and readied for battle and the men prepared themselves for a big fight. Seamus breakfasted with them this morning, leaving Horan, Brosnihan, Mulvaney and the other senior company men to the higher quality coffee and bacon in Horan's tent.

A huge artillery explosion from across the Antietam shook the ground. Some of the newer men went pale and swore. They were grateful not to be anywhere near that explosion and feared it would not be long before they were led over there. At the same time, there was a nervous energy that would quickly dissipate into unfulfilled dreams and the frustrations of what-might-have-been if they weren't to be involved.

Seamus wanted to be tested this day. He didn't feel the all-consuming hatred and lust to kill that he'd felt at Fair Oaks. Neither did he have the numbing fear he'd had before Gaines's Mill. He did feel a powerful urge to do battle. To be tested. To live in the present.

And if he survived, to come out a different person.

That above all.

***

Sounds came muffled and menacing to those inside the wagon. O'Rorke caught the eye of the corporal from the Ohio 6th who, like himself, was genuinely seeking to rejoin his regiment after being wounded, the difference being that the corporal seemed recuperated from the gunshot wound in the thigh he'd received at Chantilly. They shared recognition that the battlefield was where they needed to go to do their job and that it was near. Their travelling companions were more reticent: O'Rorke sensed their fear. One of the skulkers – a boy of seventeen from Rhode Island who claimed he'd been hiding out in Frederick because he'd been told in a letter from his mother that McClellan was going to betray them all to the rebels, who'd make slaves of them – mumbled prayers to himself which became progressively louder and faster the closer they got to the sounds of battle.

Finally, after two days of jolting, rocking and being tossed up and down while his wound continued to suppurate, they came to a halt that wasn't a scheduled food, water, or toilet stop. The tailgate was slammed down, the canvas pulled back and they were ordered to alight; they blinked in the bright sunlight as they were led away to rejoin their individual units. The surly Guards were more relaxed now that they'd chaperoned their charges from the streets of Frederick in time to be fed into the carnage taking place on the other side of Antietam creek.

An old fella, who looked too old even for the Provost Guard, began escorting him towards the Irish Brigade encampment. The man hawked tobacco wrapped in wads of black phlegm.

'Lordy, but you sure don't look fit for duty, Sonny. Didn't think we're that badly off for men that we have to kick the dying out of bed,' he slurred with a lump of tobacco pushed to the side of his cheek. 'What say, I take you to a medic and we get you a certificate out of here again? Some of those young Guards, who are perfectly capable of fighting, are too eager to bring every poor bastard back to be killed just so they can look good and continue to avoid the fighting themselves. But I've killed enough Injuns and Mexicans myself not to worry about anything like that. Would kill rebels too if they'd let me. Too old, they said. Never too old to plug a Rebel, I say.'

Every provost-guard claimed they were prevented - against their wishes - from fighting themselves. 'I want to fight, Granpa,' O'Rorke growled.

The old Provost-Guard hawked another spit and shook his head at the stupidity of young fellas but had enough experience to know it wouldn't be healthy for him to push it with this one. Instead, he quickened his pace the sooner to be rid of his disturbing charge.

They were passing across the rear of the Union Army. Couriers and staff dashed hither and thither on horseback and foot delivering and dispatching messages of troop movements, strategic shifts, news of crises and triumphs. Ambulances ferried dead, dying, and seriously wounded with such speed and disregard for the rutted ground that they could only be hastening the deterioration of their passengers. Some regiments were drilling, more to take their minds off forthcoming engagements, than any practical lessons they'd learn at this final hour. A few men came through with bulging eyes, dishevelled attire, and slight wounds; Provost Guards chased them, rounded them up like sheep and shepherded them back to their units. And all the time artillery boomed and arms crackled as smoke billowed into the background sky.

O'Rorke's blood quickened: he wanted to be past this pandemonium and beneath that battle-smoke where revenge was attainable in blood. Yet there was opportunity amidst pandemonium.

The old Indian and Mexican fighter never seemed to realise his throat was cut: he sank to his knees; a look of surprise and wonder on his experienced features, feeling for a wound around the sides of his face like a man checking to see if he needed a shave; he began to choke on tobacco juice, a soggy lump of it fell onto the grass seconds before his face. His lower legs drummed on the ground behind.

O'Rorke walked steadily on – the vicious Bowie, now smeared with red, concealed inside his shirt once more. He was anxious to get inside the battle-smoke, but on his own terms, in his own time. No Provost Guard, young or old, was going to deliver him to an officer for restrictive orders. Mikey O'Rorke would be free to spill blood his own way at Antietam. To ensure the bluebottle would alight on those of his choosing.

CHAPTER TWENTY-FIVE

Two further hours they waited. Two hours drinking coffee, munching rations, writing letters, checking, and rechecking equipment. Festering, while their comrades fought and died on the other side of the creek.

'They'll come for us when they're desperate,' Mulvaney declared and the others knowing this to be true whiled away, as carelessly as possible, what could be their last moments on earth.

'Wouldn't want to go out with fluff on me buttons,' Pat Gorman said, polishing them for the umpteenth time that morning.

'Have you got that bloody harmonica on you? Put it over your heart, that way it might take the bullet: your life would be spared and the rest of us would be spared having to listen to the wailing that comes out of it.'

'Murphy, you've no soul – that's your problem.'

'Haven't much to worry about today then, have I?'

They carried on. In the shadows of their own deaths, they carried on. Because that was all they could do.

Sunlight burned away the early morning mists to reveal the gory details of the crimping of the right flank of the Army of the Potomac. General McClellan sat on a soft chair on the lawn of the Pry farm, overlooking the battlefield from the safe side of the creek. He looked through a telescope – aligned so conveniently he didn't have to raise himself from his chair – and observed the horror unfolding beyond the Antietam. He drank English tea from the Pry family's best china and frowned intellectually for the benefit of his watching admirers.

Hooker's Corps was ground to mincemeat in The Cornfield and Mansfield's supporting Corps was stuck in the East Woods. General Sedgwick led an impetuous charge over to the West Woods and his regiments were annihilated. By nine a.m. the Army of the Potomac was bogged down in blood and gore. The situation was desperate. Time to send for the Irish Brigade.

'On the march and double quick!' Horan relayed the orders to Seamus. In short time Company L came to attention in lines of four, next to the other companies of the 88th. They were ordered to leave behind most of the equipment they had been cleaning and checking since the previous evening. Even their jackets were to be left. All they needed for now was muskets with bayonets fixed, filled cartridge belts and boxes. They would cross the Antietam and march to the top of a ridge overlooking rebel positions, halt and deliver a close-in killing blast from their smoothbores before making a headlong Celtic dash for the entrenched position and overwhelming the rebels who'd taken cover there. Seamus wanted to see if it would be suicide or glory.

'No need to worry about going out with fluff on your buttons anymore, Pat,' some of the others called to the harmonica player.

'No, and I've put my old harmonica in the pocket, to ensure it survives also.' A collective derisory groan rose from Company L.

The Brigade assembled in columns by regiment with the 88th on the left, to their right, the 63rd, then the New Englanders of the 29th Massachusetts and on the far right, the 69th. Meagher and his staff rode out in front; the General's resplendent blue uniform was adorned with a buff sash and in one of his saffron-gloved hands he brandished a blue sabre which glinted in the early morning sunlight. The Irish chieftain was leading his tribe to battle, and the world would know.

The colour bearers carried a giant United States flag and a dazzling emerald-green Irish Brigade one with the sunburst above the harp, burnished with its Gaelic motto about never retreating from the clash of spears. The regimental colour bearers were just behind. The drums rolled. Meagher dropped his arm, and the Irish went to war.

Meagher and his staff rode across the Antietam; the men waded, muskets and ammunition boxes aloft. Seamus gasped from the shock of the cold water which rose above his waist but concentrated on ensuring that his men got across safely and in good order. At the other bank they clambered shivering up a small incline, grateful to be out of the freezing water and back in the sunshine. Meagher paused while the men wrung the worst of the wet out of their socks, emptied their shoes and checked that their ammunition had not gotten damp. Then they straightened their lines again and continued their march, a little shabbier and damper after fording the creek but with senses sharpened from the cold water.

On the other side, the noise of battle became a thunderous roar rolling over the horizon to envelop them, shaking loose thoughts of home, loved ones and the future. Seamus found himself glancing at the ground and wondering if he would ever again stroll carelessly on the likes of such lush green grass.

'Close up! Close up!' He barely heard Horan's exhortations in the din and was certain his own men didn't hear him at all, though they dressed their line smartly and gathered speed in pursuit of the galloping Meagher.

They were up onto farmland once more: grass speckled with white clover, orchards dripping with fruit, corn ripening in the fields or its shaved stubble crunching underfoot. An attractive white, clapboard farmhouse with outbuildings stood off to their left. As Seamus looked, an ugly pall of black smoke rose from its upper storey: the gods of war were not discriminatory in their choice of victims.

The Brigade ran – working up a head of steam for the approaching fight.

Father Corby rode across the lines, out in front. At first, Seamus thought his gesticulations signified the chaplain had become infected with battle-fever and was exhorting the Brigade onwards. Then he realised the low murmuring coming from all around was the sound of the Act of Contrition being recited by thousands of men. Father Corby was blessing them with final absolution as he rode: bestowing on the genuinely repentant the gift of a holy death. *Oh my God I am heartily sorry for all my sins, I hate them, I detest them, I'm ashamed of them…* unbeknownst to himself, as he ran towards the fray, Seamus had begun reciting.

…I will love you always: now and at the hour of my death. Amen. He led the men after Horan who, with Brosnihan, led them after Colonel Kelly, who rode just in front of the regimental colours behind Meagher and his staff, who were directing the men towards a snake fence stretching across the top of a ridge before them, creating a marker for the horizon. Anxious to break through this obstacle barring their way to the death or glory battle beyond, the men charged; the end of their Acts of Contrition blending with a wild, ululating yell.

The fence exploded in a sheet of flame and smoke and, as if the barrier had jumped forward fifty yards or more, the leading men were thrown backwards with such violence and finality that they might have run into an immoveable obstacle. The Confederates were using the railing as a first line of defence on this part of the field and they poured lead into the advancing Irish.

Company L had not yet reached the front of the charge and so were spared this initial murderous fire. Those who had sight of the fence now knelt and poured a volley at it. It danced and shook like a wounded beast.

Splinters and chunks of wood flew into the air while grey and butternut clothed bodies flew backwards behind what was meagre shelter from such an onslaught.

The Irish roared, rose, and charged again. And were met by a second crippling volley from the rebels who had remained intact behind the fence rails. The leading chargers crumpled once more and this time lead, like metal raindrops, spattered in amidst Company L, thumping violently into flesh - gouging, splintering, and killing. John Conlon fell clutching at an opening in his neck that pumped blood; Eddie Cagney swore and screeched like a cut pig: bloody shards of shinbone protruded from his ripped trouser leg. Seamus tripped over the musket of a fresh-faced recruit whose arm had been rendered useless by a bullet in the shoulder; his look of surprise just being overtaken by that of pain.

His men were getting hit but Seamus carried on charging with those who had managed so far to dodge the violent rain. Another volley may have been loosed from behind the fence - he wasn't sure - there was fire and death coming from all sides now. The right flank of the 69th and 29th was being maimed by an enfilading fire laid down by the rebels from the safety of the barns and outhouses of one of the prosperous farms dotting the region; men of the 88th and 63rd behind poured volleys over the heads of leading men like himself that were more dangerous to their own side than to the rebels'.

With a bestial, life-affirming roar he threw himself at the fence. In one of those mysteries of life that sometimes govern the workings of men, hundreds of his comrades launched themselves at the same time and it disintegrated before their combined weight. Seamus landed on a scared looking teenager who, seconds before, had been a murdering thug; he let the weight of his falling body apply the force of his thrusting bayonet, skewering the youngster through the chest. He strained to pull it out as quickly as possible, just freeing it in time to parry a stab from an older Rebel. Someone, looked like John Mulvaney, stabbed a Confederate who was just about to take him on his exposed side. There was no time for gratitude, only selfish relief. He pressed forward. All around, men in blue did the same - cutting, thrusting, getting off the odd shot. He had a vague realisation of being at the centre of a concave line; he sensed that the right-hand end was being hammered in by enfilading fire and if he didn't progress forward quickly the hammering would reach him. He pressed and thrust with greater urgency, and miraculously, as if he was its instrument, the concave line pulsed outwards, the rebels in front gave way and the Brigade was through and running free over the ridge.

Into Hades.

Broken and twisted bodies of blue and grey littered the trampled clover, corn, and shredded orchards. Amidst the rips of battle-smoke bodies flip-flopped, twisting like landed fish, begging for water, to be shot, or both; most just lay there at impossible angles. And all over, men, both in organised units and ragged lines, moved forwards, backwards and sideways like pawns in a deadly game of chess, looks of fear and hatred twisted their faces. But the most pervasive assault on the senses came from the concussion of sound emanating from hundreds of batteries and thousands of arms. It jarred the brain, vibrating it between the eardrums.

The Irish Brigade went forward. Into hell's wall of hate-filled sound. And Seamus felt liberated. For what seemed like long moments, he was shaken free from all concerns and desires, even those relating to living or dying. Glorious, transcendent moments that he could have searched a lifetime for without knowing this was what he desired.

If he died now, he died in ecstasy.

Reality, in the form of a rolling canvas of white heat and flame, came scything out of the ground and slashed his exhilaration into ribbons of fear and self-survival.

The leading ranks of the Irish Brigade were shredded in that awesome fireball. A dreamy unreality shielded Seamus from the worst of the shock of so many of his comrades falling mortally wounded all around him. His senses numbed themselves from full acceptance of what had occurred, though not enough to forestall stirrings of irretrievable loss and the certainty that his brief moments of ecstasy were shattered irretrievably.

He stopped amidst the carnage and tried to connect himself to the reality of the moment. He knew Tom Dillon was down because he saw his head split open like an overripe tomato; Seamus's hands and the right side of his face were flecked with the blood of his Malvern Hill saviour. Pat Duignan, given up for lost at Savage Station, but later found, was now lost forever at Antietam: his chest exploding into a red pulp right in front of Seamus. James Lalor, who had miraculously recuperated from injuries received at Malvern, would surely not recover from having the side of his face blown off. There were others, many others, all around.

Was that him shouting at his men to close up, dress the line and fill the gaps? How ridiculous! How could he? He looked out at Jer Horan and, though the Tipperaryman looked pale and stunned beyond what even his indomitable spirit could endure, he clasped his mentor's survival to his consciousness as a nun would a holy relic to ward off evil. Further out, Colonel Kelly was slumped over his horse, blood from his face running down its flanks. The colours lay forlorn and dusty on the ground; the lifeless bodies of three young bearers just as forlorn and dusty nearby.

It was a lost, leaderless, moment. Though he still shouted at his men to close up, close up and dress the line, he was aware they had taken on the posture of stupefied fish: stunned, eyes agog, mouths open. If he shouted forever, they wouldn't respond and he himself wouldn't be any less fearful. They would mill here aimlessly until blasted by another thunderclap of death from the rebel line; until they were all dead or maimed. Seamus screamed unheeded orders at the prospects. The Irish Brigade had reached the end of its road.

Then, Meagher rose tall in his saddle. 'Boys, raise the colours, and follow me!' His voice rang out above the din in clear, cultured, authoritative tones and broke the spell of stunned lethargy that had ossified the Brigade.

A tall, bearded captain stepped out from the ranks of the 69th and picked up the colours. 'I will follow you, General,' he said loudly, but calmly.

Right on cue the lines dressed, the men cheered, and the advance resumed. And also, right on cue, another blast of fire emanated from the rebel front. Though it had only been seconds since the first blast, they'd been filled by an eternity.

This second volley was every bit as devastating as the first – knocking men over like skittles. The staff holding the colours was cut in two in the Captain's hands, bending down to retrieve it, the top of his hat was shredded. The young recruits who'd refused Provost duty and sent a delegation to Meagher were decimated. As if forming one solid mass in pursuit of their chief, their centre exploded in a shower of red, misting the air crimson before falling onto the devastated remnants below.

Willie Jones was knocked backwards, though it didn't seem that serious, a bone splintered in his wrist or some such area; a debilitating wound but put into perspective by what had befallen the new recruits.

'Let's give them a taste of their own medicine,' Horan called. 'Pour it into the bastards.' Under their leaders' directions the men of the Irish Brigade stood and raised their muskets. And Seamus saw that what he would previously have considered bravery personified was no more than the instinctive defensiveness of frightened men.

'Fire!' He and hundreds fired into the rebel positions entrenched behind stacked fence rails in what looked like a sunken road or track. A near perfect position. Then his line stepped back to allow others take up the fray. He reached into his pouch, took out a cartridge, bit its end off, smarted at the salty sting of gunpowder on his lips and poured a large portion into the priming basin. Beneath the overarching din, the clinking of ramrods chimed the effectiveness of parade ground drilling as men simultaneously poked cartridge, paper and ball down musket barrels, placed percussion caps on firing cones and stepped up to deliver another volley just as the other line stepped back. Six volleys, three by each line, were delivered within thirty seconds. And what remained of the Irish Brigade, charged.

To be met by a withering fire that set their thinning ranks jigging tragically; their limbs flailed with a flamboyance that would have been comic on the stage; their faces frozen with miens stranded between horror and surprise that they'd been singled out for this spectacular, but farcically brief, dance. Then, they fell. Meagher first, his horse collapsing dramatically beneath him.

Those not yet chosen by rebel lead to perform the death-dance carried on advancing. In Company L, these men continued to be miraculously led by the likes of Lieutenant Brosnihan and Sergeants Horan and Farrell.

They reached the lip of the sunken road and looked into the eyes of their tormentors. Then fell upon them with invigorated savagery. There was no room to aim a musket; Seamus grappled with a sweaty, scared looking Southerner whom he'd caught in a chokehold. Underfoot the ground felt squishy and unsteady; he glanced down to find himself fighting on a floor of dead and dying rebels. He screamed and applied ferocity to the grapple. Seamus wanted his opponent down and underfoot so that he could clamber out of the cesspit. A volley of shots peppered the road and Confederate and Union men both were hit. Then from the south, another line of rebels fired at the Irish and it was more than living flesh could bear – they were trapped with hell in front, behind, overhead, and now: underneath.

'Fall back! Fall back!' Horan shouted.

Seamus gouged desperately at his opponent's eyes, forcing contact sufficient to make the man swear and relax his grip – a fatal mistake, for the rebel received several inches of bayonet steel in his belly as a consequence. The smell of the rebel's fear and the gases escaping from his stomach, overlain by the stench of battle caused Seamus to retch and throw up a breakfast of hardtack and bacon; the last earthly sight the poor devil saw was vomit cascading from the mouth of his killer. An ignominious end for some mother's beloved son of the south.

There was no time for regret or remorse: Seamus still, somehow, had to cut his way out of the hellhole and fall back to a safer line. How to do that without being shot or slashed to pieces his only thoughts at that moment.

There was no answer, beyond giving it a go. No answer and no choice. He glanced up and saw a lunatic with a red face, bulging eyes and spittle-draped face and realised it was Martin Brosnihan calling him out of the trench. He slashed and parried furiously as he clambered out of the sunken road and led the men around him in a backwards crawl that made the advance seem like a tea-party frolic.

Seamus smashed the butt of his musket full force onto the face of a huge flop-hatted Southerner who'd come after him like a pig snuffling for apples. The man screamed as his nose and face disintegrated into mush and shards of bone, then he fell backwards onto the dead and writhing bodies in the roadbed. In more civilised times, Seamus would have been sickened at what he'd done, now he registered grim satisfaction and immediately looked for another victim. Comrades in every direction from the Irish Brigade performed similar actions, though in the chaos, he didn't recognise anyone, apart from Horan: companies and regiments had become intermingled. There was no dressing the lines now, or any calling to order. This was an individual scrap for survival.

Seamus got trapped between two sweating, heaving rebels. One managed to get an arm-lock around his head, while the other punched the air out of his stomach. Seamus knew the second man was bringing a bayonet to bear on him. It wasn't a time for dignity: it was a time for self-preservation. He wriggled like an eel and screeched like a woman for help. He thought he felt the steel enter him and he screeched louder, even more high-pitched. Then there was an 'uumph!' and amidst the noise he heard one of his tormentors sigh almost gently; immediately the other one released his grip. Seamus stabbed viciously with his own bayonet. He glanced at a corporal from the 29th who should have been over on the other flank and tipped his cap in acknowledgement of the lifesaving service he had been rendered.

'Think nothing of it, Pat,' the corporal responded in a plumy accent, 'I'm sure you'll do the same for me someday.' Regardless of their inherent racism there was no doubting the New Englanders' ability to fight, nor their willingness to help out in a tight spot.

When he was about fifty feet from the sunken road, Seamus threw himself onto the ground alongside a line of Brigade comrades and proceeded to fire back at any rebel he saw down there, rolling onto his back to load. Many Irishmen had still not extricated themselves from the road or from the melee on its embankment, finding a suitable target was difficult, and any Union fire was being returned with interest. They were still in an extremely hot spot.

Horan threw himself down alongside him. 'Great day for saving hay!' he shouted.

He looked to see if his friend was gone insane, but big white teeth sparkled amidst the black soot and grime and Seamus marvelled anew at the man's capacity for humour amidst all this carnage. He threw back his head and laughed idiotically himself. Ireland, Kathleen, Padraic, his mother, didn't matter here. There was just him. And his comrades. A rifle shot thudded into the ground inches from his face spraying him with dirt and stones, temporarily blinding him. He wiped his eyes clear and laughed again. For he was damned. He had discovered his niche was in hell and he never wanted to leave. He squeezed off a shot at a rebel who'd leaned out of the embankment to try and stab a private from the 69th.

All around him, others performed similar actions. It had been twenty minutes since they'd left their camp on the other bank and the Irish Brigade were fully engaged in the Battle of Antietam as it raged and swelled across the fertile landscape.

CHAPTER TWENTY-SIX

Bloody stalemate ensued along the sunken road. Men from Ohio, Indiana and Pennsylvania were stalled and pinned down by men from Alabama, Georgia, and Mississippi. Over on the Confederate right, near where the road took a sharp south-southeast turn, the Union Irish Brigade, with men from Massachusetts, New York, Limerick, and Cavan were stalled and pinned down by men from North Carolina, Georgia, and Mississippi. Squashing himself in his hollow, Seamus fired his smoothbore before pushing his face back into the clover.

'Christ!' he exclaimed.

'What's the matter, Sarge? Have you caught one?' Bart Collins, an Irish New Yorker, called from nearby.

'No, but the hand is burnt off me,' Seamus replied. 'Bloody rifle.'

'Hold it with the strap!' Martin Brosnihan shouted.

'The strap is smouldering.'

'We'll need to do a sortie. My own is red hot as well,' Brosnihan responded.

'I've run out of ammunition,' someone else called.

Seamus sighed. He knew what this entailed: they were going to have to raise themselves from the hollows and depressions they'd made in the lush grass and raid the dead and wounded men around them. They needed muskets and ammunition: they had used up most of the cartridges they had brought with them this morning and, as a result of the unrelenting rate of fire, muskets, like his own, were becoming too hot to hold, even by the strap, while others had become jammed by powder residue or unfired balls. Also, he and his men were parched from fear and saltpetre - if any of the dead out there had water left in their canteens it could help preserve the living.

'Collins! Moran! Condron! Murphy! Keeffe! Duffy! Follow me: we need to get as many weapons and cartridges as possible from the fellows out there. And water. But for God sake: keep your thick skulls down.'

'Sure if they're that thick there's no fear of them, Sergeant.'

'Murphy, even your thick skull would be hard pressed to stop a minie ball, so try to keep it down.' It was the kind of banter that kept them sane in an insane world.

Without looking back to see if they followed, Seamus manoeuvred forwards on his elbows and knees, keeping his head as low to the ground as possible, using his fallen comrades as cover. Immediately, the air around him came alive as he drew fire from the sunken road. Dirt and grass spattered all around; dead and wounded bodies twitched as they absorbed fire. He assumed from a sudden increase in the fury of the fusillade that the others were crawling around behind him. He reached one discarded musket: a .69 calibre smoothbore – definitely Irish Brigade – with the initials J.C. scratched into the stock. It was unlikely that J.C., whoever he was, would require the weapon again this side of his Maker. Seamus hefted it while lying on his back with lead and balls whizzing all around. It felt a decent weapon, not as heavy as his own Prussian model which he'd had since Fort Schuyler, but when he went to examine the primer and the barrel, he realised it was jammed with unfired cartridges. J.C. had been so nervous and excited that that he never primed the gun after loading and kept pulling the hammer on unfired cartridges until the weapon became jammed and useless. J.C. was gone from the battle, probably skulking somewhere to the rear right this moment. He, on the other hand, was still in the thick of it and needed to find an effective weapon fast. A rifle bullet sang past his ear and smacked into the side of a dead Irish brigadier from the 63rd causing the left arm to rise in a half salute. Cartridges rattled in the dead man's pouch. Even more arresting - water sloshed in his canteen, Seamus crawled towards the man, praying for his soul and silently thanking him for absorbing the lead that was expended in his direction.

There was no sign of a weapon – probably pilfered by another soldier in need soon after the chap's incapacitation. As the sun beat down and bullets and balls thudded all around it became too hot, in every sense of the word, for Seamus to stay out where he was; he needed to get back to the relative safety of his clover patch, where his weapon might have cooled sufficiently to handle for another while. He slipped the cartridge pouch onto his arm and stuffed others from the man's belt into his pockets; he couldn't risk raising himself even slightly to tie the pouch on properly. He pushed the canteen inside his shirt and rolled over a couple of times until he was able to begin dragging himself back towards his own line once more. He was tempted to raise his head to see if he could quickly discern how the others who had come out with him had gotten on. A piece of lead whizzed past so close it stung him, making his eyes water; he felt a trickle of blood from his numb cheek and was reminded that his world for now was best confined to the dirt and bugs that crawled beneath his nose.

He pulled himself back towards his line; nose rubbing the trampled ground.

'Sarge, help.' Amidst the din, the words were so close to being lost that if Seamus hadn't his ears inches from the speaker's mouth, he would have passed on by without hearing.

'Please…' the voice mumbled again. Seamus raised his eyes slightly and a bubble of blood perforating on the lips of young Conor McCarthy filled his vision. The youngster's eyes focussed on his sergeant; their questioning vitality replaced by a sickly grey, pleading look. Glancing along the youngster's body, Seamus felt like vomiting again. Young McCarthy no longer existed below the knees. His body ended in a mesh of bloody strings, his legs nowhere in sight. One of the brightest prospects of the Irish Brigade had been cut down before he had gotten time to blossom.

'Shoot me…' For a moment he thought young McCarthy was asking him to loot him, presumably for his ammunition and other battlefield assets. 'Please, Sarge, shoot me…please.' It was the pleading look that enabled Seamus to finally understand what the youngster wanted.

Since coming to them from a prosperous trading family in New York, swayed by Meagher's mellifluous tongue into letting their youngest son join the Irish Brigade, Conor McCarthy had thrown himself eagerly into the duties and tasks required of him by army life. A lively, intelligent lad, who looked to Seamus for leadership and guidance. The older man had enjoyed the self-esteem of being a mentor; it did his confidence no harm to believe he had something to teach a kid like this; but now it felt all the worse to look the lad in the eye, shake his head and deny him his last wish.

The youngster's look faltered and he dropped his gaze towards his musket, which he tried to push towards Seamus. 'Bayonet…' he mumbled, 'push it in…' Again, the heart wrenching plea: 'Please…'

The entire roiling, reeking, raging battlefield had, for Seamus, become condensed in this legless youngster's death plea. 'Hang in there, McCarthy – you're going to be alright.' He didn't feel any better for lying or for seeing the look in the kid's eyes that showed he knew; for a few seconds he was tempted to push the blade into young McCarthy's heart in the hope of ending both their miseries. Instead, he leant across and poured water from the dead soldier's canteen onto the youngster's lips, moistening them and wiping the blood away. Immediately, another red bubble formed. Sweat trickled down the lad's face bestowing it a yellow sheen of death.

Seamus stuffed the canteen under Conor's arm. 'Hold onto this and I'll be back with help,' he lied and crawled shamefully away. Young McCarthy sighed despairingly behind him. Seamus crawled back to his line faster – maybe he'd feel better once he'd maimed and killed more rebels.

***

Eoghan Crosby was lying low when a ghost tapped him on the shoulder and made him scream. He had seen more than his share of dead and dying this day to satiate a lifetime of nightmares, though it was a price he was willing to pay for surviving; but now it seemed the dead would not even wait for him to sleep before popping up to intimidate him.

'Where is he?' the ghost, a blanched, goggle-eyed, skewed version of Michael O'Rorke with putrid breath, hissed.

'Who?' Crosby asked – maybe if he placated this apparition it would dissipate back into the ether.

'The Limerickman,' O'Rorke's revenant specified. 'The traitor.'

Crosby looked at the others skulking behind the tree trunk to see if they were seeing this apparition also. It gave him no comfort to see Donnelly and the others staring open-eyed at the spectre of their former leader. O'Rorke no longer had that angry look – he held something more terrifying, more blood chilling within him – and Crosby would have rather turned to face a thousand screaming rebs before acknowledging it.

Hunger. The hunger of the dead for the flesh of the living. Paralysis seized Crosby's system and he thought he would be unable to respond to the Apparition's question. But he would have done anything to deflect that hunger from himself and so he pointed a quavering finger towards the lefthand side of the Brigade's battleline.

'Over there, somewhere,' he managed to say.

***

Seamus supposed it ironic that his luck finally ran out when, through sheer physical exhaustion, he'd ceased firing and rested his head in the grass. When he'd returned, his musket was still too hot to handle, but Thady Moran had somehow brought three unjammed rebel weapons back with him and passed one to his Sergeant. It was a Springfield rifle – a lot lighter and more manoeuvrable than his smoothbore. The problem was: neither his own dwindling cartridge supply nor the supply he'd acquired from the dead soldier to his front would fit the .58 calibre barrel. He realised that this was the sort of weapon young McCarthy had and that his cartridges were likely to fit; Seamus cursed himself for not having the presence of mind to relieve the dying youngster of his useless supply of cartridges. Then castigated himself for such callous thoughts about a boy he'd abandoned to an agonising fate.

He scrounged sufficient from comrades to recommence firing at the rebels in the sunken road, taking out his angst on them. Then a box of ammunition acquired down the line was passed to him; aided by the breech-loading Springfield he blindly fired and fired, breaking his own dictum – and that of all experienced soldiers – but he certainly felt better. With each shot he squeezed off, he saw the face of young McCarthy and felt he was avenging its suffering and that was far better than thinking of how he'd abandoned the young lad to his fate out there on the gory stretch before the sunken road.

Eventually, his arm and shoulder grew too numb to pull the hammer back, it was like he'd chopped down Ballinleena Wood; the Springfield was beginning to overheat and his .58s were running out. He didn't even know how many of his men were still with him. By continuing to fire blindly without a care for those around him, he would be failing in his duty as a sergeant and as a soldier. Anyway, he was physically unable to carry on. He needed to stop and collect himself. Young McCarthy was surely dead by now and there was nothing further he could do to avenge him.

He lay his head in the soft clover and as the bullets flying all around whizzed a lullaby, he dozed.

A bee sting in the shoulder startled him awake. He recollected immediately where he was, but it took a few moments to register that the pain was not caused by a bee sting but from a bullet that had finally found his range.

'Jesus!' he groaned, and pushed himself backwards with his right arm, pulling the Springfield awkwardly along. His movements and the line in general continued to attract fire, so he didn't retreat very far. The pain and disability in his shoulder prohibited movement anyway; when he felt he was out of the immediate line of fire he stopped and rolled onto his back, sweating and breathless.

'Where are you hit, Sarge?' Tom Healy, a private in Company L, crept up to him.

'My shoulder.' Seamus muttered in reply.

'Stretcher! Over here!' Healy called.

Suddenly Seamus realised he might have to leave the fight and the possibility shocked him as severely as the pain in his shoulder. He was in no state to start thinking about life beyond this battlefield.

'Just get me strapped up,' he grimaced. 'I need to stay here.'

'But you won't be able to fire your weapon, Sarge,' Healy persisted.

'Just get me strapped up, Private!'

'Sergeant Farrell, causing trouble again, I see.' It was Horan, standing tall amidst the carnage, oblivious to the lead twitching the grass all around.

'Just trying to do my job, Sergeant,' Seamus replied.

'Right now that job consists of getting yourself and the remainder of your men off the field. We have orders to pull back before we are completely annihilated. Caldwell's men are supposed to be relieving us and extending the line beyond that bend to enfilade the rebs, but they're making a pig's ear of it and we can't wait any longer.' Horan indicated a line of blue troops milling half a mile behind to their right.

'Are they Meagher's orders?' Seamus asked.

'There is no sign of Meagher or Kelly – I think they're both down. The order to retreat came from General Richardson himself via a sniffy adjutant who seemed upset he was getting dust on his white gloves. I expect the General thought Caldwell would be in place by now, but he's got a bad dose of the slows. We've virtually run out of ammunition, our weapons are overheating, and most of our best men are dead or injured. I think that gives us the licence to move. It might even hurry Caldwell up.'

'Aaagh!' Seamus screamed as the orderly poured spirits onto his wound.

'Jaysus, that's an awful waste of good alcohol,' Horan commented.

'Sergeant, shouldn't we at least wait until Caldwell is in place?' Seamus managed to say through gritted teeth.

Horan looked at him solemnly. 'James, I want to bring at least some of our men out alive. Who are you going to liberate Ireland with? An army of cripples and dead men?'

Seamus shivered with cold sweats as the orderly strapped his shoulder – he feared he was going to faint or lose consciousness, but the situation was too critical to allow himself that luxury.

Through clouds of pain and wisps of battle-smoke, he studied his friend. Over the past number of hours, they had very much maintained a chain of command relationship, but this was his best friend in the Army – right now, the world – and knowing Horan was there kept him steadfast amidst the carnage. Horan hid lionhearted courage and utmost loyalty behind a humorous front garnished with hilarious facial expressions and a constant run of quips. It wouldn't even be beyond the bounds of possibility that he dreamed up the current dilemma just to keep his friend's mind off the pain – though there was no doubting they were in straits dire enough for peremptory action. Seamus also knew that if they abandoned their lines too soon, before Caldwell was in place, Horan ran the risk of a court-martial.

'We can hold out for another fifteen to twenty minutes; Caldwell is bound to be up by then.' Seamus said.

Horan shook his head. 'In fifteen minutes the Irish Brigade may no longer exist. Company L certainly won't.'

But Seamus still did not want to retreat. 'If we pull out too soon the Rebs are going to pour out of that road and run over us. Even more of us will be killed than if we continue trying to hold our ground – they must be hurting too, we've picked off quite a few of them. Christ!' This last was addressed once more to the pain caused by the orderly as he tightened the strapping on the shoulder wound and, as it served to undermine his whole argument, Horan smiled ironically. It seemed he would have to face reality sooner than he wanted.

'Sarge!' Private Healy indicated movement to the right.

'Shit!' Horan exclaimed when he looked where Healy was pointing. 'The mad bastards!'

Seamus looked across and saw they wouldn't be leaving the battlefield anytime soon. The 29th were charging the sunken road. They were as foolhardy as the Irish after all. With a shout and a mad dash they went in – a sight to stir the blood of Celt and Puritan alike.

'Covering fire! Covering fire there!' Horan started to exclaim and he turned to exhort the able men around him to increase their fire and help prevent the 29th being raked as they advanced. Seamus turned from the orderly and, gritting his teeth against his painful shoulder, moved to get himself in a firing position.

As he turned, he saw that Horan had his battle face back on: features set grimly; eyes slitted in concentration; blood pumping so vigorously his face was violet.

For a second it seemed he stumbled as he ran forward with his sword held out before him, then a shower of red tinged with darker matter spewed up from the back of his head and his face became shocked and open-mouthed like hundreds of others Seamus had seen shot in battle. Horan made a 'mmmh' sound, like there was something he wanted to say but his vocal cords had been rendered useless. He toppled forward face down onto the ground. Dead.

***

They followed O'Rorke because they always had. Since coming into the Army, he had given them leadership and a structured outlet for their cruelties and cowardice; in his absence they had been lost and their energies had regressed into the petty ambitions and barely concealed hatreds they'd been in civilian life. This had led them to a skulking position at Antietam, which they'd sugared with a covering of self-deceit and small-mindedness that was just beginning to feel comfortable when O'Rorke came back from the dead.

Now they scuttled across the backwashes of the fighting, following their leader on his personal mission. A major from the 63rd saw them pass. 'Where are you lot going?' he shouted. 'Shouldn't you be over with the 69th?'

O'Rorke fixed him with a baleful glare and, showing his faded Sergeant's straps, mumbled: 'There…' and pointed towards the left where the 88th reputedly were.

The major frowned and wondered why a raggedy-assed sergeant and a bunch of men who looked as if they'd not been in any fighting were heading away from their regiment. Then he shrugged and waved them on. This whole battle was insane, and he had enough on his plate without bothering about men he'd never seen before scuttling towards the meat grinder at the far end of the sunken road. It was a decision that spared his life – at least for a while longer – for if he'd looked closer, he would have seen the white knuckles of the sergeant steadying to plunge the blade into his belly.

A ball split a rock close to Donnelly as he scampered along and the splinters raked the back of his hand, drawing three parallel lines of blood, he yelped like a hound being kicked. He stopped and for a moment considered dropping out of the troop. One dart of a backwards glance by O'Rorke was enough to persuade him that his healthiest option was to continue.

O'Rorke held his hand up and they paused amidst wounded men and horses whose piteous cries and groans created a bedlam exacerbated by disoriented ambulances and stretcher bearers. Fifty yards beyond the worst of the chaos, the limp, bullet ridden flag of the 88th drooped forlornly, but defiantly. O'Rorke beckoned his followers onwards again, until they were on a slight rise overlooking the rear of Company L's position.

There, he paused once more, this time lying down and, with a hand signal, bade the others to do likewise.

O'Rorke lay as if he'd died again. His eyes remained open, but his breathing was so slow it may have been non-existent. His skin so pale the blood might no longer have been coursing through its veins. For several minutes, he lay like that and the others began casting quizzical looks at each other. The stench from the wound at the back of his head had a whiff of the grave about it.

Finally Crosby ventured: 'Sergeant? Michael?'

O'Rorke swivelled his head with an alacrity that made the others start. 'It's always "Sergeant" when we're on duty,' he croaked in a dry voice appropriate to a speaking corpse.

Crosby merely nodded, like the others he wished he was back behind the log. He was even thinking that frontline battle would be preferable to being here with this insane ghost thing.

O'Rorke turned back towards the front and pointed. 'There. There's the enemy,' he said. At first, the others looked out at the grey hordes milling in the sunken road and beyond and considered this statement of the obvious further proof of their Sergeant's insanity.

'Kill them,' O'Rorke said in his husky whisper and pointed again, this time leaving no doubt that he meant soldiers in Company L and not the rebels they faced. As they looked, individual forms became distinct and they could pick out men like Jer Horan, Tim Healy, Martin Brosnihan, and the hated James Farrell, alias Captain Rock of Kilgarry, who seemed to be wounded.

O'Rorke saw his nemesis in a sitting position being attended by an orderly and surrounded by some 88th pals of his. It was a shoulder wound, obviously not fatal, which was good because he did not want to be denied the opportunity of personally offering the bluebottle a feast on the low-life's eyes.

Farrell was half-sitting and his head formed an easy target for O'Rorke's rifle as he drew a bead on the traitor. At fifty yards he would not miss; his breech-loading Enfield was good for up to half a mile. He could end it now and provide himself with the satisfaction of sending such scum to his grave; then a further thought alighted on him. Why not make him suffer first? One way was to wound him in the limbs a few times leaving him in agony before finishing him off. And that was very appealing, but then he saw a better opportunity to make Farrell's final suffering even more agonising. He would take out what was dearest to him. Jer Horan – a Tipperary gombeen man and Farrell's best friend. He didn't trust the weaklings he had with him to play their parts in a stand-up fight if Horan's death drew attention to them, but the pleasurable anticipation at what he was about to do would not be denied and he drew a bead on Horan. Then God showed he was on his side because a fracas started as some Northern units charged the positions in front, multiplying the chaos and giving O'Rorke the perfect opportunity to take Horan out unnoticed. He fired at the Tipperaryman's skull as he rose to join the charge.

And scored a direct hit.

O'Rorke emitted a wail of triumph – a victory cry from beyond the grave, chilling the neck hairs of those within earshot. Then he turned his rifle back towards Farrell.

***

Seamus's world became constricted once more: this time into a dark tunnel of hatred holding the dead Jer Horan in its centre. That hatred, and a numbing shock, held grief at a distance for the moment. Now was for action. For revenge. And on a scale far beyond what he'd attained over young McCarthy's death.

He brushed the orderly aside and, without a word to Healy or any of the men left around him, turned towards the sunken road with a low animal growl. He tripped over the orderly's knapsack, instinctively tumbled towards his right shoulder to spare his wounded left the worst of the impact. A bullet, which would surely have mashed his head, if he'd remained upright whizzed past his back as he did so. He fell to the ground with a thump that severely jolted his wound, though he'd succeeded in keeping it off the ground.

He found himself staring into Horan's glazed eyes. The back of his friend's head was covered in a bluish-black netting. Then a bullet thumped into the prone body and the netting rose indolently into the air to reveal itself as a collection of bluebottles and flies already feasting on his blood.

As they settled down again, Seamus, for the second time that morning, puked, though all that was left to commemorate his friend was bile and yellowish fluid. With the retching came a revelation: the bullet that had killed Horan and the one that would have killed him, if he hadn't tripped, had come, not from the rebels in front, but from behind. From Union men.

***

O'Rorke swore. The bullet flew past the falling Farrell to rip into fleshy resistance further down the hill. The Limerick bastard had nine lives. Well, five guns trained on him would more than half those odds. If his blurring vision and the crushed ice thickening his blood were anything to go by, he had only one more shot in him – though he was determined not to die before Farrell. It was time for the others to prove they were men and not mice, to repay their debts to him. After all, without him, they would be worthless scum like Farrell.

He pointed a shaky finger at where the Limerickman lay on his side. 'Kill him,' he commanded. 'Kill him.'

The others saw what he wanted, and to their relief, saw it was a task they would have no qualms about carrying out. They would find the courage to shoot Farrell in the back.

Except now, he seemed to be looking up the rise at them. Never mind. He'd noticed them too late. They steadied their weapons and readied to fire their first shots of the battle.

***

No one could ever properly explain what finally caused the 'impregnable' Confederate line in the sunken road to unravel. Too many things happened at once, resulting in too many claims and counterclaims to allow the course of events a logical beginning to end strand. The broad picture encompassed an impetuous charge by Colonel Joseph Barnes, 29th Mass., Irish Brigade, towards the sunken road. This so startled the battered Confederates that they began to retreat from the road in twos and threes. The trickle turned to a flood when General Posey, 16th Mississippi, first led his troops out of the lane in a doomed counterattack then back through the road to relieve overcrowding and confusion. This backwards movement was assumed to be the beginning of a general retreat by a large volume of exhausted Southerners and they began pouring out of the road, to be mowed down by exultant Yankees before they could reach the comparative safety of the Piper Orchard behind. Then the remaining forces of the Irish Brigade finally got to enfilade the southeast turn in the road and poured a devastating fire along the rebel line. To cap it all: Caldwell finally got his men in place.

But there was too much of a free-for-all; too much of a melding of Northern and Southern troops in and around the sunken road to be certain about what had precipitated what.

The only certainty was that, amidst everything, Seamus O'Farrell and Mikey O'Rorke, fellow exiles from oppression in Ireland, finalised their New World antagonism.

For the briefest of seconds, Seamus refused to believe that the scarecrow on the hilltop was O'Rorke. He fired anyway. It was an instinctive, life-preserving shot from a rifle primed to kill Confederates down the hill. The bullet exploded in O'Rorke's chest just as he squeezed his own trigger, knocking him backwards on the hilltop scattering his shot wildly and stunning his cohorts who themselves were about to fire at Seamus.

As Seamus clambered uphill, the figures at the top were flooded by a milling blue tide that swelled over the rise to flow downhill, swirling around him and the remnants of Company L, threatening to take him along in their surge.

But, in an effort to fill the screaming vacuum that had opened within him, he continued to charge against it.

He had to make certain he'd killed a scarecrow before turning to join the Northern flow.

O'Rorke lived. But as neither man nor scarecrow; rather as an entity spewed out by the hell of battle to span the divide between the living and the dead.

Red tissue and bluish-grey organs pulsed where his upper torso should have been, and the back of his head seemed to have been squashed square against the ground. Yet when Seamus bent over on the chaotic hilltop, O'Rorke's eyes focussed on him with steely hatred; he was a revenant, a shadow person, but fuelled by sufficient hatred to enable him to breathe forever. Seamus saw he'd be doing him a favour by finishing him off and for a moment was tempted to gain his revenge by leaving him live to be a pathetic wreck. A deep sensing part of him, that might be a soul, knew that if he finished his enemy off while he lay helpless, he would cross a threshold to never again be Seamus O'Farrell from Kilgarry. It would be beyond killing Flaherty. He considered for a final moment.

Then, sunk his bayonet hard past the bastard's ribs and onwards into his heart, watching as the final puffs of life gurgled out of his nemesis, before turning and running downhill to join the surging blue throng.

EPILOGUE

By one o'clock in the afternoon, the Irish Brigade's role in the Battle of Antietam was over. In a few short hours, they had created a historical reputation to resound down the years, echoing into legend. They had played a major role in overrunning the sunken road – known thereafter as The Bloody Lane – at the centre of the rebel line and pushing the killing on elsewhere. And though the battle ebbed and flowed for the remainder of the day posterity would not take from the sacrifice of the Irish. When the sun finally dropped below the horizon blotting out the worst of the carnage, the North claimed a victory, the South a draw. Both sides did agree that the bloodiest day in American history hadn't finished the war. The Northerners had succeeded in driving the Southerners from their soil, but Lee got his surviving soldiers safely across the Potomac to live to fight again. The war would drag on.

The Irish Brigade paid an irredeemable butcher's bill for their legendary reputation. Nearly half the Brigade was dead or out of action. Amongst whom, the brightest and the bravest were overrepresented. A huge proportion of those seeking martial experience to expend later on behalf of their beloved Ireland discovered, too late, that for them such a time was to be postponed indefinitely. As indefinitely as the reawakening of Fionn MacCumhaill and his warriors.

The once ebullient Meagher, who had been feared dead, was alive but broken. The following morning, he walked around his remaining regiments shaking his head at the gaps and muttering to an equally downcast Jack Gosson: 'Woefully cut up. Woefully cut up.'

Seamus O'Farrell survived. Maybe he wasn't one of the brightest or the bravest. And he certainly didn't feel lucky.

He did feel he'd arrived at a point of major significance in his life. Not a crossroads. A point. A point where feelings he couldn't quite label had birthed within him; feelings he hadn't had before – certainly not with the same texture or consistency. There seemed no doubt that they had arrived to stay and would forever be part of a different him. The one word that came close to describing this new texture and consistency was *acceptance*. Though even this was not right - implying as it did a pacification and forgiveness he did not feel.

But he accepted he had to carry on.

The night of the battle he had lain amongst hundreds of wounded in a straw barn looking out on a portion of the battlefield. Outside in the gloom and night, mists which had reclaimed the field, lights, like souls, rose and fell. They were the lanterns of women and orderlies moving amongst the dead and wounded offering succour; some undoubtedly belonging to pillagers of the same dead and wounded. There was no Horan to come to his rescue now, but to a mind befuddled with shock and morphine there was beauty in any light amidst darkness. Individuals he'd lost, living and dead, whispered to him from out of the flames, and throughout that otherwise long and terrible night filled with moans, wracking coughs and recollections of death and dismemberment, he released them. And, in turn, was released.

Released to a world he hadn't sought and didn't think he wanted to be in. But it was a world with different paths, and he had the freedom to choose. Though such freedom was a lonely thing, he could and would move on. Maybe this new path would still lead to a fight for Irish freedom, maybe not. Freedom, of whatever kind, was not something to be rushed into. It required consideration.

He accepted that.

Sept 18th, 1862

Antietam Battlefield

Dear Kathleen,

I sit against a tree of stripped bark and bare branches that yesterday morning drooped low with fruit. Today this tree stands on bloody ground. Many I held dear are buried in it. But I live and, apart from a badly mauled shoulder, should be fine as long as infection does not set in.

I received your last letter with shock and indignation and while I would like to say that the events of the past twenty-four hours have mellowed me, it would not be the truth.

I accept though that we chose a difficult, probably impossible, path in a brutal world with too many possibilities for being sidetracked, bushwhacked and terminated. To survive in such a world we should not ask too much of each other. I see now that we did.

So, I can accept that you and Padraic had to try it this way. Though I cannot say 'good luck' either, I release you from any obligation you feel towards me.

As for living my own life - I intend to, though I am not yet ready to give up on the dream of returning to Kilgarry and liberating

Ireland. Hopefully, it is possible to live for oneself and still work for a greater good. I will see.

> See you in the old dart someday,
> Seamus.

Realising he didn't want to send it after all, he crumpled the letter, stuffing it in his pocket rather than adding to the debris of the battlefield.

The following day he walked the bloody ground. Now that it was clear hostilities would not be resumed here, the dead of both sides could be buried. The fertile landscape that had seemed to glow red during the battle was now as muddy and grey as the corpses that were picked up in blankets and tossed into shallow trenches.

Seamus was unable to physically help the burial details, but in his capacity as sergeant he walked the ground they'd fought over the previous day and supervised the gathering of corpses from his company. Most of his dead charges and campfire acquaintances were placed in shallow mass graves, but he insisted that Jer Horan's body was buried individually with a wooden cross under an oak tree behind one of the Dunker farms.

He couldn't bear to watch the lively, twinkling features of his friend being covered by earth so he walked away to locate others. Along the sunken road men, who'd tried to kill him two days before, were stacking their dead like cordwood and he showed them where there were some advanced rebel bodies. His enemies politely thanked him and offered to trade tobacco for coffee.

He came across other bodies of those he'd known: Conor McCarthy, Pa Bourke, Tom Dillon and many more, including Private George Twoomey of Company K – the first Irish Brigade soldier he'd ever seen back on New York's dockside. Barney O'Sullivan, the Connemara fisherman of the 63rd and some of his cronies – most of whom had no English, only Gaelic, now silenced forever in an alien land, fighting for an alien cause by people speaking an alien tongue. He watched as the men with whom he had hoped to fight for Ireland and Kilgarry with were tossed into the soil of Maryland. Their bodies superfluous manure for an already fertile land.

Of O'Rorke, there was only shreds. Moments after he'd killed him and turned to charge downhill, dead, wounded, and able-bodied were obliterated by a Confederate shell blasting that part of the ridge to smithereens. The burial detail there said they had to scoop blue and grey rags, bone shards and fleshy bits into sacks and toss them into a trench.

Using the pain in his arm as an excuse, Seamus left that field of the dead with its grey corpses, bloated flesh, decomposing smells and internal organs intermingled with earth.

He returned to camp to find himself brevetted First-Sergeant. No treks to Meagher's quarters this time, no grand words or champagne, just a direction from Colonel Bourke of the 63rd, one of the few remaining capable field officers, who saw an urgent need to start pulling the regiments together. Martin Brosnihan, who was proving as indestructible as Seamus himself, was brevetted Captain. Seamus felt no pride at following in his dead best friend's footsteps; he had not yet moved beyond that sense of acceptance. The dream of liberating Kilgarry and Ireland seemed as dead as his comrades. He thought of Dan O'Leary's wife.

"…it will be just the usual bunch of idealistic eejits… they'll waste their energy and lifeblood fighting each other, like the Irish always do – the only difference being they'll do it thousands of miles from home this time."

And wished she had been wrong.

The brevetting did cement his instinct to carry on as a soldier. Amidst the carnage and the campfire, he had found a place that was his. And maybe that was true freedom.

The rebels buried their dead and during the night scampered across the Potomac. The Union Army slowly prepared to follow. McClellan, as ever, insisting on perfection in organisation, supplies and appearances.

The Irish Brigade closed up its ranks and recorded its depleted roster. First-Sergeant Farrell brought the remaining men of Company L together; ordered them to dress arms and prepare to march. Second-Sergeant Mulvaney sniffled indomitably while McClellan led his army out, followed by his generals, brigadiers, and regimental commanders. Drummer boys rattled a stirring beat and pipers piped. The tattered flags of the Irish Brigade caught and flew in a rising breeze. Meagher flourished his sword; Jack Gosson rode a dashing new mount. There would be battles up the road where love would remain buried but dreams might be resurrected.

The dead awaited redemption while the living marched.

Meagher dropped his sword.

Seamus O'Farrell followed the living.

ACKNOWLEDGEMENTS

Although, I wish he were here to write his own acknowledgements, I would like to thank the people who helped make publishing our dad's story a reality. Thank you to our incredibly kind and supportive patrons Liam Gordon, John McDonnell, Michael MacKenzie, Pamela Paterson, and Gerard Shiels. A massive thank you to our loving friends and family who contributed toward publishing this novel: James and Frances Barcoe, Noel Kennedy, Brendan Kennedy, Kathy English-Gordon, Kathy English, Ann Hayes and Jeff Collins, and The Forghani Family. I would also like to add our appreciation for Dad's close friend, John Whelan, whose own publication was inspiring and for whose support and advice we have been grateful.

Thank you to Andy Bridge for designing a cover that we love and cherish.

I would like to extend my infinite gratitude to James and Frances Barcoe (well-deserving of a second mention) who housed, fed, and looked after me during the initial lockdown of 2020 and in whose lovely home in

Kilkenny I spent weeks within working on editing, researching, and planning where *Rebel in Blue* could go.

To Liz, my everything, I love you and thank you for inspiring me to believe that we could make this happen.

To Mam and Clare, without the love, resilience, and support of the greatest team this story may never have been shared with the world.

Lastly, Dad, thank you for leaving us with this amazing story. We love you so much.

- Ciaran

ABOUT THE AUTHOR

Liam English studied English and History at University College Cork. This ignited his passion for writing and interest in the American Civil War – particularly the role that the Irish played in it. He worked as a head researcher for a large financial services company in the UK before moving back home to Ireland and becoming a part-time librarian.

During that time, he was able to truly dedicate his time to the research for his novel, *Rebel in Blue,* by extensively reading and road tripping all over America to visit close to every Civil War site that comes to mind. His passion for history, writing, and Ireland is felt in every page of his novel.

Sadly, Liam passed away in September 2007 at the age of forty-seven. Liam was a kind, generous man who remains a special person to so many people that he met, knew and loved in his too-short, but much-lived, time with us.

Printed in Great Britain
by Amazon